BURN DOWN SEATOWN

BURN DOWN SEATOWN

Hans Hergot

WWW.HANSHERGOT.COM

BURN DOWN SEATOWN
THE JESTER'S CURSE: BOOK TWO

Copyright © 2014 by Hans Hergot

Published by:
Bezzle Books
1492 Lake Murray Boulevard
Columbia, South Carolina 29212

Burn Down Seatown, Hans Hergot, 1st print ed., 2014

ISBN 978-0692303863

www.hanshergot.com

Table of Contents

Chapter One

S ome stories in the kingdom of Arovia began with a
kiss, others with a boot to the head.

Marius, prince among jesters, couldn't choose.
He had to have both. The curse that afflicted him
wouldn't hear otherwise. It loved the irony.

Marius floated in a pleasant dream, a dream he hoped
never to leave. There was nothing funny about it at all.
In dreams he could quit joking. He didn't have to act. In
dreams, he didn't have to sleep on the cold ground beneath a moth-eaten tent.

In his dream, he soaked his weary bones in a steam-
ing bath, drawn in the intricately tiled bathroom of
House Marcel, the richest family in Amok, filled with
bubbling, clear water as far as the eye could see. A beautiful woman swam next to him: Sybil, the promiscuous
daughter of House Marcel.

Sybil grabbed him by the shoulders playfully pulling
him beneath the surface of the bath.

When Marius emerged, he took a deep breath. The
woman in his dream had changed. They did that sometimes. Now it was Irina, the former slave of House Mar-

cel and the love of his life who lay in the water within easy reach.

The two women mixed together sometimes in his dreams, becoming one. Irina with her frizzy auburn hair often morphed into Sybil with her long, red locks. His dream girl smiled at him, looking at him with Irina's kind eyes and Sybil's mischievous smile.

She didn't pull back or act embarrassed by his closeness.

Instead, she began to choke him teasingly, as though he'd been naughty. Their bodies squeaked together from the suds filling the bath.

Irina's auburn hair fell across her face. With a flick of her head, she became Sybil again.

Sybil wore a wicked smile. Her slender fingers tightened around his throat. She took obvious pleasure in his discomfort. Sybil loved mixing pleasure and pain.

When she didn't let go, panic began to set in. Marius realized that the woman of his dreams had stopped playing. She was choking him in earnest.

He remembered too late how he'd denied Sybil his love. How she'd threatened his life. Her grip tightened, threatening to cut off his lungs.

Marius awoke from the dream with a gasp. Spittle flew from his lips. Yet the pressure on his neck didn't let up.

He hadn't been dreaming. He was being choked.

Marius's hands flew to his throat. He felt the soft leather and slender ankle of a woman's boot.

"Is that the cursed one?" a gruff voice whispered from the darkness outside the tent. "Doesn't look like much."

Marius didn't recognize the owner of the voice.

The owner of the boot he knew full well. Her face had been carved into his memory by the sheer terror of their last meeting.

By the dim light of the autumn moon, Marius saw that that a fate worse than Sybil's scorned wrath had caught up with him.

Lespa the Astor, one of the appointed guardians of the kingdom of Arovia stood over Marius. She had her boot to his throat. Her toe squeezed his windpipe.

Lespa stared down at Marius with a look of contempt, "Did you miss me, fool?"

Marius wished he was still dreaming, that this apparition might be a nightmare. But he knew she was real.

She had finally caught up with him. Lespa had come to kill him.

* * *

Marius needed to breathe.

The tent fell away from his vision as his brain shut down from lack of air.

Marius squirmed. The woman standing on top of him put more weight on the ball of her foot, pinning him down. He could smell the boot's oiled leather mixed with dirt from the road.

Marius's eyes swam in his head. He looked for an escape.

His companions in the tent were asleep. He'd been traveling with a family of poor tinkers after leaving the city of Amok. Every night they camped alongside the road.

Marius wondered whether the tinkers were really asleep. If they were pretending, he wouldn't blame them.

Astors like Lespa were the law in the kingdom of Arovia. They could dispense justice as they saw fit. Some

Astors treated the responsibility with more care than others.

Lespa let up, allowing Marius one gasp before returning her boot to his throat.

The tinkers wouldn't help him. He wasn't a member of their family. He was a slave. A runaway at that. The tinkers wouldn't be coming to his aid, even if he cried out—which he was unable to do, since the Astor's boot was making sauce out of his Adam's apple.

Lespa leaned over, staring into Marius's face.

"It's him," she whispered to her companion. "It's the jester. By the Lady, I'd forgotten how ugly he is."

A proud man might have taken offense. Marius, however, had been called ugly so many times it felt normal, like someone calling the grass green or the sky blue.

In fact, Marius was ugly. His nose shot away from his forehead as though it were ashamed to be seen with his face. The nose pushed apart his bulging, brown eyes, giving him the appearance of a fish. His long neck, which was providing a convenient footrest for Lespa's boot, sprouted from his shoulders, thin and wobbly, like a sapling carrying too much fruit.

He couldn't help being ugly. He'd been handsome once, but that was before the wizard cursed him with the Jester's Curse.

His hand gripped Lespa's boot. His gangly legs flailed under his blanket trying to gain purchase.

Lespa leaned close to Marius's head. "Come quietly. Don't give me a reason to kill you," she looked around the tent, "or your friends."

Inwardly, Marius groaned. There was no way he could exit the tent quietly, not with the Jester's Curse looking to trip him up every chance it got.

Because of the curse, Marius had been kicked out of his comfortable berth as a house slave.

He had nearly starved, till he learned that his curse could be useful. It made people laugh at him. The bigger the audience, the bigger the laugh—usually at Marius's expense.

The curse helped him make a living, but at a cost. Marius's manhood recoiled at the memory of the abuse it had taken from the curse's pranks.

Worse than the pain, the Jester's Curse delighted in depriving Marius of even the meanest pleasure. Back in Amok, he'd wanted to be with Sybil. The curse had come between them.

It acted that way sometimes, beyond his control. The curse made him do things he didn't want to do, like slighting Sybil instead of embracing her. The curse had sent her sprawling into a hot bath. She'd emerged wet and angry enough to kill him.

It was a common enough theme with the people Marius met. Many wanted him dead because of the curse, others because of his personality.

With a serious audience like Lespa, the curse would pull out all the stops to make her smile, even if it provoked her into putting a dagger between his ribs. Actually, thought Marius, cutting him open might be just the thing to put a smile on her cruel face.

Lespa removed her boot from his throat.

Marius started to rise. He had to exit the tent without causing a scene. Not only for himself, but for the tinkers. By traveling with them, he'd brought trouble on their heads. They'd been kind to him.

Marius rose to his knees.

He stood slowly.

He didn't release an ear-shattering fart. That was a good start. The curse loved the simple gags.

Marius took a faltering step toward the door of the tent. In the corner of his eye, he could see the prone bodies of the tinker family. In the center of the tent, the embers of a cooking fire winked at him. From the tent posts hung the metal tools of the tinkers' trade and samples of their wares: pots, pans, and the like.

Thankfully, none of the implements barred his way. Otherwise, the curse would have knocked his head into them, causing a din.

Marius reached the door of the tent.

He stepped out.

Nothing happened.

Standing outside the tent, without incident, was a minor miracle. His mouth fell open in mild shock. Had the Jester's Curse been healed overnight? Or was the curse still asleep, perhaps dreaming of Irina or Sybil?

By the light of the moon, Marius could see Lespa standing a few paces away. Her companion hunkered near the ground. Both wore the tell-tale sign of the Astor, a blood-red star painted onto the breastplate of their black armor. The big man pawed at something on the ground.

Marius realized that the Astor was looking through Marius's bindle—the small bag that contained all his worldly possessions.

Bindles were carried by Walkers like Marius who roved the countryside of the Arovian peninsula.

Marius whispered loudly, "H-Hey!" His curse came with an infuriating stutter. "That's m-mine."

He took a step toward the man.

His clothing snagged. Marius looked down at the side of his pants. A piece of metal had hooked itself onto the seam of his trousers. Marius traced the hook back to its source: the latch on the door to the tent. If there had been time, he would have sighed.

As it was, Marius could only watch as his pants pulled at the door latch which, in turn, pulled at a tent pole. The pole tilted precariously.

In a chain reaction, each pole holding the tent fell. Every pot and pan, and every metal tool hanging inside clanged to the ground or onto one of the sleepers. Marius wasn't sure which made more noise, the crashing metal or the tinkers' curses.

The embers of the cook fire woke up. The tent burst into flames.

Bodies rolled out from under the burning tent. Like them, Marius had the sudden urge to get as far away from the conflagration as possible.

Marius ran.

The flaming tent, attached to his pants by the door latch, raced after him like a dog on his heels. His pants ripped. The fabric fell around his knees, breaking his run into a series of short shuffles.

Marius gamboled past Lespa and her companion: his pants around his knees, the tent on fire, pots and pans falling away on every side, the shouts of the tinkers pursuing him into the night.

Lespa the Astor shook her sharp chin in disbelief. Her companion smiled. His canine teeth flashed in the moonlight.

"That's our mark all right," said Lespa. "Marius the Fool, known in Amok as Prince Pratt—the man with the Jester's Curse."

Chapter Two

The rough bark of the log on which he sat clawed at Marius's backside. He clutched at his tattered pants, keeping them modestly above his waist. The pants were a crazy quilt of colors as befitted a jester. Despite his glum face, Marius's clothing remained comical.

Lespa's hand rested on the hilt of a sword. She kept a cautious eye on the tinkers as they abandoned the campsite, leaving the forest glade to continue down the road to the coast. The tinkers had murder in their eyes.

How strange it was, thought Marius, that the Astor who had just threatened his life was now protecting it.

Overhead, the tree frogs and owls continued to sing, oblivious to the scene unfolding below.

Marius watched the family of tinkers depart. They might have spared him some cord to fix his pants. Of course, they would need the cord to fix the tent he'd just ruined. And they looked like they'd sooner use the cord to string him up by the neck.

A cold sweat ran down Marius's back as the tinkers left him alone in the forest glade with Lespa and her companion.

Though Lespa was an Astor, a sworn agent of the Arovian Empire, she worked alongside the wizards of the White Tower—wizards like Malconus, who had cursed Marius.

The Kingdom of Arovia was at war, though few of its citizens knew it. The White Tower and the Church of the Lady struggled behind the scenes for control of the empire.

Having been cursed by a wizard, Marius had aligned himself with the church.

Lespa, an agent for the wizards, must have found out. She had come to kill him.

Without turning, Lespa spoke to Marius, "Those tinkers want you dead more than I do."

"Get in line," said Marius, without a stutter. The curse must have thought the joke funny enough on its own.

He lurched forward as Lespa slapped him on the back.

She said, "That's what I like about you, fool. Most people would be soiling themselves."

Wait a few minutes, thought Marius. The curse had once made him foul his pants to avoid capture. He hoped they weren't in for a repeat performance.

Lespa's burly companion grunted. He emptied Marius's bindle onto the mossy ground of the woods. Picking up the contents piece by piece, the man counted: "One dining knife, one filthy blanket, one tin cup, one red tunic, three oversized silver rings, one pair of brass knuckles," the man examined these with an air of professional curiosity, "and various twigs."

The twigs were a collection of herbs. Marius winced as his precious spices fell to the ground. Dinners from now on, if he lived, would be bland affairs.

The rings, the cup, and the brass knuckles had been gifts from the tinkers. They had appreciated Marius's ability to gather a crowd. In the villages along the way, Marius had performed bits of juggling to bring buyers to the table.

The tinkers, eager to reward Marius for his contributions, gave him a set of metal rings for juggling. Skillful in manipulating metal, the tinkers had fashioned the rings so that they could be joined together to appear like links in a chain. The crowds appreciated the bit of fake magic in his act.

The tin cup was similarly useful. Marius employed it, not for drinking, but as a codpiece to protect his nethers from the curse's perverse sense of humor.

The brass knuckles were self-explanatory. The tinkers wanted to give Marius some protection but were perplexed as to what kind of weapon they might responsibly give to a fool. Eventually, they decided that anyone who came within arm's reach of a fool deserved what he got and had made him the set of brass knuckles.

Marius's shoulders slumped as the Astor picked up and discarded his precious belongings. He didn't have much to show for his sixteen years of life.

Interestingly, though, the man did not mention the coins that were hidden in the bindle. Perhaps he hadn't found the hidden pocket sewn into the fabric. Or perhaps, thought Marius, the big Astor had pocketed the coins.

Marius knew it was foolhardy to ask after the money. Yet, since Marius was, in fact, a fool, idiocy was expected of him.

He opened his mouth to ask after the coins, only to be interrupted by Lespa.

"No more of your stuttering, fool." She toed the contents of the bindle, separating the rust colored tunic from the blanket. "This tunic is the color of House Cervix?"

Although spoken as a question, Lespa needed no answer. She knew Marius was a runaway slave. Lespa had discovered his story when they first met, before he ever reached Amok, as he pled for his life at the point of Lespa's knife.

He'd been traveling with a fellow Walker named Asadal.

Marius's brow hardened at the memory.

Unbeknownst to Marius, Asadal spied for the church. Lespa had tracked Asadal. But the old man escaped, using Marius as a distraction. For good measure, he'd stolen Marius's bindle as well.

"Pay attention, fool," said Lespa.

She drew a curved knife out of its sheath. Moonlight glinted off the sharp edges. Marius remembered the blade vividly from their previous encounter.

"You know what we do to runaway slaves?" said Lespa. The tip of the dagger danced in front of his face.

Her large companion stood back with his arms folded, looking bored.

Marius, meanwhile, was giving Lespa, and particularly her knife, his undivided attention. In answer to her question, he nodded. He knew she had the power to kill him.

"Good." Lespa continued, "You've been busy since we last met. Quite a few people want you dead."

Marius ticked off a list in his mind. Lespa saved him the trouble.

"The majordomo at your former estate, named Sivinius, was less than complimentary. He said you were possibly the worst slave he'd ever seen." Lespa paused. "I believe him."

Marius blinked. Not at the insult. Playing the fool, he'd gotten used to that. Rather, he wondered how his rival, Sivinius, had gotten promoted over the old majordomo, Flavorus.

He'd heard that the estate where he'd been a slave had been given in dowry to the fifth son of House Polonius. Sivinius must have wormed his way into the new master's good graces.

Lespa continued, unaware of Marius's roving thoughts. "Sivinius offered us a reward for your return."

Sivinius probably wanted to finish what he'd started. After all, it had been Sivinius who had tricked the wizard into cursing Marius.

It was wise of Sivinius to want Marius dead. He'd sworn revenge.

Lespa poked the point of her dagger into a gloved finger, emphasizing the blade's sharpness. Her short brown hair swept away from her face coming to a tail behind her head as tight as the blade she held. She might have been beautiful, thought Marius, if she wasn't so evil.

Lespa continued, oblivious to the turmoil inside him. Or perhaps she was probing for a reaction: a way of poking at him without using the dagger.

"After you left House Cervix and after our brief encounter, you offended nearly every respectable citizen in the city of Amok," Lespa paused. "House Marcel has a bounty on your head."

Marius wasn't surprised that Sybil's house wanted him dead. The curse had given quite a performance at House Marcel. The curse had spurned Sybil and ruined her father's dinner party, causing the old man to overturn the head table. He'd tried to kill Marius with his bare hands while Marius ran around spouting dirty rhymes at the guests.

Marius had been lucky to escape with his head. He wouldn't have, had the High Priest of Amok not interfered on his behalf.

High Priest Campri had also helped Marius save his beloved Irina from slavery to House Marcel—not that she'd given him a second look.

"Sweet," she'd called him. After he'd risked his life for her. Being called sweet by Irina stung worse than being called ugly by Lespa.

In the end, Marius had reluctantly aligned himself with the Church of the Lady in its battle against the White Tower. Not that he believed in the Lady. That was a step too far.

Lespa poked the dagger into Marius's cheek. It stung. "I'm talking to you, fool!"

He was pretty sure she'd drawn blood. Great, he thought. All he needed was a scar to add to his already garish appearance.

"As I was saying," said Lespa. "A lot of people want you dead."

"You don't have to tell me," said Marius.

Lespa turned to her companion. The knife dangled nonchalantly in her hand, coming dangerously near Marius's eye.

"You see what I mean about this one, Bithius?" said Lespa. "He has spirit."

The big man shrugged his shoulders noncommittally.

"I'm telling you all this, fool," said Lespa, returning her attention to Marius, "because I want you to know that I own you."

Lespa put her heel on the log beside Marius. She leaned on her knee. He studiously avoided staring at her tight leather pants. Marius held his hands in his lap, begging the curse not to trigger an embarrassing reaction.

"I can find you anytime I want. I can kill you anytime I want. Or I could tell your former friends where to find you," said Lespa. "Do you know why I haven't?"

Marius couldn't begin to guess.

"I haven't killed you, fool, because you are going to help me find your friend Asadal."

"My f-friend?" Marius had been worried that Lespa had been sent to kill him for working with the church. Marius hadn't expected Lespa to ask him about Asadal. At the mention of the man's name, Marius's face clouded.

"He's not my f-friend!" Marius stammered. "He stole m-my bindle and left m-me to die while he escaped."

The side of Lespa's lip rose a fraction of an inch. It was the closest thing to a smile Marius had ever seen on her face. She appeared to be waxing nostalgic.

"I remember that night," said Lespa. "I also remember sparing your life. In return, I want you to do one thing. Tell me where he is."

It wasn't a request.

"Y-you can have him a-after I'm through with him," said Marius.

Bithius, the big Astor, laughed. "He's a fighter, eh?"

Lespa's smile continued to grow, her lips receding from her predatory teeth.

"We want him alive. Remember that, or you won't be."

Without warning, Lespa grabbed Marius by the back of the neck bringing the dagger toward his throat.

Marius waited, expecting to feel the blade bite into his exposed neck. His heart skipped a beat.

Her smile disappeared. "We saw Asadal nearby, only one night ago. Where do you think he was going?"

Marius shrugged. He didn't dare speak. The dagger's keen edge hovered just shy of his throat. Marius gulped, his Adam's apple nearly slicing itself on the knife.

Lespa released his head. Marius fell backward. His torn pants, stuck to the log, refused to come with him. He lay on his back, face up, half naked.

Lespa's companion chuckled.

"Don't encourage him, Bithius," said Lespa.

Clumsily, Marius pulled himself back onto the log.

"I'm going to catch Asadal," said Lespa, "and you're going to help me." She replaced the knife into its leather scabbard. "If you don't help me, if you don't have any news next time we meet, if you're not valuable to me, you know what happens." She slid her thumb under her chin making an ominous slicing sound.

Marius sat very still.

Lespa and her colleague turned to leave. Their leather armor protested at the sudden movement, silencing the forest animals, who sensed danger.

Though he was glad to see their backs, Marius's curiosity got the better of him. He called out, foolish though it was.

"How did you f-find me?"

Lespa shot him a look reserved for an ignorant child.

"You've been drawing signs pointing to yourself ever since you left Amok, idiot."

Marius nodded dumbly. True enough.

Walkers like Marius communicated in symbols, marks left along the wayside. Anyone with sufficient knowledge could read them. Marius had taken to adding a mark of his own, the sign of a jester's hat with an arrow pointing in his direction.

He thought Asadal might see it and come looking. When he did, Marius intended to give the old man a piece of his mind. He would make Asadal explain why he'd deserted him.

Marius hadn't thought about anyone else following the trail. His mind went to House Marcel and the very specific threats Sybil had made against certain parts of his anatomy.

If Lespa had found him, others might not be far behind.

Lespa and Bithius left. Marius breathed a sigh of relief.

They were not going in his direction, toward Seatown.

He had been told by High Priest Campri to meet Notori, an ally of the church, at the fair in Seatown.

Notori was Marius's ticket out of Arovia and maybe out of the curse. If Marius was lucky, he'd be at sea before Lespa ever missed him. No more Astors, no more House Marcel, and best of all, no more Asadal. He would start a new life.

Marius got up from the log and began to repack his bindle. He tied his meager possessions in the cloth, noting as he did that Bithius had not, in fact, stolen his hidden coins.

Marius shrugged. Though he had only sixteen years of experience in the world, Marius knew there was no explaining some people. Bithius would have stood by and let Lespa murder him, yet the Astor hadn't stolen from him.

Resting the bindle on his shoulder, Marius contemplated whether he should spend the rest of the night in the clearing or move on. If he stayed, the tinkers might come back to look for him. If he walked toward Seatown they might be waiting for him on the road.

Marius scratched his head.

"Going so soon?"

Marius nearly jumped out of his colorful jester's suit. His pants slipped.

A gentle breeze stirred the branches of the trees.

A man stepped from behind a trunk. The very man Lespa had been looking for. The man who had abandoned Marius so long ago. In the waning moonlight, in the middle of the forest glade, stood the man himself—the man Marius had been hoping and dreading to see: Asadal the Walker.

Chapter Three

Asadal stood in the glade, his dark skin looking as ancient and weathered as ever wearing his tunic of rough wool and matching bindle. His long black hair, curled in tight braids, fell over his head, ending in silver-white tips. On his swarthy face was the usual bright smile. His thin walking stick twitched up and down causing the muscles in his forearm to coil.

Marius clenched his fists. It would be a fair fight, the sixty-year-old Asadal versus the sixteen-year-old Marius. Only, Marius didn't intend to make it fair. He reached into his bindle coming away with a pair of brass knuckles and the fancy dinner knife he'd stolen from House Marcel.

His bindle fell to the ground.

Asadal raised an eyebrow.

The last Marius had seen of Asadal was the back of his head as he'd sprinted into the woods, leaving Marius at the tender mercies of Lespa.

She had threatened to end Marius's life, twice now, because of the old man.

True, Asadal had kept Marius alive after he'd been kicked out of House Cervix. Asadal saved Marius from starvation and taught him the way of the Walker. But that didn't make them even.

"Wh-what are you doing here?" Marius demanded.

The darkened woods seemed to close around Marius as his anger intensified.

Asadal raised his hands to his side. He spoke with a thick island accent untamed by his years in Arovia. "I need your help."

"You helped yourself last time I saw you."

Just a few minutes earlier, Marius had again been looking down the length of Lespa's dagger. The cut it made on his cheek was fresh. He dabbed at it with the back of his hand. It came away wet and red.

The comfortable commute to Seatown with the family of tinkers had been ruined thanks to Asadal. Marius had nearly been killed, again, for this man.

Asadal didn't react to Marius's visible frustration. "You got to sail where the sea takes you."

Marius shook his head. Asadal was forever speaking like that.

Before, traveling the roads of Arovia together, he'd been enthralled by Asadal's experience and by the stories he told. Now, Asadal's platitudes sounded foolish.

Marius had learned to survive on his own on the streets of Amok. Before, he'd owed Asadal his life. Marius considered the debt paid when Asadal left him to die.

Marius pointed up the road. "Your friend Lespa was here. I guess you were in the woods, watching her torture me?"

"Your stutter's not too bad," said Asadal, ignoring Marius's protests. He examined Marius carefully up and down. "Your curse, that's still bad."

Marius had been so mad that he hadn't noticed the absence of his vocal tic. Of course, having it pointed out to him only made the stutter worse.

"I c-could call Lespa!"

Asadal shrugged. "Then call her. I'll take the road as it comes."

By the Lady, Marius cursed, was the man mentally deficient? Was Asadal not even sorry for his betrayal or for the trouble he'd caused?

Marius stuck out a hand, "My b-bindle. Give it back."

Asadal's eyes narrowed, as though he were thinking about the request.

A bird sitting on the limb of a tree filled the silence with its gentle song.

Marius held out a hand, "My bindle."

Asadal pointed with his thin stick. "It's there, on the ground where you dropped it."

Marius grimaced. "Not that one. My o-old bindle. You s-stole it."

Asadal smiled, his accent strengthened, proportional to his mirth, "That old thing?"

"Why d-did you do it?"

The old Walker flicked his stick up and down. No answer was forthcoming.

"High Priest Campri says you're going to Seatown," said Asadal.

"Don't change the subject," said Marius. The priest has said that Marius had been touched by the Lady, that he had a destiny. Marius didn't believe in the Lady or fate.

Asadal replied in his strange accent. His vowels were too round for the Arovian peninsula. "Strange things happening in Seatown."

"So what?" said Marius.

Asadal raised an elbow toward his ear in a half-shrug. "Campri asked me to look into it; to check in on you."

"I'm doing f—fine."

Asadal nodded, "So I see."

Marius couldn't believe that this was all there was to their conversation. After all that time together and apart.

"So that's it?" he asked.

Asadal paused before responding. He drew a repetitive pattern in the dirt with his stick. "The Lady has her ways."

Marius had had enough of the Lady, "Like the w-way she let me get c-cursed? The way she l-let this happen to me?" Marius waved a hand up and down, inviting Asadal to look at what the curse had done to him, at the spectacle he'd become.

He'd been a normal teenager. Awkward, certainly, as anyone still getting used to their full growth might be. But he'd been normal. He'd had employment, albeit as a slave. He'd had friends.

Now, because of the curse, he had nothing. His legs and arms felt constantly too long. His mind worked quickly, but his tongue and mouth couldn't keep up. His words came out slurred and stuttered. Everyone thought him a fool.

And he acted the part. He had to act foolish. Acting stupid had been the only way to keep the curse from making him do something worse.

By embracing his role as a fool, Marius fought against the curse.

The wizard who had cursed him said that the Jester's Curse would eventually take over, turning him into the fool he pretended to be. Still, Marius fought it. If that's what it meant to be touched by the Lady, she could keep her hands to herself.

Asadal looked him squarely in the eyes. Marius could see the compassion behind the look. He turned away, too angry to accept Asadal's pity.

Asadal said, "The church needs your help."

"The church can go h-hang. And so can you."

Asadal continued, speaking quietly. His stick doodled in the dirt, swirling back and forth. "Course you don't have to help. But if you don't—"

"Is that a threat?" said Marius. "I didn't think the church m-made threats."

Asadal wagged his head from side to side as though weighing his response. "The church doesn't make threats. But there's Notori. He doesn't do things same as the church."

Marius swallowed. His Adam's apple bobbed in his neck. High Priest Campri had said that Notori could help him—that Notori might find a way to lift the curse, a way that didn't involve dedicating his life to the church.

Now Asadal was threatening to take that assistance away.

"What do y-you want me to do?"

Asadal grinned. His white teeth practically lit the clearing. "Keep your eyes and ears open. That's all. There's a storm brewing in Seatown. Trouble between the Lady and the White Tower."

"P-perfect," said Marius. "Lespa wants me to l-lookout for you, and you want me to l-lookout for wizards. But who's looking out for m-me?"

Asadal reached into his bindle.

Marius raised the brass knuckles. The metal ribs felt smooth and cold under his fingers.

Asadal tossed Marius a worn-out rag.

He caught it, nearly slicing himself with his knife in the process. Even in the moonlight, he recognized the rag at once. It was the bindle that a kind farmer's wife had once given him—the bindle that Asadal had stolen. It was empty but still intact. Asadal had kept it all that time.

Marius examined it, running the cloth through his fingers, not only to be sure it was his but also to make sure Asadal wasn't trying to trick him into sneaking contraband into Seatown. Marius felt nothing, no concealed pocket, no strange bulge.

Asadal spoke up. "I took your bindle because I'd hidden something in it. Something for the Lady's work. I didn't think Lespa would harm a fool." Asadal gestured toward Marius leaving the obvious unstated. Lespa hadn't killed Marius.

Asadal held up his hands to forestall Marius's protest. "I know you're not a fool. Maybe one of the only people in Arovia who does." Asadal rubbed at his chin. "There's work for us in Seatown. Dangerous work between the Lady and the White Tower. If you need my help," said Asadal, "if you find yourself in a bad way and need someone to look out for you, remember that cloth. Tie it round your arm. That will be a sign between you and me. If I see that tied round your arm, I'll come running."

Marius looked at the worn fabric again. Whatever was happening in Seatown, Marius doubted it could be any more dangerous than standing in a dark glade in the forest, a runaway slave, talking to a wanted man with a brace of Astors within hailing distance.

Marius considered Asadal's request. It sounded like something he could accept. Asadal only asked him to do what he would already be doing, keeping a close lookout for danger.

Marius nodded. "When I g-get to Seatown. I'll keep my eyes open," he said, clenching the fabric in his fist. "But you and I are th-through."

"As you like," said Asadal.

"When Lespa c-comes after me again, which she will, I w-won't give you up. We're Walkers. But I d-don't have to like you."

"What will be, will be," said Asadal holding out his hands in a beatific attitude. "The Wind and the Dove and the Fire go with you, Marius." Asadal invoked the benediction of the Lady.

"And the devil with you." Marius picked up his bindle and struck out in the direction of Seatown, any tinkers on the road be damned. It were better for them that they not encounter him that night. They had forged the brass knuckles. Marius was mad enough to use them.

* * *

Most of the night he spent walking, thinking about what Asadal had said. Now, with the first rays of the sun, Marius stopped beside a large stone on the side of the road. He had a duty to other Walkers to warn them that an Astor was nearby. Asadal had taught him his duty as a Walker, a member of the loose-knit band of vagabonds that roved the highways of the Kingdom of Arovia and the roads that spread into the Arovian Empire beyond.

He would not shirk his responsibilities as a Walker just because he hated Asadal. In fact, it wouldn't surprise him to learn that his old travelling companion had already made the same mark in whatever direction he had gone that night. Never mind that Lespa and other Astors were adept at reading Walker symbols. Forewarned, as Asadal always said, was forearmed.

A final scratch completed the sign of the Astor. Marius stood back from the rock and examined his work as the sun rose over the hills beyond the woods.

On the stone, a pair of carved eyes stared at him from atop a star. The interior of the star had been shaded, meaning that the Astor was up to no good. The eyes, which were open, meant the Astor was close by.

Any Walker worth their salt could judge the age of a mark at a glance. Fresh marks like this were white with sharp edges. Older marks were obscured over time by rain and by the dust of the road.

Marius had added his own small touch to the sign. The eyes of the Astor, instead of looking ahead, were staring toward an adjacent symbol, the sign of a jester's hat with an arrow beneath it, pointing in the direction of Seatown.

Maybe it was foolish to keep drawing his personal mark. After all, Lespa had used it to track him. Asadal had probably done the same.

On the other hand, to Marius the mark felt like a confirmation of his existence. He lived on the road without a fixed home. He had no family, no friends to speak of. Marius existed in a perpetual state of change, unsure where he would sleep that night or where his next meal might come from. Leaving his mark on the stones as he passed made him feel just a little less alone. Other Walkers would see it. Though they might not know him personally, they would come to know him by his mark. They would know that the Jester had been there, that he was alive, that he existed.

Marius brushed the dirt from his trousers and picked up his bindle. He set off down the road toward Seatown, thinking about Asadal as he walked.

The roads of the Kingdom of Arovia consisted of hard-packed dirt about ten paces wide. Stone markers on the sides of the road told the distance and occasionally pointed to a nearby village. More accurate for Marius's purposes were the Walker symbols etched onto the official markers or onto stones nearby. These symbols brought the road to life—telling a weary traveler where he might find a safe bed, a warm meal, or a place to work. The Walker symbols read like a book, written by those who had trod this path before and speaking of the wonders they had discovered along the way.

Although Marius had been born into slavery, occupying a comfortable berth as a house slave, he couldn't imagine a better life than the one he enjoyed on the road.

Marius took each day at a time, just as Asadal had taught him. The old man had so many sayings.

Asadal said that, to a hungry man, no food is rotten. He taught Marius to sleep when and where he could and to always look poorer than he actually was. Asadal also said that a Walker remembers every place he'd been but home.

Marius thought of his own home, now run by his rival, Sivinius. It was a place to which he'd never willingly return, at least not until he could extract his revenge on Sivinius for having gotten him cursed.

At least, thought Marius, Sivinius would be easy to find. Most slaves never strayed far from the estate.

Marius let his mind wander through fantasies of revenge. The thought of the horrible tortures he might inflict on Sivinius brought a smile to his lips.

But Irina wouldn't like it.

That thought brought Marius back to the present, back to the dirt road. He stepped over a pile of ox droppings.

Irina, the former slave of House Marcel, wouldn't like him taking revenge on Sivinius or on anyone for that matter.

In his mind's eye, Marius saw her dressed in the light blue tunic of House Marcel, and then, as he'd last seen her, wearing a robe of the Church of the Lady where she'd taken sanctuary.

Irina had a kind of magic that made Marius want to be a better person. Being around her had changed him, and not just because he'd fallen in love.

She wanted him to stop acting the fool. Of course, she hadn't known about his curse. She didn't know that he had to act foolish in order to prevent the curse from fully taking over.

Marius kicked a small rock off the road. It made his toe sting, but the pain was a welcome distraction from the thought of how he had disappointed Irina with his antics.

The evil wizard Malconus had threatened to kill her because she helped Marius. The wizard meant for the spell to grow inside Marius, expanding until it consumed his soul, making him entirely a fool.

Marius struggled against the spell. He'd beaten the curse at its own game, discovering that the curse couldn't take control of his body if Marius himself acted foolishly.

So, Marius played the fool.

It wasn't fair.

In his mind, he was a normal sixteen-year-old boy. But because of how he acted, others saw him as an object of ridicule, an unfortunate accident of birth.

He wanted to plead his case. He wasn't an idiot. His brain worked, but his body betrayed him. He had to act the way he did, all because of that blasted curse.

Marius let out a long sigh born of frustration.

He'd wanted to tell Irina all his troubles, but the curse wouldn't let him. He wanted to profess his love, but when he'd finally managed to say it, she'd called him "sweet."

"Sweet." The word burned its way to the bottom of his stomach.

That's all she thought of him. But why should she think otherwise? He was a fool.

Yet he had to survive, and for Marius, survival meant playing the fool.

After all, that was the first rule of the Walker: to survive. Asadal had taught him that.

The old man had certainly followed his own advice, deserting Marius, practically shoving him into Lespa's hands.

Marius's fist clenched involuntarily at the thought. Sometimes, in his daydreams he fought her and won. Sometimes in those dreams, the beautiful Astor rewarded him with a kiss, sometimes with more.

Marius shook his head to clear away the thoughts. He loved Irina. And besides, Lespa was crazy.

Crazy enough to keep track of him after all this time. And not only Lespa. A lot of people wanted Marius dead.

But things weren't so bad for all that. Like Asadal always said, bad as the horizon looks, appreciate the road under your feet.

Marius had been born into a life of slavery. As a boy, Marius wouldn't have dreamt of a life of travel as a Walker.

Not that life as a house slave had been bad. He'd been taken care of like a prize bull.

At first, he'd been so scared to walk away from that life that he'd nearly starved. If Asadal hadn't found him, Marius would have died.

Since then, he'd learned to adapt.

Thankfully Irina wouldn't have to learn the same hard lessons. High Priest Campri of Amok had not only secured her freedom but had offered her a position serving the church. She seemed happy.

Campri had also offered Marius a place with the church and had offered to remove the Jester's Curse. All Marius had to do was to swear loyalty to the Lady.

The price seemed too high.

In the end, Campri advised Marius to travel to the coast, to the city of Seatown, as much to avoid the wrath of House Marcel as to meet a certain man named Notori.

Notori ran a circus and would be in Seatown during the fair.

According to High Priest Campri, Notori might help Marius find a cure for his curse and get revenge on Malconus, the wizard who'd cursed him.

Marius knew nothing else about Notori. Not what he did for the church. Not what he looked like, except that he hated wizards.

Campri had mentioned, however, that even though Notori fought alongside the church, he did not bow his knee to the Lady or give heed to her signs: the Fire, the Dove, and the Wind.

Marius respected the man's position. The Lady had given Marius precious little help so far.

But if Asadal was to be believed, Notori would not help Marius unless Marius, in turn, helped Asadal solve the church's problem in Seatown.

Marius's mouth turned down at the corners. The battle between priests and the wizards had nothing to do with him. Yet he'd been caught up in its net. The wizard, Malconus, had cursed him, and the priest, Campri, had offered to help.

Marius stopped on the side of the road to tighten the makeshift belt he'd made for his pants.

He considered abandoning the colorful, torn pants. He could wear his old slave uniform.

However, as a runaway slave, such an outfit wouldn't be safe. He shouldn't be carrying it at all. He should have gotten rid of the rust-colored tunic of House Cervix.

Lespa had recognized it immediately when Bithius pulled it out of his bindle. Yet Marius remained loathe to part with the clothing, the last remnants of his old, beloved life as a slave.

Tightening the belt, satisfied that the curse couldn't expose him to passersby, Marius shouldered his bindle.

With any luck, he could lose himself in the city or maybe even catch a boat beyond the reach of Lespa and her hulking companion, Bithius. Or maybe things could still be salvaged between him and Notori. Only time would tell.

He heard a team of oxen approaching from behind.

Marius turned to see a cart full of vegetables being pulled to the nearest market, probably Seatown. Marius could smell the acidic tang of ripe tomatoes. His stomach rumbled.

The driver took one look at Marius and snorted derisively. "Get out of the road, Walker! The rainbow vomit you're wearing is upsetting my team."

Marius reached for a comeback.

Drivers and Walkers occupied the roads of Arovia. A rivalry had developed between them, along with a certain amount of animosity, usually on the part of the Drivers.

Marius always supposed it was because the Drivers longed to be free like the Walkers but lacked the courage. Drivers traveled, but only at the mercy of their cargo.

Marius grimaced as the cart rolled by. Had he been able to muster a suitable insult, he might've earned a ride on the back of the wagon.

That was the deal. The cleverest insult won.

Drivers appreciated a good invective. Problem was, drivers swore so vividly that Marius had difficulty beating them.

His former companion Asadal had no problems. He'd traveled the world and could always come up with a shocking retort.

And there he was. On the back of the wagon, Asadal sat grinning widely. Asadal patted the seat next to him, offering Marius a ride. Marius shook his head. He hadn't forgiven the old Walker. He never would.

The cart bearing Asadal disappeared around the next bend, bound, as was Marius, for Seatown.

With Asadal ahead of him and the Astors following behind, Marius considered sitting down in the road, simply refusing to move. But he knew that trouble would eventually find him one way or another. The Jester's Curse would see to it. The curse would never let him rest.

Chapter Four

Seatown stank. Not the kind of stink that a person could eventually get used to, like some of the farms Marius had worked on while travelling as a Walker.

No, the city of Seatown stank in new and various ways with each step he took, with each gutter he passed.

Asadal said something was wrong in Seatown. The air itself seemed a likely choice for the culprit.

Seatown was unlike any city Marius had ever seen. Amok and even Zeno, the capital of Arovia, sat on the flat plains of the peninsula. Seatown, meanwhile, fell away down a steep hill toward the ocean.

Family dwellings populated the top of the hill. Tall, narrow houses rose inside courtyards surrounded by thin walls. The walls would hardly afford any real protection, though they might deter thieves.

The houses and their walls were painted with bright colors, causing the entire city to resemble Marius's jester's tunic. From the top of the hill where Marius entered the city, the houses cascaded toward the blue ocean, looking like a set of colorful, giant steps.

Through cracks in the gates, Marius could see green-ery inside the walled courtyards. Fruit trees hung over walls into the street. Marius helped himself to an orange. No one seemed to think it strange. He took three more, sticking them into his bindle.

Larger dwellings, presumably those of the rich, sat at the very top of the hill. These he passed first, though he took his time doing so.

As he strolled down the cobblestone street, people stared at him. Marius was used to it. The Jester's Curse made him walk funny, his ankles, knees, and hips op-erating independently. He tripped along like a happy drunk. The silver rings hanging from his bindle clanked together creating a pleasant jingle.

Marius's eyes roved past the gawkers, looking for signs of the Walkers scratched into the walls of the hous-es. He looked for signs pointing to a hot meal and for warnings against angry dogs or worse.

In Seatown, he'd been warned, if you got too drunk or looked vulnerable, you might find yourself stuck on a boat working the long voyage to Machoo.

Although Marius had been a slave and liked his old job, the free life of a Walker had begun to hold some ap-peal. He'd not willingly go back into slavery.

Even working for the Lady was not something that he did willingly. Marius worked with the church because it seemed the best way to get revenge on the wizard Mal-conus, and eventually, he hoped, on his old rival Siv-inius, who had gotten him cursed, which had gotten him thrown out of House Cervix.

To do that, Marius first had to connect with the man named Notori at the fair in Seatown.

But to meet Notori, Marius had to help Asadal with whatever danger lurked in Seatown. He kept a sharp lookout for signs of trouble.

Marius scanned the walls for the sign of the Astor: a star with a pair of eyes atop it. If Lespa and Bithius were already in Seatown, he wanted to know about it.

As he passed the colorful houses, Marius found a welcoming sign: the symbol of three loaves atop a table. These pointed the way to a hot meal.

Imposing on others was part of the Walker's way of life, an art form. Like all the arts, those with talent, persistence, and a healthy dose of luck, got rewarded.

Marius's stomach rumbled at the thought of a warm meal. Of course, since Bithius hadn't stolen his money, Marius had sufficient coin to buy breakfast at a local inn. But why spend when you could beg?

He followed the symbol downhill till he spied a corresponding mark etched into a light-blue wall. The scratches lay beneath a weathered patina, indicating that the house had a long-standing reputation for hospitality to Walkers.

Had it been otherwise, the mark would have been scratched out and replaced with a curse.

To Marius's eyes, the house inside the wall looked rich. Certainly wealthy enough to spare a bowl of soup for a beggar.

Marius walked toward the gate thinking what sort of trick he might perform to gain entrance.

Before he could reach it, however, the gate opened. A woman spilled out, barreling headlong into Marius's chest. As tall and skinny as he was, Marius fell under the woman's weight like a piece of wheat hit by a scythe. They toppled together onto the stone street.

The woman looked up. The fear in her eyes went beyond concern over hitting a stranger or possibly injuring herself.

Marius, as a former slave, had learned to read people, to anticipate their wishes. He felt a sense of profound wrongness emanating from the woman. Asadal's warning of danger in Seatown leapt into his mind.

"Are y-you okay?" said Marius, wishing his stupid stutter would take the day off, especially in moments of crisis.

The woman blinked, seeming to come to her senses. She looked around, realizing that she was sitting in the street facing a stranger.

In that moment, Marius captured an impression of the woman. She was blonde and not too much older than him, in her twentieth year perhaps. Round cheekbones stood guard over a pleasant mouth.

She wore the tunic of a house slave, though he didn't recognize the aquamarine color. Perhaps she belonged to a lesser house or to a local one, one without a presence in Zeno.

Over the tunic she wore an apron. Mentally, Marius lumped her in with the kitchen slaves, which brought to mind the love of his life, Irina, who'd worked in the kitchen of House Marcel, buying goods from the market.

"My son," said the woman, "has gone missing."

Marius squinted. She didn't look old enough to have a son, much less one that could walk.

"I'm s-sure he's all right," said Marius.

The woman looked at him sideways as if recognizing him for the first time.

She didn't immediately heap verbal abuse on him. Marius took that as a good sign. He pressed his advantage.

"What's his n-name?"

"Jank," she said. "His name is Jank and he's not supposed to leave the house."

"H-how old is Jank?"

Marius had grown up in the capital of Zeno. Though a child could get lost in those labyrinthine streets, Marius failed to see how a boy could go missing in a town as small as Seatown, especially where navigation was as simple as going up or down the hill. Marius suspected the boy had gotten himself "lost" to avoid his chores.

"He's eight."

Marius blinked. If Jank was eight, then the woman had to be— He didn't get a chance to finish the calculation. The woman stood up and began looking around, obviously ready to speed off in search of Jank.

Marius hopped up, "I'll help you l-l-look."

The woman nodded her appreciation before rushing past Marius on the way to a neighbor's house or perhaps to check a favorite hiding spot.

Marius watched her as she passed. Jank's mother wasn't bad looking at all.

He made a mental note to be on the lookout for a boy named Jank wearing an aquamarine tunic. Jank would probably make it home on his own. If he didn't, a boy like that shouldn't be hard to find in a city of this size. And if his mother indeed worked in the kitchen, finding young Jank might be Marius's ticket into the pantry.

Marius rested his hand on his hips. The colorful houses stepped cheerfully down the hill. The sun glinted off the ocean. A soft wind carried several large birds inland.

He longed to breathe in the salty ocean air. But the terrible stench of rotting fish filled his nostrils.

Even so, Seatown didn't seem nearly as dangerous as Asadal had implied. Marius walked down the hill with a bounce in his awkward step.

He had hardly started again when an old woman, dressed in black and wearing a hood stepped out of a narrow alley. Marius would have paid her no attention. She didn't seem wealthy enough to be a target for his begging. But she motioned to him furtively, waving him to the place where she stood.

Marius gave her his best crooked smile.

The old woman stood in the shadow of an alley. A dark hood obscured her face. She spoke with a voice as dry as a smoldering log. "Are you a Walker?"

Marius bobbed his head up and down. He didn't feel like giving reign to his stutter.

Suddenly, the old woman grabbed his wrist. The force of her grip startled Marius. She seemed too old for so vital a strength. She looked at his hand, turning it over, bending to peer at his palm. She examined it closely. He could feel her breath on his skin.

Her head snapped back, looking into his eyes. The wrinkles on her face seemed to blend into the dark fabric of her hood, but her eyes were of a vivid blue, tinged with madness.

"You must abandon Seatown," said the woman.

Marius could only stare at the strange creature.

"I have seen the future." Her voice rattled. "Fear the new tide. For at the turn of the new tide, a Walker will die!"

Marius's mouth moved but no sound emerged.

The old woman disappeared into the shadows of the alley, leaving Marius to consider what she'd said.

The noonday sunlight suddenly didn't seem as warm. The houses didn't seem as colorful and inviting. The stench remained unchanged.

* * *

Marius walked down the hill lost in thought.

The old woman had said that a Walker would die before the new tide turned. To Marius, who had been born far from the sea, the concept of a new tide held no meaning. The old woman might have meant tonight for all he knew. Then again, she looked as crazy as a sewer rat. Maybe she spoke her dire predictions over every Walker that entered the city gates.

At the base of the hill, Marius found himself in the central hub of the city, a rotary with streets branching off like spokes on a wheel.

In front of him, a tall statue rose in the middle of the hub, an image of the Lady facing out onto the waters of the bay. A delicately carved dove rested on her outstretched hand. Her garment rippled as if blown by a steady breeze. Her other hand held a large lantern. Marius could see why a fishing village would value such a strong image of the Lady watching over them as they went to sea, giving them wind for their sails, her light guiding them home.

Beyond the statue, a lively market sprawled across the streets, leading toward the port where the masts of tall ocean-going vessels could be seen above the market stalls. Marius could make out the roofs of great warehouses that must hold merchandise from the sea. To his right, the buildings quickly gave way to a series of jagged rocks that separated the roiling ocean from land.

Marius got his first view of the ocean. The way it crashed against the rocky coast made the prospect of taking a dip decidedly unattractive, especially since Marius didn't know how to swim.

Instead, Marius strolled among the stalls in the market, looking for a bit of food and keeping an eye out for Jank.

His mood had sobered. Asadal had warned him that danger lay ahead in Seatown. Now, the woman in black had issued a dire prediction. Then again, thought Marius, she hadn't said that he would die, just that a Walker would die. He broke into a grin, she could have meant Asadal. That happy thought put a bit of the old strut back in his step.

* * *

The market in Seatown held more fish than the ocean. Stacked like cordwood, the fish stared at Marius through round, sightless eyes. Their gaping mouths hung open as though surprised at their fate.

He stared at a huge, red fish that lay in a barrel on top of hundreds of its smaller, silver kin.

He stopped to gawk at a creature with too many slimy legs and no discernable face. Nearby, buckets of water held tiny, wriggling tubes.

In a corner of the market hung a fish larger than Marius himself. The fish had hundreds of sharp teeth, though they hadn't done it much good in the end. The toothy fish hung by its tail while a burly man hacked away at its side with a sharp cleaver. Curiosity getting the better of him, Marius moved closer to examine its teeth: row upon row. The urge to touch one felt almost irresistible. He might have done it, had the teeth not looked sharp enough to cut through his skin.

A few vendors, perhaps the most desperate among them, hawked their wares at Marius as he passed.

Marius examined a bucket filled with the pink tubes.

A vendor approached him. The man wore a green vest over a blue tunic. The vest parted wide in the middle to accommodate a sizable belly. An unkempt brown mustache obscured his upper lip. He addressed Marius in a growling voice, "That," he said, "is a skin flute."

Marius took a step back. The creature looked disgusting.

"It's good for you," said the vendor. "It makes you manly." He thrust out his forearm making a low, guttural noise.

His belly jiggled with a laugh. Nearby sellers chuckled at Marius's obvious discomfort.

The vendor punched a fat fist into the bucket, returning with a single, squirming tube. "Take a bite."

Marius helps up a hand, declining the treat, "N-n-not cooked?"

"It will heal that stutter," said the smiling merchant.

Marius seriously doubted that.

But small charms had helped to ameliorate the effects of the curse before, like the grass rings Asadal used to weave for him.

Then again, Marius had learned to never refuse an offer of free food, no matter how bizarre. Having nearly starved to death, Marius had returned from the edge of the great beyond much less picky about what he ate.

"Do it," one of the other vendors urged him on.

"Mortimer's offering you a delicacy!" added another.

"You won't regret it, son."

Though he knew he was being put on, Marius couldn't turn it down. What if it did work? What if the grotesque creature had some magical power? People paid good money for the small creatures. Neither its looks nor its smell recommended it. Maybe the creature did have magic.

Marius stretched his neck to take a bite. The vendor, Mortimer, pinched the creature between his thick fingers.

"Careful," he said. "Don't let it bite your lip."

The skin flute, sensing danger through whatever passed for its eyes, suddenly shrunk away.

Marius bit the shopkeeper's thumb.

"By the Lady!" Mortimer cursed.

His friends, who'd been goading Marius, howled with laughter at the vendor's discomfort.

"What's wrong with you?" the man asked.

Marius felt the Jester's Curse taking over. He tried to resist, but the curse took charge of his tongue, "I'd tell you, b-but it would take too long to explain. You don't look too b-bright."

The vendors laughed, all except the man that he'd bitten.

His growling voice dropped even lower, "I don't take that kind of talk from the likes of you." The man grabbed a long fish by the tail, swinging it at Marius's face. Worms dropped away from its rotten flesh as it arced toward him.

Marius held up his hands, dropping his bindle. The rings on the end of his staff came away, catching on the tips of his fingers. He held them up like a shield without a center.

The fish entered the rings. On instinct, Marius twisted the rings. The fish flipped into the air.

One of the merchants gasped.

Two of the rings slipped out of Marius's grasp, following the fish into the air.

As the fish and the rings fell back toward his face, Marius tossed the third ring and held out his hands, intent on catching the fish before it crushed his nose. He felt the curse rejoicing in his discomfort, happy to have been set free once more. Marius knew this little performance wouldn't end well. He wished he had put on his codpiece before entering the city.

He grabbed at the slimy fish. It squirted free of his hands. He caught the two rings instead. Quickly, he abandoned them, tossing them back into the air, so as to be on guard against the fish and the third ring, which had reached the peak of their respective arcs and were threatening him again.

The fish he missed. It plummeted down the front of his shirt and lodged itself in his pants, sliding under the make-shift belt.

With his hands outstretched to the sky, the three rings fell in sequence around his wrists all the way up to his elbows, binding him like a slave ready for a beating.

Marius's legs squirmed. He tried not to think about the maggots abandoning the fish in favor of the nooks and crannies of his pants. The scales of the fish cut at his tender flesh. His thighs stuck together from the slime on the fish. The stench of the rotten thing struck him squarely in his nostrils.

Then his belt slipped.

Marius reached down, snagging his pants with his captured hands before they could fall to the ground.

Around him, a smattering of applause broke out. A cheer went up.

One of the vendors cupped a hand to his mouth, "A fool!"

Another slapped the disgruntled fishmonger on his back, "By the Lady, Mortimer, that was a show."

Even Mortimer couldn't remain angry at the foolish young man. Mollified by the display, a smile came to his lips.

"Well played." He offered Marius his hand. "It's not often that a gawker like you gets one over on us. What's your name, son?"

Marius took a moment to decide. According to Lespa, Marius had a bounty on his head set by House Marcel of Amok. He wouldn't be surprised if his former masters at House Cervix had offered some sort of reward for his capture as well. What if word of the bounties had already reached Seatown?

"Don't you know your own name, boy?" Mortimer stood with his hand still outstretched.

"I'm called the J-jester," said Marius. "The J-jester of Zeno." His hands still clung to his pants.

Abandoning the attempted handshake, Mortimer slapped Marius on his shoulder. "Welcome Jester of Zeno."

Marius bowed as politely as he could, what with his hands clutching his pants and a rotten fish down the front of his trousers.

Mortimer continued, "You're here for the fair?"

Marius nodded, not trusting his mouth after the curse had taken advantage of it earlier.

"You're arrived a bit early. The fair comes with the new tide."

Marius again faced that unfamiliar term. The old woman had said a Walker's death would come at the new tide.

Mortimer must have noticed his lack of comprehension. "At the close of the month, in one week's time the new tide comes. Some call it the Lady's Tide. It is followed in two weeks' time by the Tower Tide."

Their conversation ended as abruptly as it had begun. A group of servants, house slaves by the look of their tunics, entered the street. Immediately, Mortimer and the other merchants turned away from Marius, their attention on the potential customers. Shouts rang out as the vendors hawked their wares.

Marius shuffled, as discreetly as he could, toward a corner of the market.

He pulled the fish out of his pants, depositing it into an open sewer grate. Then he shook his legs till they felt like they would fall off. Marius didn't stop shaking till the squirming in his breaches stopped.

The curse had had a field day in Seatown already. Not that it hadn't been helpful.

Marius felt he'd made a favorable impression with the vendors. He might be able to establish a relationship like the one's he'd had in Amok, where he worked the crowd in return for food or a few coins.

And he'd learned that the fair would take place within a week. He might be a few days early, but that hardly mattered. The main thing was that he hadn't arrived too late. With any luck, Marius could lie low, avoid the danger supposedly infesting Seatown, meet up with Notori, and flee the Arovian peninsula.

All he had to do was to eat, sleep, and stay out of trouble. Surely he could do all that for one week.

Marius could only hope that Notori, the man he'd been sent to meet, would be able to tell him how to rid himself of the curse without resorting to taking orders in the church.

Marius moved through the market, finally gravitating toward the main hub connecting the hill to the rest of the city. He spent the afternoon observing life in the market.

In Amok, he'd made a living in the market. It was the center of any city. Little happened in town that didn't eventually make its way to the gossiping shopkeeps.

He came to a rest near a wooden board where messages were posted.

Though Marius could not read—none of the slaves from House Cervix had been burdened with education—neither could the average citizen of Arovia. Those who read, often read aloud to themselves or to their companions.

With a little patience, Marius got a general impression of the information on the board. Thankfully, it didn't contain a notice about a bounty on the head of a colorfully dressed fool. Nor was a reward posted for a runaway slave from his former house.

The message board carried little of interest to visitors passing through the port. If Asadal wanted to find evidence of danger and mystery in Seatown, he'd have to look elsewhere.

Out of the corner of his eye, Marius caught a flash of white feathers as a bird took to wing. Turning to watch, he caught sight of a boy wearing aquamarine fabric, the same color as the woman who'd previously run into him on the hillside.

When his eyes caught up to the streak of color, Marius found himself staring at a young, sandy-haired boy browsing through the vegetable stalls.

Marius supposed that he'd found the long, lost Jank.

Rising from his position beside the post, Marius shouldered his bindle. He followed the boy through the winding stalls of the market. If he could return the boy to his mother before supper, she might offer Marius a good meal and, who knew, maybe a soft bed for the night. A fool could always dream.

* * *

The boy looked left and right before stepping into a small wooden structure overhanging the ocean.

If the young boy was trying to see if he was being followed, he'd failed miserably.

Marius had tagged along at a distance as the boy passed through the market and into the warehouse district. Marius trailed him through narrow alleys carefully avoiding puddles full of offal that had missed the sewer grates.

Emerging from the warehouses near the ocean, they passed through what Marius could only assume to have been a slave market. Having been born into the profession, he'd never seen the seedier side of the business of buying and selling people. Slaves bound in chains stood in a line beside a crate. A slave atop the crate stood, looking sullen, as a merchant auctioned him off.

The sun had nearly set when Jank and Marius entered a narrow lane full of rickety wooden shops.

These were little better than shacks. The wares outside bore thick coats of grime, the accumulation of dust and sand and seawater.

Undeterred by an apparent lack of sales, the merchants had extended their shacks by building out over the sea wall. The buildings hung precariously over the water. Several of the shops were two or three stories high. Marius wondered what a tall, solid wave would do to the district. Probably clean it up a good bit, he thought.

Something about the place didn't feel right. Marius looked around. Nothing obvious stood out. It took him a few moments to realize what was bothering him: the Jester's Curse liked it here. It was as if the curse found the dilapidated shops as comfortable as a roaring hearth. Marius put a hand to his chest to see whether he was feeling all right—not that he could actually feel the curse, no more than he could feel his soul.

Marius watched as Jank stepped into one of the shops.

He marveled that the structure didn't collapse under the boy's added weight.

Outside the shop, dried fish hung from strings. Beneath them, small fish, the size of his smallest finger, were sorted into boxes on a table. A black ribbon dangling above the boxes brushed at the fish every time the breeze sprang up. The ribbon chased away the many flies who settled between gusts of wind.

The ceaseless battle between the flies and the black ribbon fascinated Marius, so much so that he didn't see Jank emerge from the shop.

The boy flew through the doorway at a dead sprint. Like his mother, Jank barreled into Marius.

An elderly woman emerged from the shack.

"Thief! Grab that boy!"

Jank struggled to shake himself free of Marius.

Marius, who recognized the situation from his long experience in the market at Amok, caught Jank firmly by the collar. The boy must have tried to steal something and been caught out.

"J-jank," he said. "I f-finally caught you. Your mother is worried sick. You forgot to take the money she gave you."

Jank went slack in his hand. The boy looked up at Marius with wide eyes.

The old shopkeeper, clothed in black, looked eerily similar to the woman who had confronted Marius when he entered Seatown. Her wrinkled face matched the dried fish she sold.

A crowd began to gather, looking for anything to enliven the otherwise dull routine.

"That boy stole from me," said the woman. She pointed a thin finger at Jank.

Marius shook his head dramatically. "The b-boy was sent to the market. B-but he forgot the money. He feared a b-b-beating, I'm sure."

The woman's eyes narrowed in a calculating manner. She recognized the chance for a negotiation.

"What d—did he take?" said Marius, careful to avoid using the word "steal."

The woman pulled at the neck of her black dress. She looked decidedly uncomfortable, as if she didn't want to mention whatever it was Jank had stolen.

"Something precious," muttered the woman. "He stole something very precious."

"How p-precious?" said Marius.

"A dukette at least," said the woman, naming one of the larger denominations. "Sentimental value, you know."

Marius was sure now that the woman was lying. He let a sigh escape his lips. He wiped the back of his free hand across his forehead. "A dukette?" he said. "I don't have a dukette. We'll have to call the l-law."

The old woman shot him a malevolent look that faded as quickly as it had arisen. "Surely we can make a deal?"

"A tiara then?" said Marius, naming the lowest coin.

The old woman shook her head. Her lips tightened. "A half-crown and not a shaving less." She looked at Jank. "I don't want to get the boy in trouble with the law, but there are other kinds of trouble in the world."

Jank instantly tensed at the threat. Marius realized that the boy was genuinely afraid of the old woman. But why? Marius glanced around. Many in the crowd wore black and had the same wrinkled visage as the shopkeeper. Their eyes pierced through his skin staring into his soul.

Marius realized with a start: the woman was a witch. The crowd was lousy with witches or friends of the White Tower. The Jester's Curse chuckled inside him. No wonder it felt so comfortable.

"You're robbing us, mother," said Marius, trying to stay calm. He let go of Jank, reaching into his bindle. He slipped a coin out of a secret pocket.

"Where did I put that m-money?" Marius asked. He palmed the coin and patted his thighs and vest. He didn't want anyone in the crowd thinking that he actually kept money in his bindle. He worked hard to look as though he had nothing worth stealing.

Finally, he pretended to pull the coin from a small pocket on his colorful vest.

"Ah," he said. "Here it is."

He held it out toward the old woman.

Jank kicked Marius in the shin, hard. The boy wiggled through the gathered circle of bodies, leaving Marius standing there, looking at the old woman, wearing a painful grin.

"K-k-kids," said Marius. "Right?"

The curse, sensing an opportunity, fumbled the coin from his hand, dropping it down the front of the old woman's shirt.

She stared at him with a look of incredulity, then she began muttering under her breath the beginnings of a powerful curse.

If Marius didn't think fast, the Jester's Curse was about to have company.

Chapter Five

The confrontation with the witch cost Marius a dukette after all.

He'd waved the large coin in front of the witch's face. Her curse died away as her lips curved into a harsh grin.

He didn't get the half-crown back in change, either.

It had been an expensive exchange. He could only hope the boy's ransom would pay for itself in free food.

After a moment's confusion, Marius had picked up the boy's trail and kept him in sight while trying to remain as inconspicuous as possible—a task rendered nearly impossible by the curse. People pointed at his colorful clothing and his awkward limp.

Marius's injured shin still smarted from where Jank had kicked it, but he'd emerged from the encounter with the witch no more cursed than he already was. He had to be thankful for the small things.

A flash of aquamarine told him that the boy was on the move again, drifting out of the shabby shacks that lined the oceanfront, making his way toward the warehouse district.

Jank paused at the mouth of an alley. The tall wooden walls of two warehouses leaned together, creating a small and rather dangerous looking passage between them.

Marius ducked behind a stall filled with rotting, purple fruit. The sour smell of the fruit made his nose twitch. He caught a sneeze in his throat.

To his right, not twenty paces away, the ocean rushed up to meet the rocky shoreline. A short wall guarded the street from the spray of waves. The cries of the sea birds as they circled overhead gave the place a melancholy air. A prodigious bird dropping narrowly missed his arm.

Jank hung around outside the alley, his weight shifting from foot to foot, anxious about something.

Marius considered his next move. He wanted to be the one to return the boy to his worried and not unattractive mother. To do that, he had to convince the boy to go home with him, willing or not. Marius had size to his advantage, and he had moral leverage, having been commissioned by the mother and having saved the boy from being cursed by the witch for stealing.

A pair of older boys squeezed out of the alley. They were a head taller than Jank. He guessed they were only a few years younger than Marius himself. Their tunics were filthy.

The bigger of the two had brown hair that fell over a protruding forehead. Freckles ranged around a mouth that hung open like one of the fish in the market.

The other boy, who Marius immediately took to be the leader of the group, had a wide, mocking grin framed by dimples that might have been precious as a baby but that looked out of place on his older face.

The leader shoved Jank. "You do what we told you?"

Marius quickly reassessed the situation. The boys were not Jank's friends. Yet Jank did not fight back.

Jank had his head down. Marius couldn't hear his reply.

The mouth-breather barked out an incredulous laugh. "He's lying, Rebius." He poked Jank in the chest with a fat finger. "You never went to the black market. You never stole from the witch!"

Jank put a hand into his pocket. He fished out what looked like a handful of dried grass.

The mouth-breather gawked. "Is that it, Rebius?"

The dimpled boy, Rebius, stood over Jank. "You stole it from the witch?" He snatched the grass.

"Give it back!" Jank pawed at his closed hand.

"Can we smoke it," said the bigger boy.

Rebius replied, "Not near this warehouse. Can't you read the signs? We'd be blown up."

Marius noticed for the first time the sheets of paper plastered to the side of the building covered with bright drawings warning against open flames.

Rebius added to Jank, "We'll know if it's real when we smoke it. If you're lying—" His sentence died away. The threat was implied. He put a hand on Jank's chest, holding him back.

The mouth-breather jumped in. "Look, Rebius, the baby wants it back." He reached out, patting Jank on the head, intentionally hard. A stupid grin creased his face. "Witchweed isn't for babies."

Rebius examined the dried grass, holding it up to the dying sunlight. "Hold him, Demari."

His big friend complied. His thick arms wrapped around Jank's shoulders and chest. Jank squirmed. Demari only held him tighter.

Anger clouded Marius's vision as he watched the boys torment Jank. It reminded Marius of the treatment he'd received as a slave at the hands of Sivinius.

Sivinius was years older than Marius and had made Marius's life a living hell. Not that slavery was all that great to begin with.

Marius hadn't been able to do anything about Sivinius. He wished that he'd at least tried to hit him. He daydreamed about it often enough. If he was going to get thrown out of House Cervix anyway, it would have been nice to have gotten a punch in.

But if he'd fought back, if he'd hit Sivinius, he might have been beaten for damaging valuable property—both his fist and Sivinius's face.

Now, watching Jank struggle against the older boys, Marius realized that nothing held him back. He didn't have to stand by and watch them bully Jank.

Marius set his bindle under the fruit stand. He left the brass knuckles and the knife. He shouldn't need them against the two smaller boys. Though they towered over Jank, Marius had a few years and a few inches on both Rebius and Demari.

Marius strolled toward them. He guessed that the presence of an adult (or near-adult) might cause them to let the boy go. If not, he was more than ready to break it up. Marius's hand flexed, forming and releasing a fist.

He whistled as he walked, drawing attention to himself, not that he needed much help. His colorful jester's clothing stood out against the gray, stone streets. His silly walk resembled something between a trip and a skip.

He expected Rebius and Demari to retreat into the alley.

They stood their ground. Demari held Jank. Rebius hardly glanced at Marius before returning his attention to the witchweed.

Marius drew himself up to his full height. Without the slouch imposed by the Jester's Curse, Marius was tall for a native-born Arovian.

He spoke to Demari. "L-let him go."

Demari's mouth opened even wider. A look of glee shone in his eyes as though someone had given him a gift-wrapped present.

"Luh-luh-look at him!" Demari mocked his stutter. "Jank, is this your boyfriend?"

Jank stopped squirming. His nose turned up as though he'd smelled something foul. Marius had thought the young boy could show a little gratitude toward his would-be liberator.

Then he too noticed the smell. The entire area around the mouth of the alley stank. The stench seemed to be seeping out of one of the warehouses whose wall formed one side of the alley.

Rebius, meanwhile, now gave Marius his full attention. His head cocked back in surprise as he took in the colorful clothing and admittedly shocking appearance of the young man people called the Jester.

Rebius's brow creased as though he were considering what to do in a scenario that had never hitherto presented itself.

Finally, he spoke.

"Go away."

"Not w-without the boy."

Rebius pocketed the witchweed. His other hand hung nonchalantly at his side. He wasn't afraid of Marius.

Demari laughed, "The way he talks—"

Rebius held up a hand, cutting him off.

"You're new in town?" he asked.

Marius nodded.

"Then you're excused."

"For what?" said Marius.

"For not knowing Sparrow territory when you see it. Now go."

"Not without J-j-jank."

Rebius put his fingers to his lips and blew a shrill whistle. A magic flute could hardly have been more effective. Young boys and girls spilled out of the alleys. Others came running up the street. A few pulled themselves over the sea wall. They surrounded Marius, putting him in the middle of a circle at least two or three heads deep.

Still, they were just children. None were as old or as big as him. Marius thought he might be able to bluff his way out. He wished he'd brought a weapon. Then he imagined punching his way through children with brass knuckles. Not good.

"I said, l-let him go." Marius pointed at Jank. He took a step toward the boy.

Demari shifted, putting Jank between them. An arm tightened around the boy's neck.

The children standing in the circle reached into their pockets, pulling out stones the size of large eggs.

Marius swore under his breath. Brass knuckles to the face might be just what some of these kids needed.

He ducked as a stone whizzed past his ear.

Chapter Six

A motley collection of children armed with stones ringed Marius, their features nearly indistinguishable under the dirt covering their faces. He could smell them over the stench of Seatown and the foul warehouse, which was saying something.

Marius was older and taller than the lot. He could see over their heads. He could see that the scene was being ignored by every adult within view. Either they knew who the Sparrows were and feared them, or, more likely, they didn't care about the affairs of children.

At the edge of the circle, the burly boy, Demari, held Jank tightly around the neck.

Inside the circle, the gang's leader, Rebius, looked Marius up and down. He was a few inches shorter than Marius but stood casually, as though he were in perfect control of the situation.

Rebius put a hand up, speaking to the children, "No more stones. Not yet." Turning to Marius, he added, "You want us to let him go?" He nodded toward Jank.

Marius considered his options. If he tried to run, he might be able to break through the circle like one of the children's games they used to play back home.

But then he'd have an army of children throwing rocks at his back. He might not be able to outrun them. Marius had no idea where he could seek sanctuary. They knew the city better than he did.

Also, he had to survive for a week on the streets of Seatown. That would be next to impossible if he didn't come to terms with the Sparrows.

Rebius continued. "Jank's the one who wanted to join the Sparrows. Why don't you ask him if he wants to go with you?"

Held in the crushing arms of Demari, Jank wasn't likely to say that he wanted to leave the Sparrows. Jank had to live in this town as well. Rebius was offering Marius a chance to save face. He could pretend to take Jank's word for it and withdraw.

But if Marius scuttled off, his tail between his legs, Rebius would know that he'd won. The thought galled Marius.

Rebius shrugged. "I'll let him go, if you say please." The fig leaf had been withdrawn. He stared at Marius. A slight breeze ruffled the front of Rebius's stained tunic. His face remained insouciant, but in his eyes a fire burned.

Marius took a deep breath. He could say please. The act of groveling might diminish his pride, but he had so little to begin with.

Even if he said please, though, Marius wasn't sure whether Jank would leave with him. He might debase himself for nothing.

There was also Jank's mother to think of. She wouldn't want her son mixed up with this bunch of street thugs.

Being in a gang was an especially stupid occupation in a land where an Astor could kill you just for thinking about stealing, which was probably why there weren't any older children in the Sparrows. An Astor might show mercy toward a child—if that Astor's name wasn't Lespa.

Marius had to find a way to separate Jank from the gang. He gave the young boy a stern look. "P-play time is over, Jank. Your m-m-mother is l-looking for you."

Demari cawed. "Jank, run along home to muh-muh-mommy."

Rebius looked at a nearby child, one of his lieutenants perhaps. "Teach him a lesson."

The boy threw a stone at Marius.

Marius moved.

The stone sailed past him, landing solidly in the stomach of a young girl standing behind Marius. They obviously had not thought their plan through very well. They were just kids—

Rebius melted through the circle, "All of you. Get him."

Just kids armed with stones. Marius covered up.

A rock hit him in the small of the back. He winced, ducking as another hurtled toward his head.

His curse laughed. It found the idea of being killed by little children amusing.

Well, if it's so funny, thought Marius, why don't you see how it feels? Mentally, he stepped aside. The Jester's Curse took over his body as though it had only been waiting for the opportunity.

A rock sped toward his face.

Marius caught it.

He tossed it gently back at the child who'd thrown it.

The child, surprised by the sudden gift, took aim and threw the stone again, as hard as its little arm could manage.

Marius caught the stone, and again tossed it back to the child.

He spun in a circle catching stones and tossing them back to the children in graceful arcs.

He moved at a speed only the curse could manage.

The children, growing increasingly frustrated, began throwing the stones even harder, with reckless abandon.

Marius's hands buzzed, snatching stones out of the air. He jerked to the side, catching a jagged rock just before it hit the face of a cherub-faced boy with blue eyes and auburn hair. Marius placed the rock gently in the child's hand.

A hush fell over the children.

The little boy grinned.

He tossed the rock lightly toward Marius who caught it and tossed it back.

The other children caught on. One by one and sometimes two or three together, they tossed their rocks in high arcs toward the colorfully dressed stranger.

Marius spun on his heels, turning in a tight circle as he caught stones and flipped them up again into the air, the center of an intense juggling ring.

The children laughed. Which is what the Jester's Curse wanted. Marius laughed with them.

He could see the grip around Jank's neck loosening as Demari, feeling left out of the game, reached into a pocket, presumably for a stone, probably one coated with glass.

"Stop!"

Rebius had re-entered the ring. He glared at the children, who shrank away from him.

"What do you think you're doing? I said teach him a lesson!"

Marius had a handful of stones. He tossed one toward Rebius.

The boy caught it and sent it hurtling toward Marius's head.

While it was still in flight, Marius underhanded another stone toward Rebius.

Marius caught the first stone, the rough edge of the stone stinging the fleshy part of his hand.

The second stone was already on its way back from Rebius.

Marius tossed the first stone and a third before catching the second.

Rebius caught the two stones and returned them with heat.

Marius loosed another two stones at Rebius, adding a final stone to the mix.

The five stones whizzed through the air, either toward or away from Marius. For the Jester's Curse, the juggling act was child's play. But he could see a look of fierce concentration on Rebius's face. The Jester's Curse was having fun at the expense of another person for once. Marius enjoyed the break.

Slowly, Marius advanced, step by step toward the gang's leader. The stones kept moving between them.

Soon he was standing almost toe to toe with the boy, catching the stones nearly as quickly as they left Rebius's hands.

The boy gave up. "Enough!"

Marius smiled. He flashed the five stones into the air all at once in a high cascade. Closing his eyes, he caught them one by one as they returned toward the ground.

Then he flashed them again, this time in Demari's direction.

On instinct, the boy pushed Jank aside to reach for the five stones.

To his credit, he caught three. The other hit him in the face. The last stone landed with a thud on his foot.

He howled in pain, dropping the rocks and hopping on one foot. Demari swore like a sailor, which wasn't surprising given their location.

The children in the circle laughed at Demari. Even little Jank joined in the fun. Rebius, however, remained silent.

Marius stepped back and bowed.

"Who are you?" said Rebius.

"The J-jester of Zeno."

Rebius nodded as though everything had been explained. "You're here for the fair?"

Marius shrugged, holding up his hands, tilting his head comically to the side.

"You're not bad," said Rebius, quickly adding. "I've seen better, mind, but you're not bad."

Marius looked toward Jank. "His m-mother asked me to l-look for the boy. Promised me d-dinner."

"I see," said Rebius thoughtfully. "She works in the kitchen at House Fluctus?"

Marius shrugged again. He didn't know the name of the house but assumed Rebius was correct.

Demari, still standing on one leg, tried to salvage his pride. "Poor Jank, his mother's a slave."

"Shut it," said Rebius.

Jank shoved Demari. He fell back onto the stone street, a look of pure hatred occluding his already freckled face.

Marius nodded his approval. Rebius chose not to interfere.

"Go home, Jank," said Rebius. "Thanks for the witchweed."

To Marius, he added, "We'll be seeing you around." Rebius's tone held no menace, but the threat was implied. Marius had made some enemies already on his first day in Seatown. He added Demari and Rebius to the names of people who wanted him dead. It was getting to the point that Marius needed a list to remember them all. If only he knew how to write.

From the scowl on the face of little Jank, it appeared that the kitchen slave's son wasn't much happier with Marius than Demari.

Marius took Jank firmly by the hand. He wasn't escaping this time. Together, they retrieved Marius's bindle.

Marius had ruined the boy's initiation into the Sparrows. He had deliberately brought up Jank's mother to embarrass the boy. The boy would be too afraid of ridicule to return to the gang anytime soon. As if being seen with the ridiculous man dressed in a jester's suit wasn't bad enough. Still, Marius didn't care what the Sparrows thought of him. And the less Jank hung out with them, the better.

Thankfully, it wasn't the good will of the son that he needed. The mother would be happy to see her boy. Happy enough, he hoped, to provide a free meal.

Marius hadn't discovered Asadal's mysterious trouble in Seatown, but he had gone a long way toward solving his own problems—getting a warm meal from a friendly face.

And he'd somewhat made up for the coins lost to the witch. Marius patted a small pocket on his vest. It rustled at his touch, filled as it was with witchweed picked from Rebius's pocket during the juggling match. He could probably resell it.

The day, having begun so poorly, was finally looking up.

* * *

The sun had tipped on its side like a copper coin, showing only its edge on the horizon. Lamps in the street were lit as Marius and Jank passed by, walking hand in hand, much to Jank's displeasure, up the hill in Seatown.

The walk to the top of the hill from the market proved more difficult than Marius had anticipated.

Although Marius walked every day, he'd been on flat land and had underestimated the hill leading to the top of Seatown. The small cobblestones under his feet felt like tall steps.

As they strolled by the large houses belonging to the city's nobility, Marius pestered Jank with questions.

The sullen boy refused to respond, even though Marius had saved him twice already, a fact that Marius pointed out on more than one occasion.

Marius inquired about the Sparrows, and whether they were some kind of vicious street gang. Jank rolled his eyes.

Used to having no one to talk to, Marius gave up the attempt at conversation and took in the surroundings. For a city of its size, Seatown retained an impressive amount of greenery. Houses hadn't simply been slammed against one another as they had in Amok or

Zeno. Trees and small parks cropped up from time to time.

The higher they walked up the hill, the more Marius could see over the tops of the buildings leading to the ocean. Bright patches of foliage dotted the landscape marking the places where parks stood. He wondered what kept people from building on what must be prime real estate.

An answer came unexpectedly. Looking with a certain amount of envy at the rich houses, Marius spied a woman standing on a railed balcony. She wore a tantalizingly thin shift tied at her hips with a red sash. Long black hair hung loose around her shoulders. Bands of gold worth more than his life circled her upper arms. She took a sip from a delicate, crystal glass while gazing over the city and the ocean, perhaps looking for the return of a merchant husband from overseas.

"Who is she?" Marius asked, not expecting an answer.

"Raza," Jank said quietly.

Marius looked at the boy who, like him, was staring at the beautiful woman. "Of House Ponti," Jank added.

Marius saw the city from her eyes. She had to look down the hill every day. Without the patches of green, a woman like that might be forced to look at the slums below. Her evening refreshment might lose its flavor.

Marius found for the first time in his young life that his interests coincided with the interests of the rich. They loved the parks, and he needed a place to sleep. He fully intended to spend the night in one of the parks if Jank's mother didn't make him a better offer. Used to life on the road, Marius felt certain that a patch of soft grass would be a welcome change.

At the light-blue wall that bordered House Fluctus, Jank twisted, breaking free of Marius's grasp. Jank darted toward the open door. Marius had been ready for just such a trick. His hand closed around the top of the boy's tunic, grabbing him by the collar. Jank pulled Marius into the courtyard.

A startled slave greeted Marius with a suspicious stare. She too wore the aquamarine tunic. Her hands were full of washing. Like Jank's mother, the slave wore the house colors well. Her auburn hair swept past her shoulders to the middle of her back. Maris got the impression that the master of the house preferred pretty slaves. Marius didn't mind. If he had to beg at a house, it didn't hurt that the help looked nice.

Marius jabbed a finger at Jank and asked the young woman, "The k-k-kitchen?"

The slave rolled her eyes. Apparently, this wasn't the first time Jank had been hauled back home by the collar.

"It's around there," she said, in a voice nearly as lovely as her face. She pointed through the courtyard, to a path that led between the wall and the house. Marius wondered whether the kitchen was in a separate building to protect the house from the extra heat, or, given the limitations of space, whether the kitchen would be attached to the main house. As a former slave, curiosity about such matters was unavoidable.

Marius had been trained so well that he could be dumped into any house on the peninsula and be serving competently within minutes. Not that he had any intention of returning to a life of slavery, especially since his former house was now being run by his old enemy, Sivinius.

With his hand still firmly on Jank's collar, Marius frog-marched the boy around the side of the building.

The kitchen, which was indeed attached to the rear of the house, was recognizable by the several chimneys sticking out of its low slung roof.

Poking his head inside, Marius's tongue erupted at the delicious smell of bread.

He spied the mother and nodded toward her, hauling her recalcitrant son into the doorway. Her blonde hair had been pulled out of her face.

A hand flew to her mouth. She reached the doorway in three long strides and struck Jank squarely on the side of his head.

The other kitchen workers turned away. From the sparkle in their eyes, Marius guessed that they liked seeing the boy punished, but the monologue afterward they found tiresome.

Marius himself soon tuned it out. Jank must have done the same, since, according to his mother, he never changed no matter what she said.

Marius's parents hadn't trusted their son's behavior to words alone. He'd been frequently and thoroughly beaten as a child.

Those lashings, far from irresponsible, had prepared him for a life of slavery, where the whip was a constant part of the landscape.

Finally, the mother turned Jank around and pushed him in whatever direction she'd ordered him to go. The boy sullenly obeyed.

As he walked away, the mother put a worried hand to a full cheek that looked softer than any bed.

Marius wondered at the heart of a boy who could put such a beautiful woman to such pains. But he had been young himself once. At sixteen years of age, those days weren't too far in the past.

Jank's mother beckoned for Marius to join her at a table in the kitchen. Heat rolled off the cooking fires, but the kitchen was not unpleasant. The fires had been reduced for the night. The cooks were busy preparing loaves of bread for the morning breakfast.

The rough-hewn table stood higher than those at which Marius normally sat. He could tell the table had been built especially for the kitchen staff. The height of the table had been arranged so that the women didn't have to strain their backs as they stood preparing meals: chopping vegetables or kneading dough.

Marius ran his fingertips over a patch in the table that had been scored by countless strokes of a knife. Small pieces of green onion came away on his fingertips and filled his nostrils with their pungent smell.

The table had only one bench, the other side of the table being reserved for standing work. The rest of the cooks continued preparing the morning meal while Marius and the mother sat. They acted deferentially toward her, sometimes bringing her a bowl of food to inspect. Marius began to think she was in charge of the kitchen. What a lucky stroke that would be.

"Thanks for bringing Jank home," she said. "I hope he wasn't too difficult to find." The woman gave him a weak smile. Worry lines radiated from the corners of her young eyes.

Marius had been prepared to list the trouble Jank had caused him, which included a half-crown lost down the witch's blouse and the dukette that followed to silence her curse. Then there was the fact that Jank had shop-lifted from the old woman and had been trying to join up with the Sparrows, having stolen some kind of drug.

Looking at the mother's kind face, Marius couldn't bring himself to mention anything that might cause her more worry. After all, his concern lay less in the boy's welfare than in his own. A happy mother might offer a warm, happy meal and perhaps more.

Marius adopted a placating tone. "Jank was f-f-fine."

The mother brushed aside a stray strand of hair. "He wasn't off getting into trouble?"

Marius sat back, raising a knowing eyebrow at the question, as though she were asking him to tell tales. "No worse than the u-usual things boys g-get into."

The mother breathed a sigh of genuine relief. She put a hand to her ample chest.

Marius thought of Irina. He loved Irina. He should be loyal to her. But she'd called him, "Sweet." The dismissal of his love still stung.

"I'm Clarion." The woman seemed to have recalled her manners. She looked apologetic.

Marius smiled, "I'm M-m-marius the Walker."

Clarion didn't laugh at his stutter. "A Walker," she said. "It must be exciting, traveling the world."

Marius nodded affably, "Exciting and h-hungering." He patted his flat stomach.

"Of course," said Clarion. She stood. Marius soon found himself the recipient of a loaf of fresh bread and some churned butter. The coarse sea salt with which the butter was seasoned had yet to dissolve into the golden fat. Marius spread a thick layer of the butter across a hunk of bread.

Clarion watched him eat.

The curse sensed an audience. Marius had to put his elbow on the table and approach the bread carefully, mouth spread wide, to keep the curse from crushing the butter against his cheek or chin.

He ignored Clarion's quizzical stare. What was he supposed to do, explain that he'd been cursed by a powerful wizard? When people found out, they acted as though the curse were a disease that could be passed person to person.

He didn't think anyone could catch his rotten luck. At least, he hoped not.

Clarion filled the awkward silence with small talk about what life as a Walker must be like and about the merits of Seatown, including frequent references to the healing properties of the sea.

Finally, she hit a topic that caused Marius's ears to prick.

"You must be careful, though. People have been disappearing lately."

Marius paused mid-bite. He asked with his mouth half-full, "Is that why you were so w-w-worried about Jank? That he'd been shipped to M-machoo?"

Clarion blinked, as though she were trying to reconcile his question to her line of thought. In a serious voice, she said, "It's not the ships. A ship would never take a house slave. Especially not Jank." She shook her head. "No. Whoever it is, is taking children. Taking anyone. People like you and me."

Marius didn't know if he—as a homeless Walker burdened with a terrible curse—belonged in the same category as a valuable slave like Clarion.

She continued, "If a ship took a slave it would never be allowed to dock at Seatown again. No, it's not the ships."

Marius tried to sound casual, "Have the Astors been called for?" He knew that two Astors, Lespa and Bithius were nearby. Perhaps they would pay a visit to Seatown, unless they were too busy hunting Asadal to pay attention to a little thing like multiple kidnappings.

Clarion shook her head. "I haven't heard. I wish they would come. Excuse me." One of the kitchen staff whispered into Clarion's ear. She rose to check the bread in the ovens.

Marius watched Clarion work. She moved with an unselfconscious grace and a pleasant efficiency as she supervised the peeling of vegetables and the other work that went into prepping for breakfast. Marius thought of the love he'd declared for Irina back in Amok and felt slightly guilty about watching Clarion so closely. Besides, she had a child, and he didn't know her situation, if she was spoken for by another slave or if the pregnancy had been of the type that sometimes happened to pretty slaves who couldn't resist the advances of their betters.

Meanwhile, Marius considered Clarion's news about the Astors—or lack of news—to be a good sign. If the always-gossipy kitchen staff hadn't heard rumors of an Astor, Marius figured it was a good bet that none of the Law-keepers were in the city.

On the other hand, he found the lack of involvement on the part of the Astors discomforting. True, he wouldn't have to dodge any of their curved daggers. Yet, as someone intending to spend the night on the streets, without a friend in the world, Marius had a vested interest in the problem of disappearing citizens.

He scraped the heel of the bread in the bowl of butter, scouring up the last bites of the thick, golden oil. He
savored it, wallowing the bread around till the butter
dissolved in his mouth.

Out of the corner of his eye, Marius saw Jank peeking
in the kitchen window. With the mother's back turned,
Marius pocketed two more rolls. He winked conspirato-
rially at young Jank. The boy scowled. He couldn't tell
on Marius without giving away his hiding spot. Marius
could practically see the wheels spinning in the boy's
head. Jank wanted the imposing jester out of his life.

Marius reached into his pocket and pulled out the
handful of witchweed.

Jank's eyes went wide. He mouthed one word,
"Where?"

Marius passed the witchweed into his other hand,
palming it as he did so, making it seem to disappear into
thin air.

He mouthed back at Jank, "Stole it." In fact, he'd
taken it out of Rebius's pocket while they were juggling
rocks back and forth, toe to toe.

"Mine," the boy mouthed.

Marius shook his head. "Mine," he shot back.

Jank's head sunk below the window, obviously fum-
ing.

Marius caught Clarion's attention. "I'll be g-going."

"Bye!" she waved from across the room.

Marius rubbed his hand over the back of his head.
"I'm n-new here. Know a g-good place to stay?"

Clarion paused. The others in the kitchen followed
her example. A lively discussion ensued as to the finer
points of various inns.

Marius had hoped for something a bit closer.

He hoped in vain.

"The Happy Mackerel," said Clarion, ending the debate. "Best place for the money. Good food."

Coming from kitchen slaves, that endorsement meant a lot. Still, he had no intention of wasting money on an inn.

Marius made his way out of the kitchen and back to the courtyard. He had done well in Seatown. He'd found the lost boy, returned him to his mother, and gotten his foot in the kitchen door. Marius thought he might also have discovered the unknown danger that Asadal feared.

Certainly, kidnappings were a troubling thing for a Walker. No one would care if a vagabond like Marius or Asadal disappeared. He resolved to be more vigilant.

Marius slipped out of the gate. He ran a hand over the smooth light-blue wall of the estate as he sauntered down the hill. His eyes went to the sign of three loaves scratched into the wall. The Walker's sign hadn't failed him. He'd gotten a good meal with some to extra bread in his pockets.

The sun had set far into the ocean, casting an orangish hue on the port below. The light of cooking fires and of candles in the growing dusk mixed with the glow cast by the street lamps. The wind had changed, bringing salty sea air inland. Marius breathed deep.

He thought that he just might enjoy the next week in Seatown.

As Marius reached the corner of the wall, hands reached out of a dark alley, pulling him in. A blow to the head knocked him to the ground. He heard the rattle of the rings as his bindle hit the paving stones. Then everything went black.

Chapter Seven

Marius awoke. Smoke seared his nostrils. He lay on a hard, wooden surface in the dark. His body swayed back and forth. He feared the blow to his head might have shaken his brains loose. The spot where he'd been struck felt tender to his touch, his hair matted with blood.

At least he was alive.

As he lay there, Marius realized that his body wasn't rocking, rather the floor moved beneath him. Marius had never been on the ocean. He had only Asadal's tales of travel for reference. He fought a sense of rising panic.

Marius began to guess at his surroundings. He must have been captured by a ship short on crew. For all he knew, the boat was moving through open seas already. Outside the wall of his dark cell, he heard the pounding of water against the sides of the vessel.

Feeling around with his hands and feet in the dark, enclosed space, Marius surmised that he'd been locked in a small cupboard. A dim, orange light came through a crack in the bottom of the door.

Acrid smoke came through the crack as well, tearing at his lungs. He resisted the urge to cough.

Marius began to sit up, to get away from the smoke, when he heard a voice speaking in the room beyond the door. Marius placed his head nearer the crack to listen, though it brought him into greater contact with the smoke.

"This witchweed is good, Barn."

"I know it, Pithy. I know it," the man called Barn replied. "Hand me the pipe."

"I seen a stack better in Machoo once."

"Who hasn't?" said Barn, "I remember this one time, me and Petrus—"

Barn's story was interrupted by the sound of a door opening.

Marius could hear the men standing quickly, though apparently less than soberly, to their feet.

The newcomer upbraided the men. "What do you mean smoking on the job?" The newcomer had a distinct accent, quite different than that of Marius's captors. Having worked as a house slave, Marius recognized a noble accent when he heard it. The newcomer had been educated.

The man paused. "Not to mention it's not strictly legal, is it?"

Pithy replied, "Well, it isn't strictly a legal job you have us doing, is it? We knocked that young fellow on the head, the one that come in the gate alone. He's lying in there now, ready for delivery."

Marius heard the scuffle of feet. Beneath the door he could make out shadows stepping hastily backward.

"No need to draw a blade," Barn said.

"Have you brainless beasts lost what little that passes for sense between you? I didn't tell you to 'knock anyone on the head' as you call it. By the Lady, man."

Barn spoke up, "You told us to get another warm body."

"Yes," said the educated man. Marius had already begun to think of him as a nobleman, a younger son of a lesser house perhaps. "You've watched me do it a dozen times. You offer the mark whatever their heart desires. Tell them the White Tower can offer them whatever they want for their service. They come willingly, you idiots."

An awkward silence followed. Finally, Barn's accomplice, Pithy, answered, "We aren't much good at lying, Master Coltic. But we're handy with a cudgel."

"We improvised," added Barn.

"Yeah, we improvised."

The man they called Coltic responded with a high-pitched, nasal laugh that sounded more nasty than amused. "You improvised?" he said. "Did you talk to the witch before you improvised?"

"Not exactly," said Barn's accomplice.

"Not exactly," Coltic repeated. His nose squeaked out another laugh that ended abruptly. "You were supposed to check with the witch." A note of rage had entered his voice and, along with it, a note of madness. A thick layer of smoke rolled under the door. The man coughed. "Not bad witchweed. Not bad," he said under his breath before resuming, a little more calmly than before. "You managed to grab a boy who is already cursed. The witch says that she spoke to him earlier today. She says that she felt the curse, felt it down to his bones."

Barn sounded crestfallen, "He's cursed?"

"And it's something more," said Coltic. "The witch said he's been touched by the Lady."

"What does that mean?"

"How should I know?" said Coltic.

Marius thought immediately of the woman in black who had confronted him at the gate. She had taken his hand and felt it, examining it. Could she have been looking for a curse?

Coltic continued, "The curse, however, is the work of Malconus. The witch says the boy reeks of it. Do you know who Malconus is?"

There was a general silence and rustling of clothing which Marius interpreted as the men either nodding their heads or shrugging their shoulders.

"Do you know what he'll do if you disrupt one of his experiments?"

Another billow of smoke snuck under the door. Marius wondered whether the experiment mentioned by Coltic meant Marius himself and the Jester's Curse, or meant interrupting whatever experiments the wizard was doing on the kidnapped people.

Coltic added decisively. "Get rid of him."

"What?" said Barn.

"The White Tower won't have him. We don't need him. Get rid of him."

The other man protested, "We aren't murderers, Master Coltic. We may nab a body, but we don't butcher them."

"Get rid of him," said Master Coltic, "and find me another. Isn't that what I'm paying you for?"

Pithy spoke up, "You haven't paid us yet—"

Barn added, "We could take him to the slave auction."

Coltic soldiered on, "Forget the auction. Kill him. Then find a poor bastard down on his luck and promise him the moon. Find an ugly woman and promise her a new face. Find someone soon. You know how those damn wizards get. They need someone willing. And, this is very important, someone not already cursed." Coltic paused. "Check with the witch next time."

"As you say," said Barn.

Coltic interrupted, "And stop smoking this foul stuff. It befuddled the mind. Here, I'm taking the rest of it so that it doesn't cloud your judgment. I've got to get back to the city. Pull up the gangplank after I leave."

Marius heard the door open and shut. So, he wasn't out to sea. The boat must be sitting in the harbor.

A low muttering punctuated by curses filtered through the crack under the door.

"Wasn't his to take," said Barn. "We stole it off the boy fair and square."

"He took my favorite pipe too," muttered Pithy.

"We should give Coltic to the White Tower," said Barn. "Nobody would miss him. Or," Barn added, "why not buy slaves instead of kidnapping?"

Pithy mocked Coltic's educated accent and nasal laugh, "Ah, ha, now, Barn. If I had money to spare on slaves do you think I'd be in cahoots with the White Tower?"

"Cahoots," Barn repeated, chuckling.

"Coltic says they have to be willing," said Pithy, resuming his normal, gruff voice. "Never knew a willing slave myself. Still, I won't be party to murder."

"Now, Pithy, I'd never make you kill the young man, especially not someone touched by the Lady."

"Not kill him?"

"Throw him in the sea," said Barn. "That's what we'll do. He might wake up when he hits the water. Or he might not. Let the Lady save him if she wants. Either way, we can't be blamed."

Pithy didn't disagree.

Marius, on the other hand, didn't find his chances to be sporting at all. He didn't know how to swim. Growing up in the capital city, he'd never learned. One didn't swim in the rivers of Zeno, filled as they were with human waste.

When Marius moved to the family's country estate, there hadn't been time to frolic in the fields and lakes. Being a slave eliminated the whole idea of free time.

He heard the shuffle of feet moving in the direction of his cupboard. Marius closed his eyes and slumped to the wooden floor, pretending to be unconscious. The men, Barn and Pithy, had already said they didn't want to kill him. He wondered whether their pacifistic resolve would hold up when he tried to escape.

The door opened, letting in a cloud of mundungus smoke from the noxious witchweed they'd been piping.

Marius stifled a cough. If they found out he was awake, the threatened dunking could take a different, more ominous direction.

A pair of rough hands grabbed him under the shoulders. Another pair took hold under his knees. Marius let his head roll back.

He couldn't help peeking at the cabin as they lifted him off the ground.

Marius had never been in a ship, so he didn't know his aft from a hole in the ground. To his unpracticed eye, Marius saw a smallish room, with walls, floor and ceiling made entirely of wood. The centerpiece of the room was a compact, pot-bellied stove. The yellow light in the room that he'd seen from under the door came from a small fire. A comforting flame wavered in the belly of the stove.

The room had a set of stools adjacent to a wooden counter. A blackened bowl filled with soot sat atop the counter where Marius assumed Barn and Pithy had been sitting, ashing their pipe, before they were interrupted by Coltic. Except for the rolling motion of the ship underfoot, Marius would have guessed they were in a strange sort of kitchen—a smaller version of the one Clarion ran back at the light-blue house.

The captor holding his legs—Marius had no way of knowing whether it was Barn or his partner Pithy—wore a simple cream homespun shirt under an orange vest. A stubbled face gave way to a stumpy nose. He was missing one eye but hadn't bothered to patch it. A gaping flap of skin stared at Marius, unblinking. His fat belly fell onto Marius's knees.

As to the man holding his arms, Marius couldn't get a clear view of him. His arms were skinny and tan. His body odor, however, rivaled the stench on the streets of Seatown. Pig farms smelled fresher in comparison. At least the pigs took a mud bath every other week. Though the man lived on the water, he didn't seem to like the stuff.

The pair carried Marius out the narrow door of the kitchen. His head, true to form, bounced off the side of the doorjamb. His captors paused, watching to see if he woke.

Marius feigned a deep snore. It satisfied Barn and Pithy who carried him up a steep stairway.

The back of his head knocked against each step.

After the third knock, seeing that Marius wasn't awakened, the pair took even less care to see that he didn't come to harm. They carried him as though they were hauling a stack of wood.

Fresh air tinged with the taste of salt hit Marius's face as they reached the top of the stairs. Stars shone overhead. The moon had risen to its zenith. A squawk arose as a surprised seagull took flight. The man supporting Marius's head almost dropped him.

Through the slits in his eyes, Marius could see the front of the ship approaching. The pair seemed to be making for a break in the railing.

Marius sensed the time had come to escape. He didn't want to find himself at the bottom of Seatown harbor. A gentle breeze blew in from the ocean, brushing against his face.

Deep inside himself, Marius willed the Jester's Curse to take over. The antics of the curse had saved him on numerous occasions. The curse had prevented his former master from beating him to death. In Amok, the curse had stymied the soldiers of House Marcel. Earlier in the evening, the curse had kept him from being stoned to death by the Sparrows. Surely the famous Jester's Curse could handle a couple of churls like Barn and Pithy.

They neared the break in the railing.

Any time now, Marius urged the curse.

In the back of his mind, the curse chuckled inaudibly.

Marius realized with rising panic that the curse found the situation funny. The curse thought it would be hilarious to see Marius flapping about in the water like a wounded duck. Didn't it realize Marius would die—that the curse would die with him?

The curse didn't seem to care.

Marius squirmed. Too late. The hands around his knees tightened to a grip of iron. The arms under his shoulders reached around his neck, taking him in a choke hold.

Before he knew what was happening, Marius found himself suddenly released, falling through the air toward the ocean.

*　*　*

Marius braced for impact. He clenched his jaw and his fists. The interminable fall ended abruptly with the shocking embrace of freezing water. Marius hadn't thought to close his mouth. The salty water poured into his sinuses, burning his nose and throat.

Marius clawed his way to the surface like a scared cat scrambling up a slippery tree. He saw the lights of Seatown and took a frantic breath before sinking back under the waves.

The dock was a stone's throw away, but it might as well have been the moon for as much as Marius could reach it.

The Jester's Curse didn't know how to swim any better than he did.

He bobbed to the surface again. He was farther away from the boat and farther from the docks. The sea was dragging him toward the rocky shore of Seatown. Marius doubted he'd make it to the rocks before he went under for the last time.

He kicked, but his leather shoes found no purchase. He clawed at the sea, but the shifting water slipped through his fingers.

Something big grabbed the back of his shirt. Marius imagined it was one of the fish from the market. Maybe the big one with hundreds of teeth had come to swallow him.

Fear animated his efforts. He splashed about wildly, drawing nearer the shore, but not close enough.

He sank again.

Something wrapped around his neck.

Marius envisioned another creature from the market, the slimy creature with the long, sinewy legs. Instinctively, he lashed out with an elbow. He connected with a solid object.

A voice called out. "Stop. You'll drown us both."

Marius hadn't expected a creature of the sea to speak. He especially hadn't expected it to sound like his old mentor, Asadal.

Marius stopped trying to swim. His body went limp.

A thin arm, strong as iron, wrapped around his chest. Marius felt himself being pulled, his head above water, toward shore.

He exulted in the sudden sense of salvation. He wasn't going to drown.

His curse sulked. Its fun had been spoiled. The curse loosed Marius's bladder. The seawater around them turned brackishly warm.

If Asadal felt the sudden change in temperature, he didn't comment.

"Stand up," the old man commanded.

Immediately, Marius flailed. The water was still too deep. He would drown again.

Then his foot caught the shore beneath the waves. When he stood, the water rose only to his waist. Marius felt more than a little embarrassed.

A wave hit him from behind, sending him sprawling into the water. He caught himself on his hands. The sharp rocks of the shoreline scraped his palms.

Asadal helped him to his feet.

He stepped out of the ocean, lifting each foot much higher than he needed to, like a newborn wearing shoes for the first time.

Marius turned to face his savior: Asadal. One of the last people on the Arovian peninsula he'd ever hoped to see.

He couldn't begin to think of what to say. Marius's brain felt thick and as waterlogged as his clothing.

"You're welcome," said Asadal, smiling. The nearly full moon brought out the best in his white teeth against his swarthy skin.

Marius's head hurt. It felt as though he were still swimming and sinking. The wound from the kidnapper's cudgel pounded with pain.

"What are you doing here?" said Marius.

"Saving your life."

"But how—?"

"I've been following you. Campri asked me to look after you, remember?"

Marius put his fists on his hips in frustration and immediately regretted it. His pants were still sopping wet and were covered in urine and sea water. His vision blurred. He vomited.

Asadal patted him on the back. "Thought I'd have to save you from that witch you ran afoul of," said Asadal, "and from that gang of urchins."

"Had that under c-control," said Marius. His stutter came not from the curse but from the chattering of his teeth.

Asadal waved a hand, "Then you get knocked on the head. Here, walk this way."

His head still hurt and his stomach felt sick. Still, Marius followed as Asadal led him along the shore. It ran under the wall that divided Seatown from the ocean. They passed under the witch's shop and those of the other merchants who'd built out over the wall. In the dark, Marius stepped in things he'd rather not imagine. The smell was enough.

When the shops ended, Asadal scampered up the side of the wall with the surefootedness of a man used to the route.

After Asadal ascended, Marius saw why he'd chosen that spot. A small gap had developed in the sea wall.

Marius struggled up after Asadal, knocking his knees and an elbow in the process. His head still hurt. His hands and feet felt a long way off.

At the top of the wall, Asadal waved him across the street and into an alley.

A noxious smell hit his nose.

"W-what is that?" Marius waved at his face as though his feeble strokes might push the smell away.

"This warehouse holds chemicals shipped to mines across the kingdom."

"Chemicals?"

"Elements of the earth that, when combined with a certain art, become useful."

Become foul, more like, thought Marius. He felt as though he could almost see the smell in the dark, like a solid wall of stink.

Asadal grabbed his arm, pulling him into the alley.

They wound through the darkened streets of Seatown. Marius quickly lost his way in the narrow passages that ran between the warehouses. He kept close to Asadal, following the Walker's gray tunic, which caught the light of the moon through the spaces between the walls overhead.

Finally, Asadal stopped. He gave a low whistle.

It echoed from the top of the roofs.

Asadal grasped Marius by the wrist and led him into a small opening. Before them lay a warehouse long abandoned to neglect. Part of the roof had caved in, perhaps done in by an enormous storm. A single red door led inside the building.

Asadal made for the door. He stepped inside, pulling Marius with him.

The candlelight that met Marius's eyes, weak as it was, wreaked havoc on Marius's sensitive sight. He held up a hand to his face. When he removed his arm, his jaw dropped.

A building that had once warehoused fish or items of commerce now housed dozens of children of all ages.

Marius saw a few familiar faces scowling at him from the shadows, including Rebius and Demari.

Demari put a hand into his pocket, no doubt reaching for a stone.

"This," said Asadal, "is the Sparrows' Nest."

He waved a hand around him, encompassing the room and its young occupants. A little girl with a smudged face looked up at Asadal with an adoring stare. A small boy no larger than Jank ran forward, taking Asadal's hand.

Asadal put his other hand to his chest, melodramatically. "And I am their king."

Marius's vision swam. His head throbbed. A falling sensation took him. He collapsed onto the floor.

As his senses deserted him, Marius heard Asadal say, "That wasn't the reaction I'd hoped for."

Marius passed out.

Chapter Eight

L ight filtering through the cracks in the ceiling walked nimbly across Marius's face, waking him even more thoroughly than a bucket of cold water.

Asadal spoke without looking up from a book. "One of the privileges of being in a city: borrowing a book from a friend." He held the book carefully—a small volume bound in a plain red cover marked with a gold stamp resembling a dove. The pages as Asadal turned them, looked impossibly thin. Holding it up so Marius could see it better, Asadal explained, "It's The Book of the Dove. One of the three volumes of the Lady."

Though Marius had never been particularly religious, he knew the book by name as well as its companion volumes, The Book of the Wind and the Book of the Flame, though some said the latter had disappeared from the face of Arovia.

Placing a thin finger, dark against the white pages, Asadal began reading: "The Dove is at all times with us and within us, guiding our steps. Though difficult to see, she is never far from us. Like our heart, which cannot be reached with our hands and yet dwells within us. So the

Dove rests within and without ever on the edge of our vision. Those who seek her, may see her. There is always a choice."

The old Walker paused, glancing over the spine of the book at Marius. "I could leave it with you while you heal."

Marius didn't respond. He didn't want to admit that he couldn't read, although Asadal must already know. Perhaps Asadal thought Marius had picked up the skill in Amok. But life on the street didn't lend itself to scholarly pursuits. He'd had enough trouble keeping himself alive and moderately well fed.

No, thought Marius, that was a lie. He wondered why he was lying to himself. He could have learned to read if he'd applied himself. Irina would certainly have offered to teach him—assuming that she herself knew. Or he could have gotten lessons from one of the merchants in the square.

Truth was, he just didn't think it worthwhile.

Once, when he'd aspired to run the affairs of House Cervix, the skill seemed important. But what was the point of a common fool knowing his letters? He put the thought aside.

"Where are we and what happened to me?" Marius put a hand to his mouth. He hadn't stuttered.

Asadal reached over and patted Marius's hand. Marius saw a familiar sight: a woven grass band wrapped around his index finger. Asadal had given him a charm against the curse.

"It can't cure the curse," Asadal nodded toward the ring, but it can help with the symptoms?"

"With the—?"

"The small things. Like your speech."

"Thank you." The words escaped his lips before he'd had time to consider them. Marius hadn't intended to thank Asadal for anything. After all, the man had abandoned Marius on the road to Amok, leaving him in the hands of Lespa, a deadly Astor.

She had come for him again not a day earlier.

Asadal smiled. His white teeth lit his swarthy face. He touched Marius on the arm. "You're welcome."

Marius laid his head back on the pillow. He didn't trust his mouth not to betray him further. His eyes looked up at the dilapidated ceiling lined with rough-hewn lumber. He remembered the warehouse they had entered and guessed that he now lay in a loft of some sort. One large wall ran from side to side. His room stretched the entire width of the building. He turned his head to take in the size of the place.

His swollen tongue caught on the roof of his mouth. He looked around for a glass of water.

Anticipating his needs, Asadal held out a wooden cup. Marius took it and drained the entire contents, finding not water but a weak soup.

Asadal spoke as Marius drank. "Campri says it's the salt in the sea that makes a man thirsty."

"What?" Marius hadn't been following the conversation. His brain still felt foggy.

"The salt water. The ocean," Asadal prompted. "You took a swim in it last night."

Marius remembered being thrown from the boat by Pithy and Barn. He remembered his head going under the waves. He realized that he was now holding his breath, as though the very thought of drowning might rob his lungs.

Marius reached toward his head feeling for the wound.

Asadal caught his hand. "You had a bad bump," he said. "We wrapped it, but it's best not to bother it."

"So that's—?"

"Why you collapsed?" Asadal finished his sentence. "I couldn't see it in the dark. Lady only knows how you made it back to the Sparrows' Nest."

"The Sparrows?" Marius became aware of the sound of children playing and fighting at the edge of his hearing.

"Yes," said Asadal, smiling and resting the red book on his crossed knee. "My merry band."

"And you're their king?" said Marius, remembering Asadal's speech from the night before.

"That I am."

"But you only just arrived." Marius didn't see how Asadal could have become king of a street gang in only one day, though, he wouldn't put anything past the old Walker. He'd seen Asadal do stranger things.

Asadal only shrugged. "I stop by from time to time. And you never stop being a Sparrow. You may grow up. You may travel the world. But you'll always be a Sparrow."

Marius considered what he knew of Asadal's past. The man had been born on a remote island and had traveled the seas to Arovia. Marius had never considering how young Asadal had been when he arrived in the kingdom, though it was difficult to think of Asadal as anything but a wise old man. Marius pushed his imagination, picturing Asadal as a boy the size of Jank escaping slavery on a ship bound for Machoo, blending into the shadows of the alleys of Seatown.

"This Nest is as much a home to me as any," said Asadal, confirming Marius's suspicions.

Marius sat up on an elbow. His vision swam just a little before coming back into focus. He looked at Asadal. "You said home is the place a Walker never goes."

"So you were listening to all those speeches back then?" Asadal sat back and regarded Marius with an appreciative smile. "True, a Walker never goes home. But that's because he calls no one place home." His wide grin slowly faded. "You find that you can't go back. That everything changed. That nothing changed, except you changed. And that changes everything. But sometimes you do go back, especially when they need you."

A small head pushed its way through a trap door in the floor. A boy's face appeared. He had round, red cheeks smudged with dirt. He spoke in a most solemn-sounding voice, "Sparrows await y-your orders, King." He too had a stutter. Marius felt an instant kinship with the boy. He looked so familiar. There was something about his blue eyes and curly, reddish hair. Marius couldn't quite put his finger on it.

Asadal nodded. "I'll be down in a moment, Iatro."

The boy disappeared as the door in the floor thumped shut.

"Well," said Asadal, making ready to rise. "I have to inspect the troops."

"No ring?" said Marius.

Asadal blinked, not understanding the question.

Marius pointed to the woven band on his finger, then toward the floor. He hadn't seen a similar ring on the boy, Iatro's, finger.

Asadal's eyes went to the hidden hole in the floor as though he could still see Iatro. "His stutter doesn't come from a curse."

"Born with a curse, you mean," said Marius.

Asadal tapped the red book with a finger, "We were known by the Lady before we were born. Yet everyone is in some way cursed."

"I disagree," said Marius, thinking of the exact moment the wizard Malconus had uttered the Jester's Curse. He'd been in the middle of a formal dinner service and had been blamed for spilling wine on the wizard's white robe. It had all been his rival, Sivinius's, doing of course. "You seem to be doing all right."

Asadal regarded Marius with a stern look in his eyes. Marius had seen the look before. He was about to be the recipient of Asadal's so-called wisdom.

"There may come a day, Marius, when you look back and see that your curse was never a curse at all but a blessing bestowed by the Lady, a help to you in a time of deepest need. You think you were not a fool until the curse, but you are wrong."

Marius interrupted before Asadal could build his argument. "The Lady helps me with a blow to the head and a kick to the groin."

Rather than responding to the lewdness of his comment as expected, Asadal nodded grimly. He stroked a stubbled chin. "The Lady's plans are not always easy to understand. With you, anyone with sight can easily see. But what's happening in Seatown on the other hand," Asadal shrugged, "is shrouded in secrecy."

Marius sat up. His heart thumped in his chest causing his head to ache with every beat of his heart. He didn't believe a word of what Asadal said about his own curse being simple to understand. But about the secrets of Seatown, he remembered some important details. "The men who knocked me out, their names were Pithy and Barn—"

Asadal stepped in. "I know who it was on the ship that took you. I'm having them watched."

"There was a third one," said Marius. He strained to recall every detail. "His name was Coltic, and he belonged to a house or to a wealthy merchant family by the sound of him, though I didn't see his face."

"It is a shame you did not see him," said Asadal. "Think, though. That they called him by the name Coltic, does that guarantee it is his real name?" He held up a hand before Marius could protest, "I will have the matter looked into. I had the man you call Coltic followed last night before I jumped in to save you." He shook his head, "He wore a dark, hooded cloak with no sign of any house upon it; and, unfortunately, the child I sent—one of my best—lost him in the alleys."

Marius lay back on the bed. His head immediately thanked him by reducing the furious pounding.

"Most unusual for one of my Sparrows to fail in streets they know by heart. But the man may have had help. Well, we will discover him in time."

Asadal moved toward the trap door.

Marius remembered more of the conversation on the boat. "Wait," Marius called to Asadal. "Coltic said that he was working for the White Tower. He knew I'd been cursed, said a witch told him." Marius recounted his encounter with the old woman at the gate of Seatown. "She said that a Walker would die before the new tide turned."

Asadal paused next to the door in the floor. He considered Marius's words before responding. "We know that they work for the White Tower," he muttered. "Did it never occur to you, though, that Coltic's witch was not the woman at the gate but the one who you confronted in the black market?"

Marius had been so sure. After all, Coltic has talked about how the witch had felt the curse inside of him, and the old woman at the gate had so thoroughly felt his hand, as though she'd been looking for something. But the woman at the gate hadn't seemed evil, just crazy. On the other hand, the shopkeeper in the black market had most definitely been both wicked and a witch.

Asadal interrupted Marius's thoughts. "There will be plenty of time to discuss these matters." He raised the door. "I must go. And you must rest. And when you are rested," said Asadal, "we will unravel this mystery together, just like the old days."

He disappeared through the floor.

Just like the old days. The thought held little comfort. Marius remembered the old days. In the old days, Asadal had turned Marius over to an Astor to save his own neck.

Marius hoped these days would not, in fact, be just like the old days.

* * *

In the Sparrows' Nest the children made more noise than a flock of migrating birds.

Rest was hard to come by. Marius finally gave up. He made his way down, through the trap door to the floor below. He discovered that his room occupied an upper story at the back of the building. Marius emerged into an enormous room and remembered his visit from the night before, when he'd collapsed. The sheer height of the ceiling had made him dizzy. Of course, thought Marius, it might have been the blow to the head that did that.

Now Marius could look into the rafters without feeling faint. His head had begun to clear. It no longer pounded with every beat of his heart. Though the backs of his eyes ached, his vision remained unclouded.

Marius beheld the organized chaos that animated the Sparrows' Nest.

In the center of the room, a group of smaller children formed a circle around a little boy and a little girl who were engaged in an energetic game of tag. The boy, who was obviously "it," hopped on one leg, chasing the girl who scrambled around on two legs trying to avoid his grasping hands. The circle kept her from straying too far. The boy moved constantly, trying to cut her off. Marius watched till the boy finally caught the girl, at which point she moved to the center of the circle, raised a leg, and took on the next challenger.

The children laughed and pointed at the pair. Their shouts of encouragement drowned each other out. Marius couldn't understand a word they were saying.

He moved away from the circle. In one corner, some of the bigger children looked to be playing a different sort of game. One child, wearing a cloak with pockets of all sizes, wound his way through a line of children like a snake through a row of corn. The other children would paw at the coat or bump into the boy, trying to throw him off balance.

Marius didn't recognize the purpose of their game at first.

Then, as Rebius threw on the coat and ran the gauntlet, weaving between the other children, his hand shot out of the cloak, capturing young Iatro by the wrist. Marius could see something shiny in Iatro's outstretched fingers. Rebius smiled triumphantly. The smaller boy winced.

Marius moved closer. Iatro held a large coin. Rebius twisted the boy's wrist, forcing him to drop the coin, which Rebius deposited back into a pocket.

Rebius held up Iatro's hand, speaking to the other children. "They'll see you coming, Iatro. You'll have to be much faster than that."

Iatro lowered his head, "B-bummer."

Marius again caught a glimpse of something familiar about Iatro—the way his head fell forward and his shoulders sagged in disappointment.

"You think that now," said Rebius. "If they catch you stealing, you'll be sorry enough." He released Iatro's wrist and, with a look of obvious distaste, wiped his hand on his tunic as though it had been soiled by coming into contact with the boy.

Rebius addressed the other children again, "We Sparrows take the scraps. Sometimes we steal to eat. A Sparrow who does not steal, does not eat."

Marius wondered what Asadal, agent of the Church of the Lady, thought about his subject's thievery. He looked around the warehouse expecting to catch a glimpse of the old man. Yet Asadal was nowhere to be seen.

The children near Rebius resumed their game, trying to pick the pockets of Rebius's cloak without getting caught.

Iatro walked away from the game, his hands at his side, his face cast toward the warehouse's dirty wood floor.

Marius felt for the boy.

After all, Marius had been picked on by Sivinius. He knew what it was like to have a stutter and for everyone to look at you like you were stupid just because you talked funny.

On impulse, Marius approached Iatro. He bumped into him.

Iatro looked up, surprised and showing a flash of anger that quickly seeped out of his face as though he were afraid to let it show.

"Hey, did you—?" Marius slapped at the pockets on his vest. "Did you just steal a coin from me?" Marius poked a finger into a small pocket. "Did you take a tiara?"

Iatro's eyebrows flew up like a startled bird. He waved his hands, protesting his innocence.

Marius wasn't buying it.

He walked over to the boy and looked down on him. Marius's gangly body and thin legs gave him the advantage of height, though Iatro had to be one of the older children in the room.

Marius wondered briefly why there weren't any older Sparrows. Maybe there was a rule about that, he thought. Or maybe young people had a healthy fear of what an Astor like Lespa might do if they discovered a gang running around the streets of Seatown. Lespa might kill the leaders, including any older children. She might sell the rest into slavery or to the salt mines. In Arovia, the rewards of crime were often not worth the risk of an early death.

In Asadal's case, hiding out with a gang made sense. He was already on the run from the Astors. The Sparrows would have lookouts, secret passages, or bolt holes where Asadal could hide.

Iatro waited patiently, expecting to be bullied.

Marius stuck his hand into the boy's pocket and drew out a tiara. The edge of the small coin peeked out from between his finger and thumb.

The boy's mouth fell open, aghast. He sputtered, "That's n-not m-mine."

"I know it's not yours," said Marius. "It's mine. You stole it when you bumped into me."

Iatro scowled at the accusation, "You b-bumped me!"

True enough, thought Marius. He'd palmed the coin when reaching into Iatro's pocket and had pretended to pull the coin out. A little fake magic.

"No matter," said Marius. He wrinkled his nose in a show of disdain. "I have my coin back, and I won't beat you. But only if you show me how you did it."

Iatro's eyes widened. He stammered, "B-but I d-didn't—"

Marius interrupted him. "Here," he said, "I'm putting the coin back into my pocket. Show me how you took it."

He stepped back. Then he walked directly into Iatro again. The boy nearly fell over.

"No, no, that's not it at all," said Marius. He reached into his pocket and removed the coin. "You can't have done it that way."

In truth, Iatro hadn't made a move toward stealing the coin.

Marius took Iatro's hand and placed the coin inside it. "Here, you put it into your pocket, and we'll try again."

Iatro stuck the small coin tentatively into the top of his pocket.

"You have to stick it in deeper," said Marius. "No one pockets a coin like that."

Iatro poked at the coin, jamming it into a pocket. Marius nodded his approval. "Much better. Now I think," said Marius, taking a step toward Iatro, "you must have done something like this." He brushed past the boy. When he turned around, Marius was holding the tiara.

Iatro hurriedly reached into his pocket, his hand sunk all the way to the wrist searching for the coin.

Marius waved it back and forth like a head of golden wheat swaying in the sun.

"You must have done something like that, right?"

Iatro shrugged. He looked confused.

"Don't toy with me," said Marius. "I'll figure out your trick." He tapped the coin on the side of his head thoughtfully. "You must have reached into my pocket at the same time your shoulder clipped me in the chest."

Marius pursed his lips. "Yes, that would do it. I've heard that if you touch a person in two places at once, they often don't feel the second, lighter touch."

He strode back toward Iatro. "Here let's try it again. Do it just like you did before. Bump into my chest while you steal the coin."

Marius put the coin in his loosest pocket, not so deep as Iatro had done. He motioned the boy toward him. "Bump the chest and take the coin. If you don't do it right, I'll know."

They walked toward each other, again colliding.

Marius turned. He patted his pockets. "There, you see! I told you I'd figure out how you did it."

Iatro held the small coin in his fingers. He stared at it in disbelief as though he'd never expected to get it.

"Bummer!" said Iatro excitedly.

"Right," said Marius. "You're still a bit sloppy though." He rubbed at the back of his head. "I certainly would have caught you if my head didn't hurt so bad."

Iatro held the coin out toward Marius.

He waived it away. "You keep that. You need the practice. The key is distraction. The mind can only think about so many things at once. The body can't feel everything. The eyes can't see everything. Just keep working, and I'm sure you'll improve."

A wide smile split the boy's face.

Marius patted him on the head.

"There are better ways to make money, though," said Marius. He was enjoying the ability to speak in complete sentences again without stuttering every other word. He could show Iatro how he'd made a living on the streets of Amok juggling and doing little tricks. Who knew how much a cute little boy like Iatro could bring in? Marius wondered that he hadn't thought to recruit younger kids to assist in his act.

"Let me get my rings," said Marius, "and I'll show you—" Marius paused in mid-sentence. His rings and his bindle. He'd dropped them last night during the attack. That small bag held all his possessions.

Marius wondered whether his attackers, Barn and Pithy, had taken the bindle. It looked filthy as though it was crawling with lice. After all, a Walker shouldn't appear to have anything worth stealing. Yet Marius's coins, not to mention his cod piece, brass knuckles, and juggling rings were in and attached to the bindle.

He had to go back to House Fluctus and retrace his steps from Clarion's kitchen. Maybe, just maybe his raggedy old bindle would still be in the alley where he'd been mugged.

Iatro ran back to join the other children, blissfully unaware of the difficult choice Marius faced.

He'd thought about hiding out in the Sparrows' Nest until the time of the fair, when he could slip out and meet Notori. He hadn't agreed to take on the White Tower and a coven of witches in Seatown. He'd agreed to keep his eyes open for danger. He'd kept that promise, not that he'd spotted the trouble before it spotted him.

Now, it looked as though he would have to go back up the hill, back to where he'd been attacked, back where he'd been warned by a witch that a Walker would die. Meanwhile, Barn and Pithy were out there somewhere, planning another abduction.

Chapter Nine

The sun hung brightly over Seatown as Marius emerged from the narrow alleys that ran through the warehouse district. The colors of the houses as he looked up the hill made less of an impression. A coat of pretty paint couldn't hide what lay underneath. At the heart of Seatown lay murder and kidnapping, dark witches, and above all, the machinations of the White Tower, that collection of wizards who had the ear of the Emperor and who helped him rule the kingdom and make war on any kingdoms that dared oppose Arovia.

Marius entered the hub at the base of the hill where a number of roads collected and then spread throughout the city. One of those roads, he knew, led to the witch's black market. Another ran to the ships at anchor where Pithy and Barn sat scheming. He skirted the edge of the rotary, remaining as inconspicuous as possible in case Barn and Pithy were looking for him, though they probably thought him drowned. Marius had others he needed to avoid as well, including the Astors, those guardians of the kingdom, Bithius and Lespa, who had put a target on Marius's back.

Marius looked at the stalls of the merchants lining the rotary. His eyes fell upon the statue in the middle of the circle, an image of the Lady with a dove and a lantern, her skirts blown by the wind, a content look on her face as she gazed out to sea.

Marius wondered for a moment what it must feel like not to be constantly fighting for your life. As a slave, he hadn't known a moment's peace. Sivinius had made his life hell. After Marius got cursed and, consequently, thrown out of his house, still a slave, but now a slave uncared for, still property that might at any moment be reclaimed—he'd nearly starved to death before meeting Asadal.

Passing near the message board, Marius paused for a moment to try to discover if any new notices had been posted. He regretted not learning to read. Asadal had wanted to teach him, and Marius felt that he needed to learn.

He thought back to those days on the road with Asadal learning to be a Walker, moving from farm to farm finding work in the harvest seasons—that had been the closest thing to happiness that Marius had known since leaving childhood and assuming his duties as a slave.

All good things come to an end.

Asadal deserted him when Lespa showed up.

No point rehashing that, Marius thought.

He'd had to make his way alone on the streets of Amok, one of the largest cities in the kingdom, and one to which he could never return unless he wanted to die at the hands of House Marcel, one of the richest and most influential families in the kingdom. Marius had insulted the master of that house and his daughter.

Correction, thought Marius, the Jester's Curse had taken a starring role in that debacle. Marius had been relegated to the sidelines of his mind, a fate he had since been trying to avoid by acting as silly as possible, not giving the curse an opening to exploit.

Looking down at the grass ring on his finger, Marius hoped it would help. But he knew from past experience that the charm would fade as the grass died and that subsequent rings would not be as effective.

As to Marius's curse, Asadal had suspected, and the evil wizard Malconus confirmed that the Jester's Curse must either be wholly driven out or wholly take over.

According to Asadal, though, Marius had been a fool before the curse ever took him. He shook his head as he thought back to their conversation that morning. He'd thought of so many clever things to say in response to the old Walker.

Marius wasn't the fool, at least not by choice. If anything, followers of the Lady like High Priest Campri in Amok and like Asadal, they were the fools for following a superstitious religion founded by a batty woman who kept birds and set a lot of fires. Not to mention that the religion had set itself against the White Tower, a collection of wizened old men who wielded actual, verifiable power, the likes of which had cursed Marius.

Yet, as he compared the wizard Malconus to Asadal and to High Priest Campri there were obvious differences between them. For one thing, the men of the church hadn't been trying to kill Marius and his friends.

Marius wondered, though, whether Malconus wasn't an exception. After all, Campri had intimated that there were good Astors that helped the work of the church. Lespa was a bad Astor. But if there could be good and bad Astors, Marius reasoned there might be good and bad wizards.

Maybe he could find a good wizard and ask for a cure. It seemed a better alternative than taking orders in the church or following a stranger named Notori around the world.

The option of a good wizard appealed to Marius, so much so that, had Barn or Pithy asked him to go with them to the White Tower, he might have followed.

Perhaps the wizards didn't know the people had been kidnapped. Maybe they really were helping people realize their dreams.

If Asadal knew what the wizards were doing in Seatown, he had not shared that information with Marius. In fact, Asadal had disappeared from the Sparrows' Nest, their gang hideout, before Marius had arisen.

Marius hoped he returned soon. He would feel better having an introduction to Notori. Not to mention, Asadal might be able to keep a handle on the Sparrows Rebius and Demari, who had both been staring daggers in Marius's direction. That Marius helped Iatro in their pick-pocket game had not earned him any thanks.

As if the boy's name held a sort of magic, Iatro appeared. He stumbled into the hub and was nearly run over by a Driver hauling a load of fish. Iatro narrowly avoided the oxen's heavy footsteps and just as deadly horns.

Seeing that he'd caught Marius's attention, the boy waved foolishly.

Marius winced. Not that he was ashamed of being seen with Iatro. The boy wasn't hideously deformed. And, Lady knew, Marius understood the boy better than most. Struggling under the Jester's Curse, he'd often craved companionship. He'd submitted to humiliation at the hands of the merchants of Amok just to fit in, to be around people who knew his name.

Iatro trotted over to him, stumbling on a raised cobblestone. He looked likely to fall but flailed his arms, arresting his momentum at the last moment. It looked as though Iatro had perfected the art of almost falling. Marius could relate.

However, now that Asadal had given Marius the charm that alleviated the Jester's Curse, he found it hard to be in the same company as a fool, reminding him of how he'd been, of how he would be without the grass ring. Such feelings were unfair to Iatro, he knew, but Marius couldn't help it.

It wasn't as though Iatro could help being who he was. Iatro's foolishness didn't come from a curse. The boy had been born that way or had suffered an injury to the head.

Marius instinctively rubbed the lump on his own head. He was lucky not to have sustained a permanent injury like that.

Wouldn't it be ironic, he thought, if he'd become a bumbling fool by a blow on the head, frustrating the Jester's Curse in its hostile takeover.

The thought made Marius smile.

Iatro misinterpreted the smile, thinking it meant Marius was happy to see him.

"H-hello!" Iatro called out a greeting. "I'm Iatro."

"I know," said Marius. "People call me the Jester"

Iatro struggled to pronounce the name, stuttering over it badly.

Marius remembered an old trick, one that Irina's brother, Ian, had taught him back in Amok. "Try saying it all at once 'Jesser.'" Marius said, "Like that, 'Jesser.'"

Iatro tried, "Jesser."

"Good." Marius smiled and this time the expression was sincerely meant. Though he had been dreading the boy's company, Marius found that he'd taken a liking to the strange young man who, several years younger than Marius, had been struggling with this condition all his life.

He thought back to Ian and Irina. He wondered whether Ian would ever become the head-slave at House Marcel. And he wondered how Irina was getting along in her new position at the church. Marius remembered that Ian and Irina had another brother, one that reminded them of Marius, one that he'd never met, having been kicked out of House Marcel for his abnormality. Marius wondered if their brother had become a Walker like him.

The thought of Irina, so lovely with her blue eyes and fair, auburn hair, sent a bitter pang through his chest. Even if he did succeed in ridding himself of the Jester's Curse, Marius wondered whether Irina would ever think of him as anything other than "sweet."

Well, there was only one way to get over the heaviness of his heart. He would visit House Fluctus and talk to the lovely kitchen slave, Clarion. It felt a bit like a betrayal of his professed love for Irina. But she had not reciprocated his love. The only attachment was on his part; so then, Marius reasoned, he ought to be able to talk to another girl if he wanted to.

Even if that girl, as he called her, was several years older than he was and had a son old enough to be Marius's not-much-younger brother.

Marius tousled Iatro's fair hair. "Let's go see about lunch."

And about his bindle, Marius thought, though he didn't hold out much hope for it. The bindle and his personal belongings were probably half-way to Machoo by now.

That didn't mean he couldn't try for a hot meal at Clarion's kitchen.

And if Iatro wanted to tag along, what was that to Marius. "Come along, then," he said. "Up the hill."

Marius adjusted the loose strap of fabric that held up his pants. It would hardly do. "Before we go, is there anyone in the market handy with a needle and thread?"

A few minutes later, Marius made his way up the steep incline, wearing pants that fit, with Iatro following close on his heels.

* * *

"Iatro," Marius whispered, "try keeping your mouth closed when you eat."

The boy grinned. Crumbs of bread the size of small stones fell from the corners of his mouth onto the raised table that sat in the middle of Clarion's kitchen.

"Bummer," said the boy, still smiling.

"Is that your thing? Saying 'bummer'? What does it even mean?" Marius had noticed that Iatro said it whenever anything good or bad happened.

Stepping away from a pot of stew, Clarion looked over at the boy. "He eats as though he's never seen food before."

"None as poor as yours I'm sure," said Marius.

Clarion waved a cutting knife at him in a mock threat before returning her attention to the stew pot.

Marius tucked into the feast she'd set before them: bread and butter along with the better half of a roasted fish in a spicy, sweet sauce served alongside chunks of vegetables. They had arrived in time to get a taste of the dinner meal before it went upstairs.

Heat swam off the fire that had long since been reduced to coals. A side of fatty pork turned on a spit in the back of the oven. At the front of the fire, Clarion tended the stew, while another one of the cooks fried fish. Clarion called out instructions to the other workers who were making the finishing touches to the dinner service. Bread that had been made the night before was steamed so that it would be warm when it hit the table. They carved carrots into intricate flowers and beets into rose petals. Clarion lent a hand, wielding her knife with a flourish that came from experience.

Clarion reached into a hanging basket. Her hand emerged with a fat, brown egg which she cracked and dumped into the stew, stirring vigorously. Reaching into a jar on the mantle above the cooking fire, she took a pinch of herbs and dropped them into the pot. The knife dangled loosely in her free hand.

Had Marius been able to smell the herbs, he probably could have named the spice right away. In Amok, he'd learned a proper appreciation for spices and the way they could turn an ordinary meal into something special.

He missed his spices. They'd been in the bindle when Bithius searched it. The big brute had scattered the precious herbs to the wind.

His bindle. Marius missed that too. His poor sack on a stick had not been in the dark alley near Clarion's house.

Marius had lost everything: his juggling rings, the brass knuckles, the tin codpiece, his old slave uniform, not to mention a fine collection of coins.

Clarion interrupted his sad reverie. "If you want more, Iatro, take your plate over to Deidre." She pointed with the knife toward one of the kitchen staff who was cleaning the cookware. Most of the remnants she brushed into a slop bucket for the animals. The better bits she held back.

Iatro's head bobbed up and down in a silly nod. Taking his thick, earthenware plate, he made his way over to the dish washer.

Marius did like the boy. Something about Iatro put Marius at ease, as though, around a foolish boy like Iatro, the Jester's Curse had no reason to assert itself. Iatro smiled no matter what Marius said as though he took simple pleasure in his company. Marius knew how it felt to be accepted by someone. Irina had befriended him in Amok despite the Jester's Curse. Perhaps he could be that same kind of friend to Iatro.

Clarion took Iatro's seat beside Marius.

True, she wasn't Irina. But she was sitting very close to him. Marius noticed a hint of spices about her, as though she'd spent so much time around cloves and lemon peels that their essence had ground their way into her skin.

She smiled, "I'm glad you brought him along. He seems like a nice boy. Oh!" Clarion exclaimed.

Marius glanced over at Iatro. He'd spilled his plate down the front of Deidre's tunic. Covered in food waste as she already was, it made little difference.

Clarion laughed. The kitchen staff tittered. Even Deidre didn't stay mad at Iatro. He apologized so poorly and so profusely, that she finally forgave him, giving him the last scrapings of a pudding just to get him away. The boy, too, looked as dirty as any of the Sparrows. Marius wished he'd cleaned Iatro up a bit before bringing him into the kitchen. Thankfully, Clarion hadn't objected.

"He is nice," Marius finally agreed. "Tragic, though. He lost his parents." Marius lied. He didn't know a thing about Iatro's lineage. But the story seemed sympathetic. "I've been looking after him a bit." Which was technically true, if by "a bit" one meant a quick lesson in pick-pocketing and a stroll around town.

Clarion regarded Marius warmly, with a look of open admiration on her pretty face—which was the exact effect he'd been going for.

He smiled.

She leaned forward. Her eyes narrowed. "You like children?"

Marius sensed a sudden, dangerous turn in the conversation. He felt as though he were back in the ocean currents, dangerously afloat and in danger of drowning. Marius wondered how one was expected to respond to an attractive mother who asked whether you liked children, especially one holding a knife.

Thankfully, Iatro returned to the table at that moment, breaking the tension. Clarion stood up to make room for him.

Marius patted the boy on the shoulder. "Well, of course. Who doesn't like children?"

Iatro looked up, his eyebrows raised in a sort of startled confusion, obviously wondering if a response was expected from him. Marius noted that the boy wore that expression a lot.

He tried to reassure Iatro by changing the subject, "Save me a bit of that pudding okay?"

"Um-kuh," Iatro responded through a mouth full of food.

Clarion turned her head, looking down and to the side, away from Marius. Her cheeks flushed.

"Not everyone likes children," she said. "My master for instance—"

She let the sentence drift, letting the thought float away on the tide of the conversation.

Marius didn't try to rescue it. He didn't know what to say.

Clarion leaned over, across Iatro's back, and kissed Marius on the cheek. Blood rushed into his face. His head began to pound a little as a result of the injury, the sudden change in his heart rate, and a sense of elation at Clarion's inexplicable touch.

"I didn't get a chance to thank you properly for finding Jank yesterday." She fumbled with her apron, wiping her knife clean on it. "It's so rare to find a nice man in Seatown." She looked shyly away from him.

I'm not that nice, thought Marius. But he added aloud, struggling to keep his voice normal, "I had noticed that you don't seem to have any male slaves?"

"A few," said Clarion. "Our Master prefers—"

"I understand." Marius had been a slave long enough to know what happened to the pretty ones. Thankfully, the male slaves were rarely propositioned, especially ones as young as Marius had been before he'd been thrown out of House Cervix. His hawkish nose might also have had something to do with it.

An awkward silence ensued as Marius struggled to think of something to say.

Iatro, amazingly enough, came to their rescue. "I w-was a s-slave wuh-wuh-wuh—"

Marius helped him along with his story, "Once? You were?"

Iatro nodded, "L-lived in the k-kitchen. B-bummer."

Marius wondered what had happened to young Iatro. Perhaps he, like Marius, had been expelled due to his speech impediment and clumsy manner. Or perhaps he'd gotten fed up at being the brunt of every joke and had run away.

It was also entirely possible, thought Marius, that the boy had left the house on an errand one day and had simply gotten lost. He didn't seem possessed of an enormous intellect. Then again, people thought the same of Marius when his curse manifested or when he acted the fool, trying to keep the curse at bay.

"Well," Clarion seemed to have recovered herself. "Dinner has to be served. It has been nice talking with you," she said. "And, really, thanks for helping with Jank. He's—" Clarion struggled to find the words.

A handful, thought Marius, along with some other choice phrases that might describe young Jank. He didn't suggest any of them to the boy's mother.

She continued, "If anything had happened to him, our master. He. Well, Jank, you see—" Her forehead wrinkled. She looked as though she wanted to tell Marius something but didn't know how to say it.

Marius thought he understood. The children of slaves, as Marius himself had been, were valuable in the same way a calf or a baby goat might be—as a beast of burden or one that might be sold for a profit.

Jank might be prized in that way, but Marius didn't think so.

Children of slaves might also hold a place in a master's heart if the child carried the same blood that flowed through that heart.

Clarion had said that their master hated children. Yet he would have been upset had anything amiss happened to Jank. That only admitted one conclusion: Jank was the bastard son of the master of House Fluctus.

It would explain why Clarion had been so upset at his having gone missing the day before. She'd been more worried than a parent ought to be about a child that had wandered off, especially a boy as old as Jank.

She must have been equally concerned for her child and terrified at what their master might do if any harm came to his offspring.

Marius looked at Clarion in a new light. He scanned the room again, noting for the first time how the kitchen staff watched her out of the corners of their eyes.

He experienced another epiphany. Clarion wasn't the head of the kitchen by years or by skill. The others deferred to her because of the favor shown to her by their master.

It suddenly dawned on Marius what a lonely existence Clarion must lead, held at arm's length by the slaves as though she were mistress of the house—and yet she was not the mistress of House Fluctus. Rather, Clarion was a slave, regarded for her sexuality, not seen as a partner in the management and rearing of a household, nor of a family.

Clarion's hand rested on Iatro's back. He happily obliterated the last remaining bite of pudding, oblivious to the drama unfolding and to Marius's previous request.

Marius wanted to do something, to show that he understood, that he cared.

He wanted to take her hand.

He began to reach out. His resolve faltered.

Marius felt the Jester's Curse rising inside of him. It sensed a weakness, an opportunity it might exploit.

Through force of will and with the help of the grass ring, the charm woven by Asadal, Marius suppressed the curse. It wouldn't be ruining the moment in the kitchen. Marius could ruin it well enough on his own.

Though he buried the curse, still Marius stammered a bit as he spoke, which was the natural state of a teenage boy, though he hardly knew it, having lived with the curse for so long, "I could, uh, help with the, uh, the dinner service," he said. "With the heavy trays."

Clarion looked him up and down, appraising both him and his offer.

"We have guests tonight," she said. "I thank you but something could go wrong."

"I've served at dinner many times," he said, admitting part of the truth but leaving out the bit about how he was a runaway slave.

Sure, technically, thought Marius, he hadn't run away. He had gotten thrown out and then had to leave to find food. But they never gave him his freedom, therefore—

Clarion snapped him back to reality. "All right. You can help, though I don't know how I'll explain it to our master."

"Tell him someone fell ill," Marius suggested, "and that you borrowed a hand from a neighbor."

Clarion tapped a finger to her lips. The knife swished back and forth by her side, keeping a steady rhythm. "He might believe it."

Marius pressed his advantage, "It looks like Deidre could do with a night off."

The poor girl was covered in muck from the washing. She'd take forever cleaning up and might get a beating if her appearance wasn't sufficient, especially with a master who liked looking at his slaves.

Marius followed up on the thought, "He won't look twice at a male slave."

Clarion barked out a little laugh. "True enough. Though one of the guests might. Still—" She walked back to her stew pot. She put down the knife and began to ladle the stew into a serving dish.

Apparently the knife hitting the table was the signal everyone had been waiting for. The kitchen burst into activity as plates were loaded and carried up a set of steps leading into the main house.

"Follow Deidre and get a tunic. You can't serve looking like that."

Clarion meant looking like a rainbow had thrown up on him. Marius's colorful jester's outfit, tailor made for him by the creepy Old Huttle back in Amok, was a patchwork riot of colors.

He wouldn't mind wearing something normal for a change. So long as he didn't get forced into assuming the role of a slave permanently.

Marius patted Iatro on the shoulder, "I'm going to help serve dinner."

Iatro nodded and started to rise along with Marius.

"You stay here," said Marius, pointing at the table.

"I can h-help," said Iatro.

Marius smiled. He couldn't imagine Clarion would sanction that.

In fact, Marius was actually looking forward to doing something that had once been so routine. His life and his vocational calling had been interrupted by the Jester's Curse.

If it wasn't for the way Asadal's charm helped contain the curse, Marius would never have chanced waiting at table. Especially not during an important occasion with guests.

Now, he could help without having to worry about the Jester's Curse making a botch of the affair. He wouldn't be spilling hot stew on the guests.

"Iatro," said Clarion, "why don't you help Deidre with the dishes. She'd appreciate an experienced kitchen boy's help."

Marius admired the clever way Clarion handled the boy. Then again, she'd had a lifetime handling her difficult son, Jank.

Deidre returned with a tunic made of aquamarine fabric. Marius found a private place in the pantry to don the outfit.

As soon as he stepped out of the pantry, Clarion loaded up his arms with the roast pork. It smelled heavenly. The roast had turned a subtle brown as the fire caramelized the fat. He hoped there would be a bit left after dinner for the kitchen staff to pick at.

Marius followed one of the other slaves up the flight of stairs. He recognized her from the previous afternoon. She'd pointed him in the direction of the kitchen. There was no time for a reunion, however. They emerged from the stairs into a short hallway and turned into a room already lit with candles despite the early hour.

Marius recognized the master of House Fluctus by the aquamarine fabric draped over his morbidly-corpulent frame. The man was huge. Marius avoided eye contact.

The other guests had their backs to Marius. The three of them sat across the table from the master, yet they took up only a smidgen more space.

Marius's appetite fled. The fat on the pig lost its appeal. He quickly set it on the table and turned to retrieve the next course.

Then he heard it, a high-pitched nasal laugh. He'd heard that same laugh the night before, while he lay in the cupboard aboard the ship. It belonged to the man called Coltic.

Marius turned. Three people sat across from the master of House Fluctus. Two men and one woman. The woman had long black hair and a red sash around her waist. Marius recognized her even from the back as Raza of House Ponti, the beautiful woman he'd seen on the balcony. She didn't look bad from behind either.

Recovering himself, he focused on the two men. One wore a red tunic matching Rasa's sash. He had the smooth hair and bearing of a young man who let the servants handle the hard work. His lean shoulders and arms lacked musculature. He had, all in all, an air of feminine grace about him—like the way his hands cupped his dinner goblet. Marius suspected that he might look as pretty as Raza, which was perhaps why House Fluctus had invited the pair to dinner. Coltic wasn't entirely weak, however. A rapier in a well-oiled scabbard hung from the back of his chair.

The third man—

Marius froze. The third man wore a tunic of white marking him, undoubtedly, as a wizard.

Marius's heart stopped in his chest. The man stabbed a fork into the side of the pork roast. Marius caught the profile of his face. He had a long crooked nose that looked like a crushed potato.

Malconus, the wizard that had cursed Marius, sat a few steps in front of him, calmly eating dinner.

Marius looked frantically for a knife. If only he had his bindle.

The kitchen, thought Marius. He would find one in the kitchen. Clarion had a knife. He would take Clarion's knife and take his revenge.

Chapter Ten

The knife lay on a small table next to the fire. Marius took it. He felt the handle, a thin metal tang clasped between two pieces of wood worn smooth by a familiar hand, by Clarion's hand. The fire had kept the grip warm as though she'd just released it.

"Marius, what are you doing?" Clarion's hand clasped his wrist.

He could tell from the widening of her irises that Clarion was afraid of him, afraid of the look in his eyes and of the knife in his hand.

"Jesser?" Iatro called to Marius it seemed from a long way off. A part of his mind registered the boy's calming presence calling him back to reason. Marius didn't want to be reasonable. He wanted to kill Malconus.

A haze occluded his vision. His arms felt heavy. He could see only what lay directly in front of him. The fire. The window. A white bird sitting on the sill.

Pain registered in his mind. His cheek stung. Clarion had slapped him.

The world swam back into focus.

"Marius, what are you doing?"

He gripped the handle of the knife.

"I'm going to kill someone." He said it quietly, calmly even.

"What are you talking about?"

The kitchen had grown uncomfortably quiet. The serving staff stood gazing at Marius with dishes held in their hands, growing cold.

Clarion shouted at them to serve the food. Hesitantly, they slunk out of the room, perhaps fearful of what Marius might do to Clarion, though he hardly saw how a bunch of pretty serving girls might stop him if he decided to do something crazy.

Clarion's hand still grasped his wrist.

In other circumstances, he might have found the contact pleasant. Now he struggled to free his arm. She had an iron grip, developed after years of wrestling heavy pots over the fire. Her fingers felt rough and calloused on the soft underbelly of his wrist.

She pleaded with him, "Marius, talk to me!" The flash of her eyes challenged him, urging him to confide in her.

Since he was about to accomplish the thing he wanted most in life, he didn't see how sparing a moment to tell her could hurt.

"I am going to kill the wizard in the dining room. I'm going to sneak up and stab him in the back. He's the one who cursed me. He's going to die."

"What do you mean, cursed?" Clarion glanced at him from head to foot. "You don't look cursed."

Marius nearly laughed. He felt the charmed ring on his finger holding the curse at bay. If only she knew.

Clarion had seen him only once before, and he'd been very careful not to let the curse come out. She hadn't even asked why he wasn't stuttering anymore and may not have even remembered his debilitating speech impediment.

That was one of the benefits of moving to a new town, thought Marius. No one here knew him as Marius the runaway slave or as Prince Pratt of Amok Square, the man with the Jester's Curse. In Seatown, he was simply Marius or the Jester of Zeno.

If he killed the wizard, Malconus, he hoped that the Jester's Curse would die with him. Even if it didn't, Marius could pursue a cure at his leisure, having gotten revenge.

He explained, "The wizard, Malconus, is evil. He cursed me and many others. He deserves to die."

"That's as may be," Clarion pleaded, "but must he die today, in the dining room, killed by my knife?"

Marius blinked. What did it matter how the wizard died? Even if it got messy, even if he had to cut up the wizard's body and burn it in the cooking fire to do the job, the important thing was to make sure the wizard died.

"You can't kill here, please," said Clarion.

Marius used his free hand to grip her shoulder. He looked Clarion in the eyes, meeting her fierce gaze. "He uses magic to change people, to warp them. He takes their natural inclinations and manipulates them, turning them into bent, broken things." Marius paused a moment, letting his words sink in. "That's how magic works. That's why he's so wicked. He could have used his skills for good, to make people better, to bring out their true nature."

Clarion stiffened. "None can show men their true nature but the Lady."

Marius was slightly taken aback. He didn't take Clarion for a religious person. He hadn't noticed any signs of the Lady in the kitchen, but he hadn't really been looking. Perhaps her master didn't allow the slaves such foolish baubles. Lady knew, slaves had so few comforts.

Marius didn't want to argue theology. "They could have made people a little bit better. And they didn't."

Hadn't High Priest Campri, the leader of the Church of the Lady in Amok, said the same thing to Marius? Campri had explained why the church so vehemently opposed the machinations of the White Tower.

"But Marius, you can't kill him."

"Why not?" Marius broke free of her grip. He held the knife away, evading her grasping hands. He held her by her shoulder at arm's length. His gangly arms were much longer than hers.

"Think of me. Think of the others. We are the ones who'll be blamed if you kill him. We'll be beaten. We'll be killed."

Marius hesitated. He hadn't thought of anything beyond his immediate thirst for revenge. He hadn't thought of what would happen after the killing, of how he would escape, or of what might happen to those who remained behind.

Thinking of escape, Marius looked toward the kitchen door. The white bird that had been sitting on the window sill prowled the ground outside, hunting in the dirt for its supper.

A thought rose unbidden in his mind as though a small voice, not his own, whispered in his ear, trying to reason with him. He could leave. He could walk out the door. He didn't have to kill, didn't have to seek revenge.

He could seek a cure for the curse and live out his life. The Lady would cure him if he asked.

He shook his head. No. He had waited too long, planned too long. The wizard had to die.

The small voice spoke again: but what of Clarion and her son? What of the others.

"Marius," said Clarion. "We gave you the tunic. I let you serve at table. We will be blamed. Please don't do this thing."

Marius let the knife drop to his side.

He took a deep breath and let it out.

Clarion took his wrist again, more gently this time, and he let her.

"The wizard took everything from me," he said. The words tumbled out now that the frenzy had run its course. "I was a slave at a house in Zeno. I might have become majordomo till he came." Marius hung his head. "After he cursed me, I was thrown out. Left on my own to live or to die. I don't think they expected me to live. Who would help a disgraced slave? This may be my only chance."

Marius's eyes burned. He didn't want to cry in front of this woman. He had never cried about his fate.

"I survived though. I—" Marius didn't want to talk about what it had taken to survive, the humiliations he'd borne in order to eat. He had become a fool in the eyes of the world.

Clarion touched his cheek. "I'm sorry."

A tear escaped the corner of his eye. He didn't touch it. Thankfully, neither did she.

"A man helped me," said Marius. He had nearly said "a friend." Perhaps Asadal was his friend, as High Priest Campri had tried to tell him. "He made me this ring, to help fight the curse." Marius held up his hand, showing her the grass ring woven around his lanky finger. "But it won't last. The grass is dying. With every passing moment the charm fades. The wizard said his curse will eventually consume my soul, making me a fool. I try to fight it, but—" Marius's voice trailed away.

"Kill him then."

Clarion released his wrist.

Marius blinked. He wiped at his cheek with the back of his knife hand. "What?"

Clarion regarded him calmly. Her hands clasped in front of her apron. Her mouth was set in a look of steady determination. "You said this might be your only chance."

"Yes," Marius agreed.

"Then you must take it. Kill him."

"I can't," Marius admitted. His muscles, previously tensed for action, loosened. Warmth washed over his skin from the top of his shoulders down through his forearms and belly.

Clarion knitted her brows, "I don't understand. You said—"

"I know what I said," said Marius. He now took her hand. "But you were right. If I kill him, you will be punished."

"I'm prepared. My master favors me, I might—"

Marius doubted the master liked her that much. He might spare Jank, but the White Tower would demand vengeance for the death of a wizard. The whole house might even be destroyed, including the master.

Marius placed the knife in Clarion's hand.

"I will wait for him outside, on the streets of Seatown. I'll find a place unconnected with you. But I need your help"

Clarion nodded.

"The man sitting beside Lady Raza, what's his name?"

"He is Secundus, the second—"

Marius finished her sentence, "second son of House Ponti."

Clarion nodded again.

"Has he ever gone by the name Coltic? Do you recognize that name?"

Clarion shook her head. A strand of blonde hair fell across her forehead. Marius nearly brushed it back before he caught himself.

"I think he's the one behind the disappearances."

He could see the knuckles on her hand turn white. Clarion clenched her jaw.

"Be careful around him, okay?"

"What are you going to do?" Clarion pursed her lips, blowing the strand of hair out of her face.

Marius couldn't help but like her.

"I'm going to expose Coltic—I mean Secundus. And I'm going to kill the wizard."

"And become Emperor of Zeno too?" She smiled.

Clarion was right. It did sound like an outlandish plan for one man, a former slave, to accomplish. But she didn't know that he had help. He had Asadal and a whole, diminutive gang at his back.

He had to reach them. He considered leaving Iatro behind with instructions to follow the wizard, then thought better of it.

He spoke quickly to Clarion. "See if you can find where the wizard is staying." Kitchen staff gossiped among themselves. Perhaps she knew someone she could ask at House Ponti. "I've got to go."

She ran a hand down his arm, "Be safe."

"And you," he said.

Calling to Iatro, Marius grabbed his colorful rags and left the kitchen, startling the white bird into flight.

Outside the walls of House Fluctus, Marius turned to Iatro. He kept walking, pulling the boy along. "I need you to show me the quickest way to the Sparrows' Nest."

Iatro nodded, showing that he understood.

A figure emerged from an alley.

Marius flinched. His hand went to the back of his head where the raised bump stood out.

"Are you a Walker?"

The witch in the black cloak stood before them, barring their way. Her blue eyes looked piercingly into his own.

He didn't have time for this. "Yes," said Marius, fighting a growing sense of frustration. He had to get back to the Sparrows' Nest before Coltic and the wizard finished dinner. He had to warn Asadal and form a plan.

"A Walker will-"

Marius interrupted. "We've been through this before. Yesterday in fact. Do you have an update? Is the dead Walker young our old? A native Arovian or a foreigner? Does he have a name, like, Asawan or Asadal," said Marius. "But honestly, if you're a seer you should know whether I'm a Walker or not anyway, right?"

Marius reveled in the fact that he could speak entire sentences, spilling the contents of his mind, without a stutter. He could say the clever things he always meant to say but couldn't because of the curse. He felt smug at having put the old woman in her place.

She reached for his hand and, opening it, examined his palm.

"Look, really, I'm in a hurry—"

The words died in his mouth as she stuck a stick into his upturned hand.

She continued the sentence he'd so rudely interrupted. "A Walker will always be needing his bindle."

He stared at her wrinkled face and then at his hand, which held the stout stick that bore his bindle. The sack hung on the end of the stick and the rings as well. He swung it onto his shoulder.

Marius felt like ox dung. He had insulted her. And here the old witch had rescued his bindle and returned it to him.

"Remember," she said. "At the turn of the new tide—"

Marius completed her prophecy, "a Walker will die."

"Bummer," said Iatro.

The witch nodded, patting Marius's hand. She stepped back into the alley. Marius hesitated only for a moment before resuming his quick walk toward the Sparrows' Nest.

* * *

"What do you mean he's not here?" said Marius.

Rebius stood in front of him with his hands planted on his hips. His dimples creased into a sneer. "I mean," said Rebius, "that he left this morning. He does that. Drops in and out. He might be gone for a month or maybe a year."

Darkness had set on Seatown as Marius and Iatro threaded their way through the narrow alleys back to the Sparrows' Nest. Marius was glad to have brought Iatro along. He might not have been able to find the hideout without the boy's help.

When they'd neared the Sparrows' Nest, Iatro had issued a series of low whistles that were picked up and passed on by the lookouts on the roofs above. The signal Iatro had given differed from the one Asadal had used the night before. Marius wondered whether the passcode changed every day. He suspected that a hail of stones would land on the heads of anyone who tried to pass at night without giving the proper signal and was even more grateful that Iatro had tagged along.

Back in the Sparrows' Nest, a motley assortment of candles had been arranged throughout the warehouse out of reach of the smallest children. The flame from a cooking fire added its light to theirs.

The candles, which ranged from one as fat as Marius's leg, to a tiny candle no bigger than his smallest finger, ranged in color from deep red to light green. Some were little better than large lumps, as though they'd been set out in the sun and forgotten. Marius suspected they'd been filched from the chandler's scrap bin. The weak light they gave off didn't reach the ceiling of the broken-down warehouse. Tendrils of smoke wreathed the rafters. Whiffs of burning tallow rendered perhaps from the oil of some great fish, filled Marius's nostrils.

The foul smell didn't improve his mood. Marius took a step toward Rebius.

Demari appeared at the boy's shoulder, his fists bunched, ready for a fight. Marius thought he could take both of them together. But he wasn't sure. Despite his height advantage, the boys' combined weight had to exceed his. Marius resembled and weighed about the same as a scarecrow.

"Asadal won't be gone long," said Marius. "He has business in Seatown."

"He's never run out on you before?" said Rebius. The boy's sneer faltered, only briefly, but enough for Marius to realize that he wasn't the only person Asadal had disappointed in the past.

Marius felt his anger fade. Marius wasn't planning on staying in Seatown. If he challenged Rebius and won, the Sparrows would be left without a leader when Marius met up with Notori at the fair.

Marius sighed. "Fine. I need a few Sparrows to follow some people."

Rebius didn't budge. He shook his head, "Sorry, but we don't take orders from you. You aren't a Sparrow. In fact, I think you should leave the Nest."

"Hoi, you!" Iatro shouted.

Rebius looked as startled as Marius to hear the usually quiet boy speak out.

Iatro came to stand between Marius and Rebius. "The k-king let him s-stay. S-so he s-stays." He stumbled on the last word, nearly swallowing it. But Iatro had his say.

The other children, who had been playing in the background, stopped to see what Rebius would do, whether he would obey the king in his absence.

Thankfully, Rebius had the good sense not to push the matter.

He motioned toward the warehouse full of children. "Pick whichever Sparrow you want."

Marius was a bit taken aback. He'd expected Rebius to make the selection. Marius didn't know the children well enough to know which of them were trustworthy and which weren't. If only Asadal were there, he thought. But the old man wasn't around. He had abandoned Marius once again, but this time Asadal hadn't left him in the clutches of Lespa the Astor. No, thought Marius, it might actually be worse. Asadal had abandoned him while he was within reach of the evil wizard Malconus. Marius wondered whether Malconus had been told by Coltic that a man with the Jester's Curse had been spotted. Perhaps not. As he'd said on the ship, no one in their right mind would tamper with one of Malconus's pet projects—of which Marius was one. And Coltic had ordered his murder.

Marius called out, "Which one of you followed the man from the boat last night?"

A slender girl with brown hair raised her hand. Marius couldn't see through the tangled hair that spilled over her face. Her dirty tunic blended into the wooden walls.

"You then," he said, "time to make up for last night. Secundus, the second son of House Ponti is having dinner at House Fluctus. I want him followed. I want to know where he goes and who he speaks to. I don't want you losing him this time."

The girl gave a little squeak in the affirmative and darted through the red door that separated the Sparrows' Nest from the city of Seatown.

"Rebius and Demari," Marius spoke to the leaders.

Rebius turned his head. A look of surprise flitted across his eyes.

"There's a wizard dining at House Fluctus as well. A dangerous wizard. I want to know where he's staying."

Rebius opened his mouth to object, "I'm not—"

Marius stopped him. "You said pick whichever Sparrow I want. Well, I want you and Demari to trail the wizard. But I have to warn you," said Marius. "He's dangerous. He curses without mercy. And he can change his appearance. He can take on the face of another without wearing a mask."

Marius remembered the banquet at House Marcel in Amok where Malconus had disguised himself as one of the slaves in order to keep a better eye on the progress of the Jester's Curse.

Rebius pointed over his shoulder with a thumb. "Good luck getting this lot to bed."

He and Demari slunk out of the warehouse, leaving the red door open. Iatro tripped over and slammed it behind them. The entire wall rattled as though it might come down. Marius took a few steps back. The other children didn't seem to notice the quake, as though they saw the door rattle every other day.

Marius hoped the Sparrows would arrive in time. He would have preferred to watch the house himself, but he feared Malconus might recognize him. In order to kill the wizard, he'd need the element of surprise.

He'd attacked the wizard twice before. During the infamous party at House Marcel, he'd made a frontal assault with the dinner knife that was now wrapped inside his bindle. The wizard had seen it coming and had paralyzed Marius, amplifying his weariness after the dinner performance till it felt like his legs and arms were made of stone. However, Marius later caught the wizard unawares. He'd nearly stuck the knife in Malconus's back.

His fingers itched. Perhaps he should have killed Malconus during dinner at House Fluctus, but as Clarion said, even if Marius escaped, she would be punished, likely killed, for letting him into the house wearing the tunic of a house slave.

Marius realized he was still wearing the tunic. Taking a thick purple candle bent like an elbow, Marius walked toward the ladder that led to his loft. He had to change and get some rest. His head ached. And he couldn't be seen around town in the garb of a slave of House Fluctus, mostly because House Fluctus had few if any male slaves.

As he climbed the ladder to the loft, wax from the bent candle dripped onto his knuckles while splinters from the rungs bit into his fingers. Ignoring these minor pains, Marius thought of Clarion, of her blonde hair and soft cheekbones. He could see why the master of House Fluctus favored her. She was so different than the black-haired beauties native to the Arovian peninsula—women like Raza of House Ponti.

Remembering the undulating fat of the master under his voluminous robes, Marius shuddered, suppressing a bilious revolt from his stomach. He couldn't imagine having to submit to a master like that, doing the things he required of his slaves. Marius was surprised one of the female slaves hadn't murdered the man already. Of course, if they had, and depending on the disposition of his estate, they might find themselves working for the eight-year-old Jank.

As he began to change out of the aquamarine tunic, Marius noticed that he wasn't alone. Iatro had quietly climbed the ladder and entered the room.

"Yes?"

The lad shuffled from foot to foot. "The k-king and Rebius are gone," he said. "Awaiting o-orders."

Marius realized that the children needed tending. They needed to be tucked into bed. He didn't have a clue about their nightly routine. He'd just have to hope that the older ones could look after the younger.

"Everyone to bed, candles out," said Marius. "We have a big day tomorrow. We're going to kill a wizard."

Chapter Eleven

The noontide sun finally burned through the mist that had settled on the port city of Seatown, draping the streets in a shroud. Marius sat in the hub of the city, near the message board, watching the morning grow old. The shadow cast by the statue of the Lady had practically walked the length of the rotary while he waited. Marius wore a band of dark fabric tied around his arm.

He wore his old bindle, the one Asadal had stolen and returned to him. Asadal had said that if Marius ran into trouble in Seatown, he should wear the bindle around his arm and Asadal would come running.

Marius had never intended to do it. He'd hoped at the time never to see Asadal again. But with Malconus in Seatown and in league with the kidnappers, Marius felt he had little choice but to put the call out for the old Walker.

Iatro sat against the wall next to him. The boy had become Marius's shadow, always hanging around nearby, hovering in the background. Marius hoped the boy wouldn't be too heartbroken when he departed with

Notori. Better yet, he'd have to make sure the boy didn't try to stow away aboard the ship.

Marius knew little about Notori except that he ran a circus and that he traveled a great deal, moving from port to port, from country to country. It was a life that a Walker like Marius could appreciate.

Speaking of Walkers, Marius had seen several enter the hub carrying bindles: two men and a skinny girl traveling alone. At least, he supposed they were Walkers. Marius thought of introducing himself. He practiced the secret handshakes in his mind but didn't know what exactly to say. Aside from Asadal, Marius hadn't met many Walkers. He didn't know what they talked about, maybe about Seatown and where one might find a safe place to sleep and a warm meal.

Marius knew where good food could be found, but so would any other Walker who could use their eyes. The sign scratched into the wall outside House Fluctus shone plain as day. Besides, he felt a little possessive over that house, what with Clarion in the kitchen. He didn't fancy any other Walkers intruding into his space. He might have scratched out the sign on the wall if that didn't go against every code the Walkers had.

Instead, Marius contented himself in watching the Walkers who arrived that day. He wondered whether they had come, as he had, for the fair. It seemed a good opportunity for people like Marius, who performed for their livelihood. It also seemed a good opportunity for pick-pockets. Marius felt sure that Rebius and the Sparrows would be plying their trade during the festivities.

He noticed something else about the Walkers who entered the hub, especially the skinny girl. Their faces all wore a uniform look of concern.

Marius wondered whether he'd looked the same way not two days earlier. He suspected the cause was the same. The Walkers (and probably numerous non-Walkers) had surely been assaulted by the witch on the hill with her dire prophecy about the death of a Walker before the new tide turned.

Marius smiled. The witch was obviously out of her mind. However, if her dire predictions were true, it meant that each newly arrived Walker tilted the odds in his favor. Any one of them might die. One of the male Walkers looked ancient. He might pass away from old age.

Marius passed the time as best he could, carving a small symbol of a tri-cornered jester's hat into the post of the message board. He didn't scratch an arrow to himself. It should be obvious based on his outlandish attire.

Meanwhile, Marius waited for Asadal to appear, supposing he bothered to show up at all. While he waited, Marius mulled over the morning's activity.

The slender Sparrow he'd sent to follow Coltic had reported back before heading to bed to sleep through the day. She had followed Coltic to House Ponti's villa in the city, not far from House Fluctus. She had then waited, blending into the shadows of the alley across from the house. Coltic emerged a little while later, wearing the dark cloak from the night before. He'd gone back to the docks and boarded the ship belonging to Barn and Pithy. Her report was corroborated by two of the other Sparrows who'd been posted by Asadal to watch the boat.

She'd followed Coltic back to House Ponti, indicating that he'd taken a circuitous route through the black market. That was how he'd lost her last time. She'd nearly lost him again when he unexpectedly ducked into a shop.

Marius wondered whether Coltic had dropped in on the witch in the black market, the one Jank had stolen from. Perhaps Coltic had developed a taste for her witch-weed. Or, more likely, as Asadal suspected, she was in league with the kidnappers and the White Tower.

Two Sparrows, a boy and a girl, had been sent to watch House Ponti with instructions to send the girl to Marius in the rotary if Coltic should leave home that morning. As the girl had yet to arrive, Marius concluded that the second son of House Ponti was having a bit of a lie in after such a late night roaming the darker corners of the city.

Marius spat onto the pavement in frustration. He ground the spittle into the paving stone with the toe of his shoe.

Unlike the slender girl following Coltic, Rebius and Demari had failed to follow the wizard. Marius wondered whether the pair had even tried. He realized belatedly it had been foolish to give the two boys the most important duty as a sort of punishment. They were bound to muck it up.

They made up a story, at least it sounded made up, about how Malconus had entered one of the public parks. Speaking words of power that, according to the boys, had burned their ears, the wizard transformed into an enormous white bird and flew off into the night sky.

If they were telling the truth, Marius wondered why it had taken the pair of them so long to return to the Spar-rows' Nest that night. Sleep had been a long time coming for him. Marius had paced the length of the loft more times than he could count before he heard Demari's laughter and felt the shudder as the red door slammed shut, waking half the warehouse.

Marius had wished for an instant that the wall would collapse on the oaf. Instead, Marius had to listen to their remarkable story as the sleepy children looked on in fright and admiration at the bravery of their leaders. He resisted the urge to roll his eyes.

Marius didn't doubt that Malconus could transform. He just didn't think the wizard had done such a trick last night. The man was undoubtedly staying in Seatown. Such a remarkable transformation to save a few steps seemed outlandish and unlike the meanness of spirit Marius had come to expect from the evil wizard.

The pair had probably been smoking witchweed again.

Yes, it had been foolish to entrust the duty to Rebius and Demari. But the job had been dangerous. Marius didn't want to risk any of the younger Sparrows. If the wizard had noticed them, he might have cursed them or killed them. His curses could sometimes feel worse than death.

Marius fingered the grass ring that Asadal had given him. Already the green had started to fade from the grass. Marius felt the curse rearing its ugly head, felt it struggling against the charm in the weakening ring.

Several times that morning, he'd found himself on the verge of stuttering. He fought to keep control over his tongue and to suppress the panic rising in his chest. He didn't want to go back to the way things had been. He wanted to be free of the curse. To do that, he had to kill Malconus.

To kill the wizard, it seemed Marius needed Asadal's help. So he sat in the hub of Seatown, in the rotary, near the message board, as the sun cleared away the fog and began to beat down on his head. He sat there like a fool, which he was, with a scrap of old bindle cloth tied around his arm.

Asadal had yet to show. Marius had been foolish to trust him.

He had to act. But what should he do? Marius stared into the sky seeking some answer.

He had no idea how to go about finding the wizard, but the kidnappers were a different story. Marius had already been on the ship controlled by Barn and Pithy. There didn't seem to be much more he could learn there, and the two men were being watched and followed by the Sparrows. That left only the villa of House Ponti.

Marius thought of the beautiful Lady Raza standing on the balcony.

He would pay them a visit tonight, after the sun went down.

Coltic was sure to leave the house. If he did, the Sparrows could follow the man. The slender girl might be back on the job by then.

Marius would then be free to steal in unobserved and search the house for clues about the kidnappings and about the whereabouts of the wizard. Maybe he would even run across Lady Raza and force her to reveal the family's secrets. Maybe she would reveal them of her own accord, he fantasized. Maybe she would willingly reveal more.

It took a few moments for his head to clear. When it did, he realized that, to accomplish his goal, he'd have to observe the villa carefully. The practiced eye of a former slave could tell much about the layout of a house from the movement of the slaves throughout the day.

The time had come to leave the rotary.

"Excuse me."

A gruff voice spoke to him.

Marius raised a hand to shield his face from the sun and waited for his eyes to adjust. He wondered whether the speaker might be one of the Walkers, the skinny girl was ruled out unless she had an unfortunately low voice.

Instead of a Walker, Marius saw the green vest, bulging belly, and bushy mustache of the merchant named Mortimer, the one who'd tried to hit Marius with a rotten fish a few days earlier.

He wondered what the man might want. "Yes?"

"Ahem," Mortimer cleared his throat. "Some of the boys and me were wondering, well, we were wondering if you'd favor us with another show."

Marius considered the request. As a Walker, he had a rule about never passing up an opportunity. The merchants might pay, and the spectators might chime in with a few coins.

He felt the Jester's Curse wiggle with glee. It wanted Marius to perform. Even if it couldn't make him appear foolish directly, it enjoyed Marius doing it himself. His act might best be described as a sort of unfortunate mix between juggling and self-harm.

The curse's desire helped Marius reach a decision. "You'll have to wait a few days till the fair."

The merchant frowned. He must have been wanting to chuck another fish at Marius's face badly.

"At the fair, I'll put on the show of a lifetime," Marius added. "If you want, you can help."

Mortimer's face broke into a wide grin. "All right, then," Mortimer agreed.

"Save me a big fish or two, and I'll show you what I can do," said Marius.

Mollified, Mortimer started to waddle off. He turned back, pinching at his chin, considering something, "You wouldn't be interested in any skin flutes? I'd give you a good price."

Marius remembered the small, pink squirt-like things at the bottom of the fishmonger's bucket.

He shook his head, "Not today."

"Shame," said Mortimer. "They were starting to turn, starting to bite each other. Fierce little creatures. Maybe I can sell 'em as bait."

Marius watched as the merchant return to his stall, feeling a shudder of revulsion at the thought of the skin flutes as well as a stab of guilt about his refusal to perform. Not that long ago Marius had been starving on the streets of Amok. He regretted the lost coins he might have made.

But there were more important things to do today. Marius had a kidnapping ring to break up, a wizard to kill, and a house to burgle.

*   *   *

Across the street from House Ponti, Marius watched and waited for Coltic to leave. The sun had long since retired from the sky. Beside him, Iatro and the slender girl, whose name he'd learned was Fira, played a game of one, two, three. They slapped their hands together quietly in a rhythmic succession. Gasps of laughter or groans of frustration punctuated the game.

The moon rose high over Seatown, looking swollen and pregnant. It would soon give birth to the new tide, the Lady's tide.

Only a few days remained until the fair. Marius could have stayed in the Sparrows' Nest, biding his time till he could sail with Notori.

He might have done so, had he not needed to retrieve his bindle from House Fluctus and had he not seen his worst enemy.

Malconus, the wizard who'd cursed him, had ultimately been the reason Marius left the safety of the Sparrows' Nest. If he had a chance to get his revenge on the wizard, even a slim chance, Marius had to take it.

He turned to Fira and Iatro. Their hands slammed into their upturned palms. Fira won.

"B-bummer," said Iatro.

Marius couldn't resist asking, "Why do you keep saying that?"

Iatro shrugged.

Fira, ever taciturn, said nothing.

"I don't think Coltic is leaving the house tonight," Marius said. "I'm going in anyway."

Fira nodded. Iatro looked confused.

Marius pointed at House Ponti. The lights inside had long since been extinguished. "Iatro, I'm going into the h-house. S-stay here."

Marius put a hand to his mouth. His curse had begun to return, not as bad as before. The worst of it hid under the surface peering out at him.

Fira spoke in a strange, northern accent that elongated her vowels. As always, she spoke directly and to the point. "Shouldn't make fun of Iatro."

"I'm nuh-not," said Marius. He tried to think of a way to explain that didn't involve telling the Sparrows that he was under a powerful curse. "When I get nuh-nervous, I—"

Iatro patted Marius on the shoulder and smiled. He nodded, a look of understanding on his face.

He really was a nice boy, thought Marius. Marius felt as though his curse might actually be better when Iatro was around. The boy exerted a calming influence on him, maybe because he had someone to look after.

Iatro couldn't follow Marius into the house though. If they caught Marius, he'd end up in prison or worse. They might find out about his status as a runaway slave. His former rival at his old house, Sivinius, must have put a price on his head by now. There was also the possibility that his captors would try to collect on the bounty that Sybil from House Marcel had put out on him. Marius couldn't put Iatro in that kind of danger.

He held up a hand and focused on his words, willing himself not to stutter, concentrating on the charmed ring on his finger. "Stay here. I'll be back."

Removing the brass knuckles, Marius handed his bindle to Iatro for safekeeping. He hurried across the street walking heel to toe to dampen any noise from his footfall.

When he reached the wall that surrounded the court-yard of House Ponti, he gave a little leap. Catching the lip of the wall, he hoisted one leg over followed by the other.

Marius dropped silently onto the other side of the wall, something he never would have been able to do with the curse intact.

Then he farted, loudly.

Marius clapped both hands to his buttocks. Obvious-ly, he hadn't meant to do it.

Somewhere deep inside him, where his soul and heart met, the Jester's Curse chuckled and stretched as though it'd just awoken from a nice long nap.

Marius looked at his hand. One of the grass strands that made up the band of the ring had been severed. It must have torn on the wall as he climbed over. The ring hung on his finger by a thin strip of dried grass. Marius silently cursed fate.

He had no chance of carrying out his search silently if the Jester's Curse had its way. He didn't dare risk trying to scale the wall again. The rest of the ring might tear. Or the curse might land him on his head for a laugh.

It would be one thing if no one was watching. He might be able to suppress the curse. But Iatro and Fira stood in an alley across the street observing the house. The curse loved an audience.

He thought of the main gate leading out of the house. It might be locked from the outside, but from the inside, he should be able to lift the latch and escape.

Marius tip-toed toward the gate, squeezing as close to the wall as possible, feeling along its rough exterior with the tips of his fingers.

Finally, he found the metal edge of the gate. Marius shuffled in front of it, looking for a handle or a knob.

"Hoi! Who's that?"

Marius turned.

He heard the squeak of rusty metal. Light from a previously-shielded lantern spilled onto the courtyard. A guard had been set, and Marius's attempts to open the door had gotten the man's attention.

He turned back toward the door, frantically searching for a latch. The light from the lamp had nearly blinded him.

Then the man's hands were on him, dragging Marius backwards. He was tossed into darkness. He fell onto a pile of stacked wood. A door closed. The lantern shone through thin slats in the side of a rough little building. Marius realized that he'd been locked in the wood shed.

The guard took the lantern and moved away from the shack. He was going to wake up the house.

Marius had been captured. His fears rushed in on him. He would be sent back to slavery at House Cervix or to his death in Amok. He'd failed to get revenge.

A slight breeze stirred through a crack in the wooden slats, brushing past Marius's cheek.

He looked down at the offending crack, putting his hand to the hole to feel the current of the wind, amazed that such a simple thing could distract him when his life hung in the balance.

Below the crack, Marius saw the glint of metal. Reaching down, his hand hit a thick handle. Marius lifted it and felt a heavy weight at the other end. He brought it nearer his face.

He couldn't believe his eyes. They had put him in the firewood shack, which was made out of wood, with the axe still inside.

Marius chopped the air with the axe, elated. He thought of waiting on his captors and attacking them when they arrived, but that seemed pointless. Marius was no warrior.

He turned the axe on the door instead. The flimsy handle came away at one chop. It might have even broken had he punched it with the brass knuckles, though it never would have occurred to him to do so.

Marius stepped out of the shack. He started to rush toward the gate, then thought better of it. They would return soon. The lantern was gone and, with it, the only useful light. He still had no clue how to open the door. He couldn't do it without light. Perhaps the door had been magicked shut. Again he thought of scaling the wall and what the curse might do if he tried.

Marius decided on a less obvious course of action. He dropped the axe beside the gate. Seeing the axe and the broken door to the wood shed, they would think he'd fled.

Instead, Marius would go into the house, find somewhere to hide. They'd never expect it. He could slip out unobtrusively when the gate opened the next morning.

It seemed like a boring, though possibly effective plan, provided the curse didn't find some way to betray his hiding place. Marius clutched the ring safely in his hand. Next chance he got, he'd tie a cloth around it, to keep it in place.

Marius entered the house and listened, wanting to avoid running into the guard with the lantern. He heard a commotion arising from the servant's quarters. Marius took the stairs leading up to the family's rooms.

While watching the estate all afternoon, Marius had developed a rudimentary layout of the house. He tested his hypotheses now. There were no lights in the hallways. Marius followed the map in his mind down the dark corridors. He counted doors as he went and tried to match them to the rooms he'd seen from outside.

He reached the room that led to the balcony where he'd seen Raza. She would most certainly be home, perhaps asleep in a soft bed on the other side of the door.

As for the rest of the family, Marius assumed that Raza and Coltic were in sole possession of the house.

Otherwise, he reasoned, the master of House Ponti—if he'd been present in Seatown—would have attended the dinner with House Fluctus and the wizard from the White Tower. To do otherwise, barring sickness or emergency, would have been a breach of etiquette.

Marius's hand ran across an open doorway, which he assumed led to the dining hall. He couldn't hide there. The servants would be in that room early, preparing breakfast. He didn't want them raising a hue and cry.

Marius headed instead toward the eastern sitting room. Facing the rising sun as it did, the family would likely avoid it in the morning, tending to use it in the late afternoon or for entertaining after dinner. Marius thought he should be reasonably safe in the sitting room.

He opened and closed the door as noiselessly as he could. Marius scanned the room. The fire had burned down to coals, lending precious little light to the room. He moved around with his arms extended, shuffling his feet so as to avoid bashing his shins against any unseen furniture. The curse would love to knock his small toe against the leg of some heavy wooden object. Lucky for Marius, the curse didn't have an audience at present.

He groped blindly around the room. In his mind, he reviewed childhood games of hide-and-seek in his master's house in the capital city of Zeno. The city villa of House Cervix had not been large by the standards of Zeno, but it seemed a palace to young Marius. Now, he needed to find a cabinet to slip into or a set of drapes to hide behind.

Marius saw the flame of the candle before his mind registered what it must mean.

Someone was standing next to the fireplace. They'd used the coals to light a candle.

Marius froze in place, one leg raised, arms outstretched, like a poor Pantomime acting out the word "sneak."

Only his eyes moved.

He saw Raza standing by the fireplace, one hand holding the candle, the other holding a rapier. The point of the delicate sword quivered in the air.

"Please don't scream," said Marius, speaking to himself as much as to her.

* * *

Lady Raza of House Ponti stood next to the mantle. A candle in her hand shown like a small sun, casting the sitting room in its wan light. Her other hand held a thin rapier. The point of the sword wobbled in feminine arms that were not adapted to its use.

Raza wore a simple white shift that, though loose, managed to convey a tantalizing outline of her body. The shift was tied at the waist with her signature red sash. Black hair cascaded over her shoulders coming to rest above her bosom. And, now that Marius could see her face up close, he realized how much beauty she truly possessed. Her nose, which, like her black hair, was classically Arovian, sailed away from her face at a sharp angle. But rather than giving her an equine appearance, the rest of her features balanced the nose in proportion. The statue of the Lady that stood in the rotary at the base of the hill could have been modeled on Lady Raza.

The flame on the candle flickered.

Marius slowly extended his hands toward Raza, fingers outspread, urging her to relax. "Please don't scream. I'm a f-friend. A friend of your brother."

To his amazement, Raza didn't scream. Nor did she look terribly surprised by his statement. She must have fallen asleep in the sitting room after dinner, only to be awoken by him, a complete stranger. If so, Marius wondered how many strangers came and went from their house that she wasn't more frightened by his appearance.

"Your brother asked me to come," Marius lied.

Raza arched her eyebrows provocatively, asking an obvious question.

"N-no," Marius responded immediately. "N-not like that. He didn't— We're b-business friends."

Raza pursed her lips and nodded, as though she didn't believe a word Marius said. She motioned toward the couch, inviting Marius to sit.

He wondered whether Coltic often had male visitors over at odd hours in the night. Coltic's own nocturnal ramblings suggested the man might engage in all manner of clandestine activities. Not that Marius cared what the man got up to, except for the kidnappings of course, and consorting with the wizard Malconus.

Coltic's personal proclivities were none of Marius's business and, better yet, appeared at that moment to be saving Marius's life.

He moved carefully to the couch, keeping a close eye on the Lady Raza and on her sword. The Jester's Curse found the situation full of the sort of awkward hilarity it liked. It appeared content to stand by and watch what happened next.

Lady Raza set the candle in a stand on a nearby table and took a seat next to Marius. She rested the sword in between them with her hand upon its hilt, ready to move the blade at a moment's notice. Marius wondered whether such a beautiful woman had it in her to run him through. He didn't want to test her. He'd known beautiful women before, like Sybil of House Marcel, who could kill as easily as breathe.

Raza indicated with a slight tilt of her head that Marius should explain himself.

Through the window, Marius could see the light of lanterns in the courtyard. The house guards were looking for him. She could call to them. She could kill him with her sword.

Marius cursed the stutter that had reasserted itself, preventing him from speaking plainly. Though the stutter wasn't yet as bad as it had once been, Marius thought about how wonderful it had been to spend a day without it, nearly a whole day without the Jester's Curse ruining his life.

Marius rubbed his moistened palms nervously across his colorful pants. Perhaps he could turn the situation to his advantage. He might be able to elicit information about Coltic from his sister.

"Are you and your b-brother very close?"

Lady Raza shook her head, yes. She stifled a giggle with the back of her hand.

Marius wondered what she found so funny. Her continued refusal to speak began to unnerve him.

"Does he tell you where he g-goes at night?"

Raza responded by raising an eyebrow. She waved a finger in his direction as though he were being naughty.

Marius understood the gesture. "I'm not jealous."

Her eyebrows wrinkled and her lips drew tight as though she wanted to laugh and had to try very hard to suppress it.

"What about the w-wizard? I meant to pay my respects. Do you know where he's staying?"

Raza broke out in a nasal, high-pitched laugh that sounded remarkably like her brother. No wonder she tried to suppress her laughter, thought Marius. The cackle stood at odds with her natural beauty.

Raza finally spoke, "I just can't do this anymore." Her voice, too, sounded remarkably like that of her brother.

Marius's stomach sank into his legs. He began to think he'd made a terrible mistake. "Coltic?"

"Please," said his companion, "in my own house you may address me as Secundus."

Marius started to rise from the couch.

The rapier darted toward his chest. "I don't think so," said Secundus, who was called in less elevated circles, by people like Barn and Pithy, by the name Coltic.

Marius sat back.

"What is this?" said Marius.

"Don't I look pretty?" said Secundus.

"You l-look like Raza."

Secundus brushed the thick, black hair off his shoulders. "Yes, I do."

"But h-how?" He wondered whether Secundus had tricked him with a simple wig and clothing. The man had seemed rather dainty at the dinner party.

"How? You of all people might well ask how," Secundus laughed his high-pitched laugh. As on the boat, when he'd grown angry at Barn and Pithy, Secundus sounded less than sane. He was becoming hysterical. "It is you I have to thank for this new body."

Marius stared at him in disbelief.

"You are the man with the Jester's Curse?" Secundus examined Marius's colorful rags before continuing. "The wizard Malconus, I think you know him, found out that I ordered you to be executed." He sniffed. "Obviously you survived."

Marius remembered the desperate swim in the ocean. He would have drowned had Asadal not pulled him to shore.

Secundus spoke again, "Those fools Pithy and Barn must have squealed on me." He tapped a painted fingernail on the hilt of the rapier. "I should have paid them, I suppose."

"But what did Malconus—?"

"What did he do?" said Secundus. "Isn't it obvious?" He spread out his arms, giving Marius a good look at the outline of the body under the shift. Marius hadn't been fooled by a trick of the light. The man clearly had breasts. "You know how magic works," said Secundus. "The wizard cursed me. He took my natural inclinations and," he waved a hand up and down, "poof, made this."

Marius tried not to look at the way the candlelight played on the white shift. He found the effect oddly discomfiting.

"Like what you see?"

"Yes," said the Jester's Curse before Marius could answer. "I mean no," said Marius, blushing. "I mean—" Marius said, seeking to change the subject. He had a sudden inspiration. "If Malconus cursed you, like he cursed me, we could k-kill him. Together."

"Kill him?" Secundus looked down the length of the rapier, considering. "Whatever for?"

The question confused Marius. What did he mean, whatever for? Because they'd been cursed. Because Malconus had ruined their lives. "Because," said Marius, "we could be rid of these c-curses!"

Secundus toyed absentmindedly with the red sash arranging it to display his hips to their best advantage. "I'm not sure that's how it works, young man."

Marius didn't care. "I'm g-going after him. If you're too afraid—"

"You mistake me." Secundus met Marius's earnest gaze. "And you mistake the wizard. He will be expecting you, I'm sure. As for me," said Secundus, "I'm not sure that I want to be rid of the curse."

Marius's mouth fell open. The man was insane.

Secundus explained, "As you know, there are certain amulets that can counter a curse."

Marius did not know.

"They are expensive, of course, but if it ever comes to that—" Secundus's voice trailed away as he crossed and uncrossed his slim legs, seeking a more seductive pose. "I thought I might try out this new body. See if I like it."

He smiled pleasantly at Marius. He looked so much like the Lady Raza. "Do you want to help me test it?" He laid a finger on Marius's knee. "You could be my first."

Marius clenched his jaws before the Jester's Curse could accept the offer. He shook his head.

"No?" said Secundus. He placed his hand fully on Marius's knee. "I hate to insist. It feels a little rapier," Secundus smirked as though he'd made a terrible joke. "Do you get it? Rapier?"

He tapped the tip of the sword against Marius's leg, sliding it up his thigh. Marius scooted back.

Secundus laughed. "Don't play coy. And call me, Carra." The point of the rapier slid up Marius's chest, stopping near his heart.

"C-Carra?" said Marius.

"Yes, I think I like that. I shall call myself Carra from now on. Now," said Carra. "Kiss me. I insist." The point of the rapier also insisted.

Marius saw no way out. He looked to the curse for help but knew he'd not get it. The curse was on Carra's side. It found Marius's discomfort amusing.

Carra leaned forward, presenting her lips: her red, luscious lips that belonged, Marius reminded himself, to a man. Or was Secundus still a man if he had the body of a woman?

The tip of the rapier pressed itself into Marius's chest, threatening to puncture his shirt and his flesh.

Marius rested his lips on Carra's.

Carra pressed the kiss home.

Marius squirmed. The point of the rapier remained quite insistent.

Carra relaxed into the kiss.

Marius acted almost without thinking.

He pushed the blade aside. The tip caught him in shoulder. He registered a wave of pain but didn't stop. Marius vaulted over the couch. Carra grasped at him. He felt her nails rake across his neck.

She caught hold of his collar. A colorful bit of cloth came away in her hand.

Marius hit the door running.

Carra's high-pitched laugh trailed after him. "I'll send the wizard your regards!"

Marius fled down the stairs, past the startled guard at the gate, and hurled himself over the wall, landing disastrously on his ass. He jumped to his feet, feeling the tip of his backbone to make sure it hadn't compressed into his kidneys.

Across the street he saw Iatro and Fira standing in the alley, their mouths wide open. He could see a word forming on Iatro's mouth and knew with a certainty what the boy would say. Bummer.

Marius heard the gate to House Ponti open, wondered briefly how they'd done it, then he turned and ran down the hill, not waiting to see if Iatro and Fira followed.

With a pack of armed guards on his heels, Marius sallied forth into the night.

Chapter Twelve

The ability to sit still while in considerable pain was an act that Marius, as an amateur performer, had not mastered.

"Don't be a baby," said Clarion. "It's not that bad."

Clarion daubed at his shoulder with a sponge. The healing solution found its way into his wound, burning as it went. But the pain from his shoulder was nothing to that of his tailbone. The simple act of sitting caused excruciating pain. He tried to ignore it.

The morning light filtered through the kitchen window. The outside world looked sunny and pleasant. A good day for the fishermen of Seatown.

Marius tried to concentrate on the beautiful day. The first rule of the Walker was to appreciate every breath, to remember the good things, such as not dying last night. He'd gotten away from Secundus, or should he say Carra, yet he still felt miserable.

Marius was no closer to finding the whereabouts of Malconus. Asadal had yet to reappear at the Sparrows' Nest. And the grass ring had nearly been lost.

His speech was becoming as stupid as young Iatro's who sat beside him at the kitchen table, having a breakfast of bread dipped in thick, strawberry jam. Clarion spoiled the young Sparrow.

Jank, meanwhile, had left the kitchen as soon as Marius entered, giving him an elbow in the hip as he went. He didn't like Marius visiting his mother. Not that Marius could blame him. After all, Marius had ruined Jank's budding life of crime with the Sparrows. Jank would be enduring taunts of being a mother's boy for a few months at least. Of course, Marius could put in a good word for Jank now that he was living at the Sparrows' Nest, the run-down warehouse that served as a hideout for the youthful gang.

For his mother's sake, though, Marius didn't want Jank getting involved with the Sparrows. Most of the Sparrows were homeless. They broke the law by stealing. They were in constant danger of being arrested by the city or by an Astor. If enough merchants complained about their criminal activities, an Astor was sure to come. It might be a maniac like Lespa or her brute enforcer Bithius. Marius imagined Lespa's carved knife slicing through the ranks of children, Iatro and Fira included.

Marius winced as Clarion tied up the wound on his shoulder.

"We see plenty of knife wounds in the kitchen," she said. "It doesn't look infected. Just a scratch really."

Thank the Lady for small blessings, Marius thought. Heaven knew the Lady had heaped enough bad luck on him to last a lifetime.

Clarion picked up her own knife and resumed her work at the table prepping vegetables for the noontide meal. "So you say Secundus is now a she?"

"Carra," said Marius. "He's using the name Carra now." He had told Clarion almost everything. How he suspected Secundus had been working with the kidnappers. How Marius himself had nearly disappeared the night after he left her kitchen.

She'd looked incredulous that he'd kept such information from her, but he hadn't come the other day to find a shoulder to cry on. He'd come back to House Fluctus hoping to find his bindle lying somewhere in the alley where the kidnappers, Barn and Pithy, had cudgeled him.

It just so happened that Clarion had been really decent to him that day, even if she later prevented him from taking revenge on the wizard Malconus.

She'd made him see reason, made him see that nothing good could come from murdering Malconus in her house.

Marius had tried to track the wizard but had failed to find his hideout or where the kidnapping victims were being held, if they were still in Seatown at all. Unfortunately, he'd put the leaders of the Sparrows on the job trailing the wizard: Rebius and Demari, the two people in the city, besides Jank, who hated him most.

He'd broken into House Ponti hoping for information only to come away feeling strangely violated by Carra's insistent kiss. That she'd been Secundus just a few hours earlier bothered Marius less than he cared to admit.

Of course, he omitted the kiss from the story he told Clarion. That and the fact that he was a runaway slave with at least two bounties on his head and a brace of insane Astors on his tail.

"And this curse of yours," Clarion interrupted Marius's mental tangent, "it makes you act foolishly?"

Marius didn't know whether to nod or shake his head. He ended up moving his chin in a small circle. "Yes and no," he said.

He'd told her about the curse when trying to convince her to let him kill Malconus.

"The Jester's Curse m-makes me act foolish. Which I t-try to prevent by acting foolish m-myself."

"Because—" Clarion prompted.

"Otherwise," said Marius, "the curse will take over c-completely." He slashed his hand sideways in the air, emphasizing his point. He narrowly avoided slapping Clarion in the backside. Marius quickly sat on his hands to avoid the curse making him do anything stupid.

It had done the same thing to Irina once, and though she'd forgiven him, he wouldn't like to think what Clarion would think of him if he harassed her, even accidentally, not with what she'd been through with her master.

"Your curse doesn't seem so bad."

"This ring is a charm that helps me." Marius held up his hand. The grass ring was barely visible through a strip of cloth Marius had used to secure it after nearly losing it while breaking into House Ponti.

"You could join the church." Clarion looked at a small statue of the Lady that sat unobtrusively in a small nook in the kitchen.

Marius hadn't noticed the statue before, but Clarion had already revealed her spirituality the day she refused to let Marius kill the wizard.

"I c-could," said Marius, feeling slightly uncomfortable since he, in fact, didn't intend to join the church. And he did intend to come back to Clarion's kitchen to visit her and her cooking. He hoped she wouldn't revoke the invitation over a little thing like religion.

"Or you could go with this man Notori—"

Marius nodded.

"—who you've never met and know nothing about."

Marius nodded again, grimacing.

She had a point. Supposedly Notori ran a circus, but he might be a smuggler or worse for all Marius knew. High Priest Campri from Amok had recommended that Marius seek out Notori at the fair in Seatown. He'd said that, like Marius, Notori worked with the church, though he didn't subscribe to the Lady's teachings.

"Or," Marius suggested in a hopeful tone, "I could k-kill the wizard?"

Clarion frowned. He knew she wouldn't like that idea. She brushed a strand of blonde hair out of her face with the back of her knife hand.

She pointed the knife at him, making a suggestion. "I think you should consider the Lady."

Marius looked at the knife. He smiled, "Is that a threat?"

Awareness dawned on Clarion of how she must look, proselytizing him on behalf of the Lady at knife-point. She smiled too, before turning the knife back on the vegetables. The morning sun caught the lines on her face, adding its warmth to her smile. She stood for a moment in Marius's mind like a painting on a rich man's wall.

"You would s-say that," said Marius, hoping to continue the levity. "After all, you follow the Lady."

"And why not you?"

Marius waved a hand from his head to his waist. "If the Lady w-wanted me, she shouldn't have cursed me."

Clarion stopped her work. She gave him a look as though she were about to lecture her wayward son. "She's not the one who cursed you. Didn't the Lady herself suffer?" said Clarion. "Didn't she die bringing the good news to us? That we don't have to live like this."

Before Marius could reply, Iatro cut in. He sounded genuinely interested. "L-like what?"

Marius sighed. That's what a full belly got you: a full ear of preaching. He wondered if the Walker's sign of the three loaves had remained on House Fluctus for so long because Clarion saw it as a good way to bend a few ears about the Lady.

Clarion smiled as she spoke to Iatro. A bit of Marius's defenses crumbled. Clarion was so pretty and so sincere. If he could believe in the Lady, he would, for her sake.

"We don't have to live like animals," said Clarion.

"Aren't we animals?" Marius asked innocently.

"We are the dove and the wind and the flame," said Clarion in earnest, as though that explained everything. "The Lady taught us to reach beyond the animal. She taught us the way to be like God."

Marius had a ready response. The curse let him speak uninterrupted by the stutter. It liked the fact that he was dressing her down. "Isn't that what the wizards do? Make people better versions of themselves?"

Marius couldn't believe he was arguing on the side of the wizards.

Clarion looked at him with a pained expression on her face. "As they've done for you?"

Marius felt like he'd been punched. That was a low blow and totally unexpected from someone as nice as Clarion.

He started to stand up.

Clarion touched his shoulder, his good shoulder.

He could see that she hadn't meant any offense and that she felt sorry to have caused it.

"What the wizards do is a poor imitation," she said. "They can only alter what God already made; yet they think they are gods. What they do was permitted for a time. But no longer. Since the Lady came they are without excuse. There can be only the Lady. In the end, She will prevail."

Marius remembered that High Priest Campri had said something similar. To hear the same speech from a house slave made Marius think that the idea must be spread from church to church, from congregation to congregation, with every follower of the church being taught to question the wizards' power.

No wonder Arovia was undergoing a silent civil war. If the church could not compromise, there was no alternative to an all-out battle between the church and the wizards for control of the kingdom and for the hearts of the people. Marius suddenly wondered whether he'd chosen to do the right thing when he'd agreed to help the church.

"Marius," said Clarion as though she were reading his thoughts, "what have the wizards ever done for you?"

The question needed no answer. He'd been cursed. Dramatically and tragically cursed. The life of someone he loved, Irina, had been threatened by Malconus. She'd been saved, in part, based on Marius's agreement to work alongside the Lady.

"Now, think," said Clarion. "What has the Lady ever done to you?"

"Besides getting me cursed?" His anger at the Lady, at the unfairness of life, overwhelmed his stutter.

"She didn't do that," said Clarion. "A wizard did."

"She could have stopped it."

"Good may yet come of it," she said. "Again, I ask you, what has the Lady done for you?"

Marius considered her question. He thought of the servants of the Lady and what they had done—though he didn't know if he could ascribe their actions to a fictional being like the Lady.

Asadal, a spy for the Lady, had saved Marius from starvation and taught him how to survive as a Walker.

Asadal had also abandoned him, leaving him at the mercy of Lespa. But High Priest Campri had said there must have been a reason, and Asadal had tried to explain.

Marius didn't know what to think about that anymore.

Then there had been High Priest Campri, who'd distracted the guards of House Marcel allowing Marius to make an unlikely escape. The High Priest had been good to Marius. He'd rescued Irina from the life of a house slave and from subjugation to Malconus who'd been a guest at House Marcel and who'd threatened to take certain privileges with her.

Campri had also helped Marius escape the city and put a few coins in his pocket for the road. Of course, Marius had also implicitly agreed to work for the church against the wizards of the White Tower. Perhaps the coins came with the job.

Now, Clarion had taken him in and served him meals and been kind to him, while the servants of the White Tower had knocked him on the head, abducted him, tried to drown him, had sliced his shoulder, and given him a very uncomfortable kiss.

Seen in that light, Marius wondered why he didn't follow the Lady.

Certainly, however, there were decent people like Notori who fought the wizards without giving themselves over to the church. Presumably, for all Marius knew, there might even be a few decent wizards in the world. Marius took a deep breath.

"I'll think about it," he said.

"Good." Clarion smiled.

"Me t-too," said Iatro.

"That's a good boy," said Clarion, rustling his auburn hair. "Now, get out of my kitchen you two. Unless you want to be put to work." She placed several small loaves of bread on the table as she spoke and didn't bat an eye as Marius and Iatro pocketed them.

Marius had his own work to do. Patched up and with a good meal in his belly, he felt vaguely optimistic about his chances of finding the wizard.

He put a hand on Iatro's shoulder, guiding him through the gate and past the light-blue wall that guarded House Fluctus.

The sun had risen over the hill and shone on their backs as they walked down the street toward the rotary. The colorfully painted houses caught the light of the sun. The morning felt fresh and new and full of possibilities.

A thought suddenly occurred to him. Marius paused in the street.

"Iatro," Marius spoke to his young charge, "did you learn the p-pass code for today?" He worried that they'd left too early for the young boy to learn the whistle that would let them enter the Sparrows' Nest.

Iatro nodded.

"Could you t-teach it to me?"

Iatro shook his head.

"Why not?" said Marius.

"Only Sparrows," Iatro replied.

"B-but—" Marius sputtered. He realized they looked a right mess, stuttering at each other in the street. Marius smiled.

"Are you a Walker?"

Suddenly, the tumbled-down witch appeared before him. Her blue eyes searched his face. Even her wrinkles had wrinkles.

"Yes, I am a Walker," Marius nodded in the direction of the bindle held over his shoulder on a stout stick.

She began her speech, "Before the new tide turns—"

"I know," said Marius, "a Walker will die. We've been through this before, you remember?" He muttered, "Or maybe you don't." He added aloud, "I'll be sure to be safe."

She had been kind in returning her bindle. Marius didn't want to be rude.

The witch caught his forearm in her vice-like grip. She seemed to weigh so little, Marius wondered if he lifted his arm, whether he could move her whole body out of the way.

"Yes, beware," said the witch. "The assassins come. The assassins are here. In Seatown. Beware, Walker. Beware!"

She released his arm and sidled back into the dark alley that Marius had begun to think of as her home.

Iatro opened his mouth to speak.

"Don't say it, Iatro."

That was a new one, thought Marius. Beware the assassins.

But of course, her mind might be slipping, imagining new and more dire threats. He wouldn't at all be surprised if her predictions grew even more ominous over the coming days before the new tide. Tomorrow, she might warn him about the dangers of ghosts and spectral spirits returning from beyond the grave, of the dead who could not die.

Marius smiled. He felt increasingly sure that the woman was loony.

He turned his mind and his feet toward the search for the wizard. Perhaps the Sparrows he'd sent to scour the city had found something by now. Perhaps he would finally have a bit of luck.

As if that would happen, thought Marius, shaking his head sadly. Right. And just maybe the Lady was real and Irina actually loved him back. No one could blame a fool for dreaming. Only, he wasn't as crazy as all that. For instance, he wasn't as crazy as the witch who lived in the alley.

Assassins indeed.

Chapter Thirteen

Marius sat upright in bed. Something had woken him. It might have been the wind, howling through the rafters coming in through large gaps in the warehouse's ramshackle ceiling.

Marius couldn't see the stars or the full moon through the cracks. He wondered whether a storm had blown in. If it began to rain, he hoped his bed would avoid the worst of the inevitable dripping.

Marius heard one of the children cry out in their sleep.

He'd been surprised at first that with so many sleeping together, scattered over the floor of the common area, anyone could get a moment's rest. Yet the children, resilient as they were, didn't seem to mind. Of course, one could get used to almost anything. People were so adaptable. The children had even gotten used to Demari's snoring, which Marius could usually hear from the loft.

That snore was absent. In fact, neither Rebius nor Demari had been in the Sparrows' Nest when he'd returned from an unsuccessful day hunting the wizard through the streets of Seatown.

The children he'd sent to watch the city hadn't reported a sighting of a wizard dressed in white robes much less one with a crooked nose.

That didn't signify anything. The wizard had the ability to change his appearance. Even changing his white robe for something more inconspicuous would create a serious challenge to their ability to find him.

Or maybe Malconus had, like Rebius and Demari claimed, changed into a great white bird and flown away from Seatown. Maybe he'd only been in town for a day or two, checking up on his minions and punishing Coltic's incompetence by changing him into Carra.

Marius wiped his mouth with the back of his hand. He'd drooled during the night.

The wind picked up. Droning. Insistent. Marius doubted whether he'd be able to get back to sleep. He would've liked to have asked Asadal how to find the wizard. Asadal might have contacts in Seatown or, as a spy for the church, might know a thing or two about where a wizard might stay.

The Lady had the church. Marius wondered whether the White Tower had a similar meeting place, a lodge perhaps or a coven, though those were for witches, he remembered.

Another child cried out and then went silent.

Absent Rebius and Demari, Marius had been responsible for making sure the younger children had gotten off to bed.

He'd checked that they'd eaten for the day and insisted that they fetch water to wash their hands and faces. It was little more than a nod to hygiene, but the Sparrows living in the warehouse were so dirty. They hadn't any mothers or fathers. Someone had to explain things to them. If he got time, Marius would institute a bathing policy. He wondered why Asadal hadn't seen to it. Then again, the old Walker hadn't been seen in days. Perhaps he never stayed long enough to care for the children in his charge. It seemed like, if Asadal really cared about the children, he would use his contacts in the church to find them all homes in a nice orphanage or something.

Marius put them to bed with tales about Prince Pratt of Market Square (his title in Amok) and how the Prince of Jesters had foiled the infamous master of House Marcel who cruelly beat his slaves and who got his come-uppance at the hands and tongue of the lively jester. He told how the Prince rescued the girl from Marcel's cruel clutches. Of course, he skipped the more ribald limericks that the curse had unleashed on Marcel. And he'd ended the story with the girl gratefully kissing the jester. Not dismissing him by calling him "sweet."

The children seemed to love the story and were eager to hear more. Marius wasn't entirely sure it was a good idea to tell them more about the life of a Walker. Surely they should be trained to take up a local profession like sailor or fishmonger.

Marius thought he heard a slight commotion in the floor below, though it was difficult to discern with the wind howling overhead.

He considered lighting a candle.

Marius heard, more than saw, the trapdoor opening in the floor. A small form crawled through the hole, dropping the door lightly back in place. Whoever it was, hurried toward the side of Marius's bed.

He reached into the bindle under his head, grabbing his knife by its handle.

"Who is it?" he whispered.

"Marius?" A young girl's voice called back quietly. It sounded like Fira, the slender girl with the bird's nest of brown hair. As she drew close, however, he realized that he could see her face. He recoiled. Fear radiated from her eyes.

She whispered, "Strange men sneaking among the children."

"Who?"

"Don't know."

"How did they get past the l-lookouts?"

Fira shrugged.

The children stationed on the roofs of the nearby buildings should have spotted any intruders. The narrow alleys made it impossible that anyone could sneak up on the Sparrows' Nest. Anyone nearing the building had to perform the right whistle. The sequence changed each day.

Maybe the lookouts had been sleeping. Maybe they were dead.

Marius remembered the witch's warning about assassins. But surely she'd been talking crazy.

He rolled out of bed. One thing was certain. If someone had broken into the Sparrows' Nest, they weren't there for the children. They'd come to find Asadal, or they'd come to find Marius.

Marius had at least two bounties on his head. That might be why Asadal didn't stay long with the Sparrows. His very presence put the children at risk.

Grabbing his knife and brass knuckles, Marius kicked the bindle under the bed in case he actually came out of this alive.

He fought the urge to run. Surely Asadal had installed a back door in the loft in case he needed to make a quick escape. If Marius left the Nest, the intruders might leave the children alone. But he couldn't leave the children with a group of potential assassins. He felt a responsibility toward them.

A scream split the night.

Marius made for the trapdoor and dropped to the floor below leaving Fira in the relative safety of the loft.

The entire warehouse was in a state of panic. Children scrambled everywhere screaming and shouting. Among them, tall, dark forms tossed children aside, making their way toward Marius.

An enterprising child threw a log onto the cooking fire. Light sprang up illuminating the scene. Marius could see the glint of swords in the men's hands. He glimpsed a Sparrow grappling with one of the invaders. Marius recognized Iatro's auburn hair.

One of the assassins pointed at Marius and shouted, "There he is!"

A shrill whistle nearly deafened him.

Beside him, Fira pulled a hand from her lips, "Sparrows fly!"

She grabbed his hand.

"W-what are you d-doing?"

"What Sparrows do," said Fira. "We run."

* * *

Their flight through the dark alleys of the warehouse district was a blur. Fira drug him by the hand. Marius wanted to go back, to help Iatro. But after a few turnings, he became hopelessly lost.

He relied entirely on Fira's sense of direction. Asadal had trusted the girl, said she was one of the best when it came to tailing people through the city.

Scared, shaken, and with a pounding heart, Marius emerged from the labyrinthine alleys a step behind Fira.

She crossed the street and crouched next to the sea wall. Fira beckoned for Marius to follow.

A noxious smell crashed into his nose. He recognized their surroundings at once. They were near the same alley where Marius had rescued Jank that first day and where Asadal had led him into the alleys. It was the warehouse that held the chemicals used for mining.

Fira slipped over the sea wall, and Marius followed her, finding the crack in the wall with his feet, lowering himself to the shore below. They skimmed along the sharp rocks, their hands pressed to the wall for support.

Soon, they came beneath the shacks that had been built over the sea wall, marking the boundary of the black market. A new and different scent of foulness clogged his nostrils. Seatown was offering samples of her finest perfumes. First the overall smell of dead fish, then the chemical warehouse, and now the decay of human feces mixed with whatever small carcasses the tide washed up.

Fira stopped.

"Hide here." She panted, putting her hands on her knees.

Marius asked, "The others? Will they c-come?"

Fira shrugged her shoulders.

The Sparrows appeared to have an every-child-for-themselves policy when it came to fleeing terrors in the night.

"Those men won't come here," she said. "There's the smell and—" she paused.

"The witches." Marius finished her thought. Fira didn't talk much and, when she did, used as few words as possible.

Anyone who disturbed a witch's slumber was likely to be on the receiving end of a rather nasty curse.

"Who were they? What'd they want with you?" Fira asked. Her eyes were wide with the shock that came from having her home violated. She also looked as though she blamed Marius.

It was Marius's turn to shrug. He didn't know who they were. "Assassins I think," he said. "Asadal and I—" he thought of how best to explain it. "We have enemies."

Marius thought back to the warning from the witch. He hadn't believed her about the assassins. Even if he had, what precautions could he have taken? He didn't know they were coming for him specifically or that they would strike the Sparrows' Nest.

If he'd have known, he wouldn't have stayed there. He wouldn't have knowingly put the children in danger.

He thought of how Asadal had disappeared and vowed to do likewise. He couldn't have the children's blood on his hands. He would never return to the Sparrows' Nest if he could help it, except once more, to check on Iatro.

Marius wondered how the boy had fared. Last he'd seen, Iatro had thrown himself on the back of an assassin.

Thankfully, it didn't look to Marius as though the assassins were striking down the children. The shine of their blades had not been dulled by blood. Good news, he thought, but more evidence that the assassins were looking for someone. After all, they'd cried out "there he is" upon spying Marius. His colorful, quilted clothing stood out. The men had been making their way toward the loft when the alarm sounded.

The only thing Marius couldn't figure out is how the assassins had known that he would be staying in the Nest and in the loft?

Fira confirmed his suspicions. "Someone told."

"T-told what?"

"The whistle," said Fira.

Marius realized what she meant. Anyone who knew the code could pass the sentries unchallenged. No alarm had been raised. Unless the lookouts were dead, and that would take a coordinated strike on the roofs of several buildings at once, then one of the Sparrows had revealed the day's whistle.

"M-maybe they f-forced someone," Marius suggested. He didn't like to think that one of the Sparrows would've betrayed them intentionally. Though, poor as the Sparrows were, it wouldn't have taken much to buy the information.

"Don't think so," said Fira. She looked certain, as though she knew something but didn't want to tell.

Marius didn't ask what the girl suspected. He waited for the laconic girl to tell him, if she wanted to. He kicked a rock with his foot, wishing he could knock it into the nearby surf without causing a noise that would alert any passersby to their hiding place. Surely the assassins were roaming the streets of Seatown, looking for Marius.

Fira spoke quietly. "I saw something."

Marius nodded, encouraging her to continue.

"Night I followed Coltic from House Ponti," she continued to speak, gathering speed and conviction as she went. "When Coltic doubled back in the black market to meet the witch," she looked up as though she could see through the shacks to the building where the witch worked. "Saw them talking to the man in white."

"Them w-who?" Marius prompted.

"Rebius and Demari."

His initial reaction was disbelief. "But they said—"

"They lied," she said. "Didn't know why they lied, but they were Sparrows."

Marius followed her to the natural conclusion: he was not a Sparrow. Fira hadn't told him about Rebius and Demari talking to the wizard out of a sense of loyalty.

Then, as though the torch of the Lady shone in his mind, Marius understood what Fira was getting at. "They weren't there tonight."

She nodded, her lips pulled tight in a look of fierce determination.

Marius repeated, "Rebius and Demari weren't at the Sparrows' Nest."

Rebius and Demari had betrayed him to the wizard, Marius realized. Worse, they had betrayed the Sparrows and their Nest. How many had been injured so that Rebius could have his revenge? Marius hadn't insulted the boy. He'd only stood up to Rebius, something the little children were too frightened to do. He hadn't demeaned Rebius in the eyes of the Sparrows or publicly challenged his authority. He'd stolen the witchweed out of Rebius's pocket, sure, but betraying Marius to Malconus seemed out of all proportion to any supposed wrongs Marius had ever done.

For some people, though, like his old rival Sivinius, the fact of Marius's continued existence seemed offensive enough to justify any amount of rotten behavior.

He added Rebius and Demari to the list of people he owed payback.

* * *

Marius and Fira hid under the shacks of the black market. They kept their thoughts to themselves. The wait was more tedious and odiferous than Marius would ever admit.

Fira spent the time examining and assembling a small collection of sharp rocks that lined the shore. Marius wondered whether she made a hobby of it.

When dawn broke, without a word they slipped back down the sea wall. They found the small break in the wall, same as he and Asadal had done, and used it to gain the road.

From there, they wove their way past the smelly warehouse full of chemicals and through the narrow alleys.

Fira put a hand up, urging Marius to wait.

She advanced a few steps to a four-way intersection.

She blew a combination of low and high whistles.

A challenge came back. "Who is it?"

Even in the daylight no whistler was being left un-challenged. That was smart, thought Marius.

Marius could see faces appearing on the roofs over-head. Small hands held large rocks over the edge.

Fira cupped her hands to her mouth and called up to the lookouts, "It's me."

The rocks were pulled back from the edge of the roof. Marius could hear the word being spread.

"It's Fira," said one.

"Knew she'd make it."

"Someone with her."

Fira called again, "Got the Jester with me."

Again the message spread like fire across the rooftops.

A reply came back, "Take him to the Nest."

Fira wrinkled her forehead, as though she didn't like the tone of the message. Neither did Marius. It sounded like an order.

She asked the lookouts, "Is it safe?"

"Safe enough."

"Bad men still there?" Fira sought to clarify. Marius was glad that she did. It could be safe enough for the Sparrows, yet Marius could be walking into a trap.

"They're gone."

Fira returned to Marius's side.

"Don't like it," she said. "Don't trust them."

"But they're Sparrows," said Marius.

Fira shrugged, glancing down the alley toward the Nest. She bit at a dirty thumbnail. "What you want to do?"

"You should go ahead," said Marius. "Check on Iatro."

She shook her head, "Staying with you."

Then they had no choice. Marius had to go forward. He needed to know about Iatro's condition, whether the boy had survived the fight. He cared about all the Sparrows in a general way, but Marius had formed a connection with the fresh-faced boy.

He thought of asking the lookouts for information about Iatro's fate. But, as Fira had said, they weren't to be trusted. It was entirely possible that the assassins had taken captives and were forcing the lookouts to draw Marius into a trap.

Marius decided, "Let's go to the nest," he said. "I've got to see Iatro and get my bindle."

Fira shrugged again, feigning indifference. She ran her hand through her hair, messing it up, covering her face.

"Why make yourself look l-like that?" asked Marius. She didn't look hideous underneath.

Fira responded with complete sincerity, "Like what?"

* * *

They walked together through the alleys. A troop of lookouts followed them along the rooftops.

Fira and Marius arrived at last in the open square that led to the red door, the main entrance to the Sparrows' Nest.

The door opened. Children poured out, gathering in the square the way they'd spilled out of the alley on the first day he'd met them in Seatown.

Now, he could put a few names to the faces that had once thrown rocks at him. The children looked excited, as though something important was about to happen.

The door closed. Then it opened again. Rebius stepped out followed by Demari. The big oaf slammed the door shut as usual, making the whole side of the building waffle. This time, though, Demari carried a sword that must have belonged to one of the assassins.

The two boys came to a halt in front of Marius.

Rebius spoke first, "Step aside, Fira."

"Make me," she shot back.

Rebius commanded several children, "Take her."

"Better not," said Fira.

They couldn't see the expression on her face, but they heard the tone of her voice. Nobody moved.

Rebius let the matter drop, adopting a sneer instead. "Look what you've done. Killers, assassins in the Sparrows' Nest. And who were they after?" Rebius pointed an accusing finger at Marius, "You!"

He held his arms out to his sides dramatically. "Sparrows, what do we do with traitors?" He let his hands hang in the air.

The children looked at the paving stones, shuffling their feet.

"Stone him!" shouted Demari, waving the sword over his head, whipping up the crowd.

"Stone him," Rebius replied. "Stone him! Stone him!"

The chant was picked up by some of the lookouts. "Stone him! Stone him!"

Marius needed to act before the first rock got thrown, before Rebius turned the children into a mob.

Marius gripped the handle of the knife and the brass knuckles he'd taken from the bindle during the assassin's attack.

He hadn't seen Iatro in the crowd. Checking on the boy was his first priority. He walked toward the red door as though he intended to go inside.

Rebius dropped the chant to challenge him. He stood in front of Marius with his head back, as though Rebius were trying to look down his nose at the much taller young man.

"Where do you think you're going?" He put his fingers on Marius's chest and pushed.

Demari stood behind Rebius with the sword. He kept his eyes on Marius's knife-hand. Ready for an attack.

But neither Demari nor Rebius had seen the brass knuckles.

Marius slammed his fist into Rebius's stomach. They boy collapsed.

Demari raised the sword. It was a mistake. Marius was quicker. He had the knife to Demari's throat before the blade reached its full height.

For once, the Jester's Curse didn't interfere. It urged him on, wanting him to kill the boy, wanting to see what he would become if he did.

Marius looked toward Fira. He raised his voice as loud as he could and in his broken speech said, "Sparrows, what d-do we do with t-traitors?"

He nodded at Fira. She walked forward, pointing an accusing finger at Rebius.

"Stone them," she said. "Saw them speaking to the wizard. Making a deal."

Rebius tried to stand up straight, to catch his breath. "No," he said. "The Jester did it."

"Couldn't have," said Fira.

Rebius looked confused, Demari scared. Demari tried to back away. Marius followed him with the knife, pinning him against the wall.

"Tell them how you know I didn't do it, Fira," said Marius.

"The whistle," she said. "Only Sparrows know the whistle."

Rebius's jaw dropped. Marius grabbed Demari by his tunic and threw him into Rebius.

The pair collapsed onto the street. Demari dropped the sword. It clattered to the paving stones.

Marius motioned for Fira to pick it up.

He grabbed Rebius by the collar, hauling him to his feet. Marius spoke to the Fira, "I need to talk to Rebius. As for him," he pointed with his knife toward Demari.

Fira called out to the children. "You know what to do." Reaching into her pocket, she pulled out one of the sharp rocks she'd collected at the shore. It now occurred to Marius why she'd collected them. Fira threw it at Demari's head. It connected with his temple.

Demari cried out. He got to his feet and tried to run. The children took it as an admission of guilt.

Stones rained down. Demari staggered. Stones hit him from all sides and from the rooftops as the lookouts turned on Demari, having realized that he'd been the one who betrayed the secret pass code.

Marius caught a glimpse of a white bird circling close to the fray as though begging for a place to land and rest its wings. Marius ignored it, just as he ignored Demari's cries.

The Jester's Curse inside him laughed. It liked this new Marius. It considered pain and cruelty the pinnacle of humor, as Marius could well attest from the many blows he'd taken.

A stone hit Demari below the belt.

At least he wasn't on the receiving end this time, thought Marius.

He didn't wait to see whether they boy made it out of the square alive. He hauled Rebius by his collar through the red door and into the Sparrows' Nest.

Chapter Fourteen

Tied to a chair in the Sparrows' Nest, Rebius looked so much smaller than he had in Marius's mind when he'd decided that hitting Rebius in the stomach with brass knuckles was a good idea.

"How's Iatro," Marius asked Fira.

The small boy lay on a mat on the far side of the room. He'd taken a nasty slice to his side during the fight with the assassins. The attacker's blade had been stopped by Iatro's ribs. The Sparrows had managed to stop the bleeding and bandage the wound.

"Needs a doctor," said Fira.

The slender girl still wore her brown hair in a mess in front of her face. She bit a grimy thumbnail. Marius could tell she was anxious about Iatro.

Fira snorted. "Better than Demari, though."

"Check on him again," said Marius, "Then go to House Fluctus. Ask for C-clarion. Tell her Iatro's hurt."

Now that the confrontation had subsided and his heart rate slowed, Marius had begun to see Fira in a new light.

She'd rescued him from the assassins, and had been the first to cast a stone at Demari. Fira was clever and dangerous, just the sort Asadal would choose to aid in the struggle against the White Tower.

Marius had also seen something in her face that night, before she'd covered it again with her messy hair. Something about her eyes had made her look older.

He thought about Fira throwing the rock.

What had possessed him to leave Demari at the mercy of Sparrow's stones? The memory felt hazy. Marius didn't want to think about it. Demari has brought it on himself. He had betrayed the nest. A Sparrow lay dying. Every Sparrow knew the punishment. Demari shouldn't have been surprised. But when Fira's rock hit him, the shocked look on his face— Marius wondered whether the Sparrow's stone punishment had ever been carried out before. Of course, they'd tried it on him only a few days earlier, but not in earnest.

He thought of asking Rebius about the history of the Sparrow's stones, but the boy was staring at him with such a mixture of fear and anger that it didn't seem wise to stray too far from what Marius really needed to know.

"What did you tell Malconus?"

Rebius pressed his lips together, refusing to talk.

"Take him outside."

Fira nodded. A couple of the larger boys who she'd recruited as guards grabbed the back of Rebius's chair and began dragging their former captain toward the red door. The children were waiting outside with stones in hand. The legs of the chair left a trail in the dirty floor.

"No!" Rebius pleaded.

The boys stopped, waiting to see what Marius would do.

He stood with his arms folded, staring into the condemned boy's eyes.

"I-iatro could die because of you," said Marius. "Throw him out." He waved his hand in an air of disgust.

The guards began hauling the chair.

Rebius's dimples contorted into a look of pure misery. He started to cry.

"I told the wizard the exact day you showed up in Seatown," he said, "and how you survived the kidnappers who tried to kill you. That's all he wanted to know."

"Stop." Marius called to the boys. "Did you t-tell the wizard about Asadal?"

Rebius shook his head, adamant in his innocence. Good, thought Marius. Rebius had betrayed only Marius, an interloper, not their king.

Meanwhile, Marius processed what Rebius had said to the wizard. Rebius had told the wizard about Marius's brush with death at the hands of the kidnappers.

So, thought Marius, Carra had Rebius to blame for her condition.

That meant, however, that Malconus must have already known that Carra's attempt on Marius's life had failed. Malconus punished her for even making the attempt. The wizard was even more twisted than Marius realized.

However, something about the story didn't make sense. If Malconus had cursed Carra for trying to kill Marius, he would hardly have sent assassins to finish the job.

"Go on, then, keep talking." he told Rebius.

Fira interrupted. "Talk to Iatro first."

Marius looked over at the spot where Iatro lay. The boy looked back at him, expectantly.

Marius instructed the guards, "Keep Rebius t-tied up."

He walked over and knelt next to Iatro. Although a blanket covered the wound, the floor was stained from their attempts at patching him up. He'd lost a lot of blood.

"B-bummer," said Iatro.

Marius nodded. Wasn't it just?

Iatro reached into his tunic, he fumbled inside a pocket. Marius wanted to help but didn't know what the boy was after.

Iatro removed a tanned leather scroll covered in his own blood. He put it in Marius's hand.

Marius examined it. The scroll looked like the sort of device used to transport documents.

"I stole it during—" Iatro coughed. His body convulsed with pain at the movement. "Did it j-just like you t-taught me. Have to t-touch them in t-two places." Iatro smiled. His lips were too dark, thought Marius, his skin too pale.

Marius remembered the lesson he'd taught Iatro several days earlier. The older boys had been giving him a hard time, so Marius had taught Iatro a thing or two about how to pick a pocket.

Iatro must have been trying to touch the assassin so that he could steal whatever was in the man's pockets. Marius nearly slapped his own forehead. So that was why Iatro had fought when the rest of the Sparrows had fled. His action had been both incredibly stupid and brave.

The scroll was fastened in the front with a seal and tied up with a knot of leather.

Slipping off the cumbersome brass knuckles, Marius untied the thongs. He broke the seal and unrolled the message.

He gazed at the contents expectantly. Immediately, he felt foolish. Marius didn't know how to read. But he didn't want the Sparrows to know that.

"What d-do you m-make of it?" Marius handed the note to Fira.

She examined it carefully, mouthing words as she went.

"Hoi!" said Marius. "Read out loud for Iatro."

"Says," Fira began. She then read the letter, speaking more words in a row than he'd ever heard her speak. And she used full sentences. She stumbled over the larger words. Marius forgave her. He couldn't read himself. He guessed those were words she'd never heard pronounced before.

The letter read as follows:

"To the Warden at Seatown from the Honorable House Marcel of Amok, A notice. These assassins have been contracted by this House in accordance with customs and laws. They should not be hindered in their work. They are to kill and only kill one Marius of House Cervix, runaway slave and wandering troubadour, also known as Prince Pratt of Market Square Amok and by many other names, the man with the Jester's Curse. Recompense for any damaged goods may be made upon receipt to our bursar, one Ian of House Marcel."

When she finished, Fira looked confused. "Who's Prince Pratt? Who's Marius."

Fira didn't know his real name. In Seatown he'd been using the name Jester. Very few knew his actual name.

Marius spoke to Fira, "Don't look at m-me for an answer."

Fira examined the letter. Reading it again silently. "Think we can ask for damage money?" She looked around at the Sparrows' Nest, which had been trashed during the melee.

To Marius's eye, it didn't appear too different than normal.

"D-don't count on it," he said.

To Marius, the letter had meant something else. Despite the serious nature—assassins coming to kill him and all—Marius nearly smiled at the mention of Ian's name. It seemed that Irina's brother was moving up in the world. Already a bursar, he would likely become majordomo when the current slave died, became incapacitated, or simply fell out of favor.

That had been the career path Marius himself had chosen before the curse, not that one got much say as a slave.

Taking the letter from Fira, he rolled it up, deciding to keep it.

The letter might come in handy one day if he ever needed to prove that House Marcel tried to have him killed. If nothing else, the letter was a symbol of Sybil's deep and abiding hatred. At least he knew that she still thought about him from time to time.

The letter seemed like a trophy of sorts, something to taken out and appreciated every once in a while.

Iatro gasped in pain. He clutched at the wound. Marius turned his attention back to where it belonged.

"Find Clarion," Marius told Fira.

Fira slipped out of the warehouse.

He hoped Clarion would come in time and that she'd know what to do. She'd mended his shoulder easily enough. But his wound hadn't been so severe.

Marius walked back to Rebius. He waved the scroll under Rebius's nose.

"Who else did you t-tell?"

"No one."

Marius slid the brass knuckles back onto his fingers. "Who else?" He held out his arm, measuring the distance between his fist and the bridge of Rebius's nose.

"Some people." Rebius squirmed. "They said they were looking for someone dressed like you. We told them where they could find you—for a price. They weren't supposed to hurt any Sparrows." Rebius tried to hold up his hands not remembering they were still tied. "The wizard gave us witchweed. The others gave us so much money," said Rebius. "You'd have done the same. Any Sparrow would have done the same."

"Asadal wouldn't," said Marius. "One last thing. Where's the w-wizard?"

Rebius's face drew a blank. He began to panic, "I don't know."

Marius pulled his fist back.

"I don't know, by the Lady, I don't know."

Marius considered Rebius's words carefully. He looked up into the rafters. A breeze blew in from the sea, making the dust dance through the sunlight. He could see the sun's fiery face through the cracks in the roof above. It had such little concern for their small affairs.

Marius looked down. Rebius seemed to be telling the truth. But he had to be sure.

He punched Rebius in the nose. He felt it break under his fist. A sudden gush of blood moistened his knuckles.

"Where is the w-wizard?"

Rebius wailed. The broken nose affected his speech, "I dohd gnow!"

He'd heard enough. The pair of them, Rebius and Demari must have spoken to the wizard in the black market exactly has Fira said, but they would not have followed him home afterward. As for the assassins, that was simply bad luck. They must have tracked Marius to Seatown just like Lespa the Astor, by following the stupid Walker signs he insisted on carving as his legacy: the jester's hat, his personal symbol.

Marius let out a deep breath. He shrunk inside as the anger seeped out of him. He didn't want to look at Rebius's face. Marius was older than the boy and weighed more. To have hit Rebius with the brass knuckles felt wrong. He told himself he'd been forced to do it.

"Untie him."

The guards shot Marius a questioning glance, checking to see if he really meant it.

"He won't betray the Sparrows again," said Marius. "Isn't that r-right?" He asked Rebius.

The boy shook his head adamantly.

"He's g-gonna leave Seatown," said Marius. He looked at Rebius. "If the wizard finds out about the assassins, he'll k-kill you, or worse."

The guards loosened Rebius's ropes.

Marius pointed with his thumb over his shoulder. "The b-back d-door."

Rebius wasted no time in escaping.

Marius knelt beside Iatro. "Help's c-coming," he said. "Hold on." If here were a religious man, he might have prayed.

* * *

The wound under the bandage opened like an angry, empty eye-socket. The needle flashed in Clarion's hand as she sewed Iatro up like she might dress a turkey. Iatro moaned and thrashed. Marius sat on his arms. Several Sparrows sprawled across his knees.

Jank, dressed in the aquamarine tunic of House Fluctus, leaned against the wall, sulking. His first trip to the Sparrows' Nest had been with his mother. A few of the children recognized the irony. Their pointing and giggling didn't improve the boy's mood.

Fira hurried the children along with a threatening wave of her fist.

Clarion's needle was too large for use on a person, the twine too thick and rough for human skin. Marius knew that the physicians of Zeno had better stuff. But they were not in Zeno. Clarion used the tools of the kitchen, the tools she knew.

"There," she said. "It's done."

"Will he l-live?" said Marius.

Clarion who had been kneeling on the floor beside Iatro, sat back on her feet. She wiped the back of a bloodied hand across her forehead, cajoling and blowing strands of blonde hair out of her face.

She looked tired, as though the short process of sewing Iatro's wound had cost her several night's sleep.

"He'll live," she said, "if the wound doesn't fester."

"If it d-does," said Marius.

Iatro groaned.

"He'll need a physic or magic."

Marius took his knees off Iatro's arms. The boy put them to his side.

Clarion bent down, brushing his hair. She whispered, "Try not to touch it."

Marius got Fira's attention, "Get my bindle from the loft."

She nodded. The mess of hair that passed for her head bobbed as she trotted toward the ladder in the back of the warehouse.

"Was it the wizard?"

Marius considered what he should tell her. He'd trusted her with so much of his story. But there were certain things that might scare her away, and he needed her friendship more than she needed the truth.

"The w-witch outside your house—"

"Mad Old Maude?" said Clarion.

Marius didn't even blink. The moniker fit.

Clarion continued, "I don't think she's a witch."

Marius interjected, "She t-told me assassins were hunting a Walker."

Clarion's head tilted to the side, considering, "You think they were after you?"

Marius didn't add how the assassins had pointed him out or how Rebius had said they were looking for someone dressed exactly like Marius. There weren't many people in the kingdom of Arovia wearing a colorful silk patchwork that looked like the masterpiece of a blind, epileptic painter.

"Do you think they're still out there, looking for you?"

Marius hadn't thought that far ahead. Of course, the assassins had to be in Seatown. They wouldn't go home after being contracted by the leading house of a major city. They'd stay till they finished the job.

Marius didn't like it, but he would have to change his clothes. He had to don the wine-colored tunic of House Cervix. It wouldn't be safe to walk the streets in his jester's garb.

"What are you going to do?" Clarion asked.

The woman was full of questions, thought Marius.

He checked his irritation, followed it back to its source. Truth was, he didn't know what to do.

Clarion cleaned her hands on her apron. "There's something different about you today," she said. "When you first visited us, you were so carefree. Now—"

Many things had happened since that first day in Seatown, thought Marius.

"Maybe," said Jank, giving his words a sarcastic twist, "He's more interested in seducing noble daughters than talking to us slaves."

Marius glared at Jank only to find Clarion doing the same to Marius.

"Everyone on the hill is talking about it," said Jank. "The guards of House Ponti chasing him," he pointed at Marius, "down the hill last night."

"I-" he stammered. "Th-that was not a daughter."

"Oh-ho," said Jank triumphantly, "a son then."

"Jank!" said Clarion.

Marius folded his arms, "I didn't seduce her. She seduced me."

"Really?" said Clarion. She looked at him accusatorily.

He didn't see why she should. It wasn't as though he and Clarion were a couple. They'd just met.

Clarion broke into a friendly smile; a hand flew to her mouth. The tension that had been holding the room in suspense broke. "Look at your face. I was only teasing you."

His face, that had grown as sour and pinched as an old grape, now flushed beet red.

"Jank," said Clarion, "he told me all about his late night liaison with Carra the guest of House Ponti." She looked at Marius quite seriously, "Sorry. Part of that rumor might have started in our kitchen. One of our slaves overheard."

Marius held up a hand. Say no more, he thought. The gossiping kitchen slave was a stereotype for a reason.

He hadn't mentioned kissing Carra. But she might have told her own slaves. She seemed like the type to brag about her conquests. And she had to tell the guards something when they asked about the strange man who burst out of the family rooms and vaulted the wall. Marius would be surprised if her story stopped at a simple kiss.

He sighed and ran a hand through his unkempt hair.

Then again, thought Marius, "Jank has a point."

The boy looked shocked.

"I need to talk to Carra or to one of her m-minions." Marius considered the walls around House Ponti and the guards within. Carra was too well guarded. Of the other kidnappers, the witch in the black market might curse him. He would have to settle for Barn or Pithy, or both. "The kidnappers are the only ones in the city who might know where the wizard is."

"Let the wizard go," said Clarion. "Revenge isn't worth your life."

"Like y-you've never thought of it." The words came out before he'd thought them through.

Clarion's hands flew to her stomach as though he'd punched her as hard as he'd hit Rebius. She collapsed in on herself.

He shouldn't have brought up her past. Her pain.

Marius felt each tear that formed in the corners of her eyes.

"I'm s-sorry," he said.

Marius reached for a hand. She withdrew them and took a deep, composing breath.

"No, you're right," she said quietly. "I did think of revenge."

She sat in silence with neither Marius nor Jank interrupting. Marius wondered if Jank knew what offense his mother had suffered that would drive her to vengeance. She couldn't have been more than fourteen when Jank was born. Had the boy never counted the years?

"But the Lady saved me. The very knife you would have used to kill the wizard—I had it in hand. He was napping. It would have been so easy. Then the dove appeared, suspended in flight against the window, the sun illuminating each feather. And I knew—"

Jank said, "Mother, what—?"

Marius gave him a threatening look. Jank fell silent.

Marius prompted her. "Knew what?"

"That I could live a different way. The way She did."

Marius nodded. What she said confirmed his impression of the church as a refuge for the weak. "I suppose suffering in silence can be heroic for a woman."

Clarion shook her head, her eyebrows crinkled as though she were astonished that he could misunderstand her so completely. "The Lady was just the messenger. She told us that we can be like God. We can love the most undeserving, just like we are undeserving of His love."

Marius had never heard the dual nature of the religion of the Lady. "But you worship the statues of the woman, the Lady."

Clarion laughed again. The lines of care that had gathered around her eyes disappeared. "Is that what you think?" she said. "Have you never been to church?"

Marius shook his head, no.

"Has no one ever told you?" Clarion stood. "We worship God and the Lady. Not the statues. God and the Lady are alive and they are one."

Marius shook his head. She might have been speaking a foreign language.

She pointed at Iatro and spoke, as though she'd perfectly concluded the previous conversation, "He'll need to come with me. He can't stay here, in this," Clarion glanced around, "filth."

Marius thought he heard a low growl arising behind Fira's mess of brown hair. He didn't want the girl to attack.

"Fira," he said. "My bindle."

She brought it to him.

Marius reached into the secret pocket, removing his entire stash of coins. He hated to part with them, but Iatro needed them more. And he could always find work as a jester, especially with the fair approaching.

He handed them to Clarion. "Take them, please," he said, "and take care of Iatro."

She looked from the coins to Marius. "You are a constant surprise Walker."

"Call me Marius," he said.

Fira put a hand to her mouth, but was blocked by her hair. He nodded, knowing she would understand that it had been him the assassins' letter had mentioned.

"Go with her, Fira," he said. "Look after Iatro."

Fira reached for the sword that had belonged to the assassins.

"Leave it," said Marius.

Fira paused with her hand next to the hilt, as if deciding whether to listen to him or not. She might have been considering striking him for bringing the assassins down upon them. Finally, she nodded, "What will you do?"

He handed her his knife out of the bindle, hilt first. The blade pointed toward his belly. She held it in both hands.

Well, you had to trust somebody, thought Marius. And Asadal had trusted Fira. Though Asadal had also stolen from Marius.

As for what he intended to do, "I'm going to find the kidnappers and ask them some q-questions."

Marius took his old tunic out of the bindle. He would be returning to his role as a slave. Perhaps he'd never left it, enslaved as he was to killing the wizard, Malconus, and earning his freedom from the Jester's Curse.

Chapter Fifteen

Witchweed makes a man do strange things, see strange sights. Barn and Pithy loved the stuff, as Marius knew full well. He remembered the acrid smoke coming under the cupboard door as he lay trapped on the boat.

"Go now," Marius patted a Sparrow on the back. The boy, with another of his friends, ran toward the shabby shack that hung over the water's edge in the middle of the black market.

Simple plans could sometimes be the best.

The children brushed past a surly witch wearing a dull gray tunic. Dust puffed off the dingy fabric as a small elbow bounced off her back.

She shook a haggard fist, "Watch it, you!"

The pair were already by her. They ran headlong into the shop from which Jank had stolen.

They emerged a moment later with their hands full. Full of what, Marius couldn't tell. Mushrooms and withered roots dropped from their pockets. One of the boys crashed into the trays of dried fish that were displayed in front of the witch's shack. The other boy carried a lacy pink undergarment high above his head like a flag.

The witch herself emerged from the shop, chasing after the boys, hurling shrieks and curses at their backs. They dodged through the crowd, darting in and out of the shoppers in the black market.

Marius made his move. He walked into the witch's shack.

It took his eyes a moment to adjust to the dim lighting. A smell like the scent of burnt incense lingered in the room. From a shelf on the wall, the skulls of small animals stared vacantly at Marius. He shuddered.

Moving behind the lacquered counter, Marius pulled open drawer after drawer. In one he found a black box containing a stack of coins. Two of those coins had been his.

Marius didn't try to retrieve them. A curse might be laid on the witch's money box. He didn't want to risk losing a hand for a few coins.

The drawer below the coins held what he'd come for. A pile of dried seaweed, pulled from the ocean under the full moon and imbued by the power of arcane incantations with the ability to alter the minds of men. Witchweed. She had loads of it.

Marius heaped it into his bindle, filling the small bag to the brim. He pulled out his old bindle, the one Asadal had stolen, and filled that one as well. Then, with a final, wistful look at the money box, Marius shut the drawers and walked out of the shack.

He looked down the street. The witch was nowhere in sight, probably still chasing the boys.

By now the boys would have taken to the alleys of the warehouse district. The witch would do better not to follow them into the alleys unless her head could withstand a paving stone dropped from a roof.

Marius put his fingers to his lips and blew a shrill whistle.

When he'd seen Fira do it, it had seemed easy enough. Yet it had taken Marius most of the morning to perfect it, much to the annoyance of the Sparrows.

He heard the steady fall of axes. Marius stood back and waited. He listened to the rhythmic work, though he could not see the workmen. Sparrows on the other side of the sea wall hacked away at the foundations to the shack.

Eventually, the chopping ceased, leaving the gentle hum of the market in the background. Marius munched on a loaf of bread that he'd gotten from Clarion, what was it? Two days before?

The bread wasn't too bad, he thought. A bit dry but still edible. He'd had worse.

The witch came trudging up the street. She looked angrier than usual. Her black robes rose and fell as she took great lungfuls of air. The chase had winded her. Too bad for her.

As she walked into the shop, Marius again put his fingers to his lips and blew.

The effect was immediate. The shop lurched, drooping and tilting to the side, the way a drunk might bend to evacuate his bowels.

The Sparrows below had put ropes around the weakened support beams and were now pulling them down.

The shack slowly collapsed. The floor went first, sucking the front steps in like a piece of pasta.

The witch shrieked as she fell. The thin walls of the shack followed her in short succession.

Finding neither walls nor floor beneath it, the roof gave up.

The witch's shack had been built precariously over the sea wall. It collapsed, taking with it the sides of the adjoining buildings. One, a launderer, sent a collection of soiled clothing tumbling after the shack.

The collapse of the neighboring building revealed a man and a witch caught practicing the oldest profession in the kingdom. The look of surprise on the man's face caused Marius to smile.

The Jester's Curse trapped inside him smiled too. Finally, they agreed on something.

* * *

"Witchweed?" The little boy held out a hand out containing a wisp of dried grass.

Two men paused beside the boy who had set up shop on the edge of the warehouse district near enough to the black market to get business but far enough away to avoid the curses that often fell on the competition.

"Bit young aren't you?" An orange vest extended around the man's considerable waist.

"Best witchweed in Seatown," said the boy.

"Give it here," said the other, a thin man with a powerful odor. He pawed at the boy's pockets and hollered when he received a bite.

"I don't have it on me, stupid," said the boy. "You want it, you have to buy it. This witchweed came straight from Machoo."

The fat man put finger and thumb to his gristled chin. "It never did."

He stooped over to look at the witchweed with his one good eye.

The boy continued his sales pitch, unperturbed, "Came off the Brown Lady when she put in last night. This is the best witchweed in the kingdom."

"We'll be the judge of that," said the fat man. "Give us a taste."

"Nothing's free," said the boy. "Show me money and you can stuff your pipe."

The fat man pulled a coin out of his orange vest. His empty eye socket flapped as he spoke, the other eye shone with desire, "Show us then, little man."

They followed the boy into the narrow alley that separated the warehouses, carefully avoiding any puddles. It had not rained in a week. Whatever water had gathered in the alley wasn't healthy.

They arrived at a small square across from which stood a dilapidated warehouse with a bright, red door.

Marius stepped out.

"Barn, Pithy, good to see you again."

They might not have recognized his clothing, but they must've recognized his face, as they immediately began to back into the alley.

They turned only to find their way blocked by several rows of children. Small children, but ones holding nasty-looking rocks.

A whistle sounded overhead.

The men looked up to see large stones being held over their heads by tiny little hands.

Not trusting the small fingers not to slip, the men moved into the square where Marius stood ready to meet them. He balanced the assassin's blade nonchalantly on his shoulder.

"As I s-said, gentleman," he used the term very loosely, "I am happy to see you again. We're going to take a

w-walk together to your ship. You first. I'll f-follow. If
you try to escape, I'll cut you down from behind."

Barn ran his hand over the stubble on his chin. His
good eye flitted from Marius to the children.

"I can see wh-what you're thinking," said Marius. "If
you run, I might not be able to kill you both, but I will
certainly kill one of you."

Marius lifted the blade and examined its edge. "I'm
already a w-wanted man. I've been c-cursed, as you
know. I have n-nothing to lose."

"Now, walk." Marius waved the sword.

It might have been the keen blade of the sword as it
whistled over his head, or it might have been the slightly
mad look in Marius's eye. Either way, the pair of kidnappers, Barn and Pithy, joined by the oddest procession, a
motley collection of children, paraded down the wharf to
their small ship.

*　*　*

Neither Barn nor Pithy could see much out of the
small cupboard. Marius was sure of that. He'd been in
there himself earlier in the week, unsure of his fate, fearful that he'd been captured by a ship bound for Machoo,
fearful for his life.

Now his captors shared his fate. Even if they had their
faces to the floor, as he felt sure they must, they could see
little more than his shoes.

"Where's the w-wizard," said Marius.

Barn replied, his voice muffled as it filtered through
the small crack in the door. "We don't know."

"I think you d-do."

"It'd be more than our lives to tell you."

"Funny you should mention that." Marius lit the first
bit of weed and placed it on a small metal plate on the

floor. He waved a fan over the witchweed, causing it to glow a dull red and moving its smoke into the cupboard.

Marius turned to the Sparrow near the door. "Whatever you hear, d-don't come in that door," he said. "When I come out, no matter what I say, I w-want you to follow the orders I've already given. D-do you understand me? We don't know wh-what the w-witchweed will do."

The girl nodded. Though she could only be eight or nine years old, she already had a solid, maternal bearing. Marius could sense her disapproval.

Marius examined the flame dancing on the witchweed. It wavered back and forth like a tongue trying to speak, trying to warn him.

The witchweed was already working.

He heard coughing coming from inside the cupboard.

"What is that?" said Barn.

"You k-know what it is."

Barn laughed. Pithy, who'd been quiet since their arrest, joined in with a weak titter.

"If this is your idea of torture, then I say give us your worst."

Marius added another lump of witchweed to the pile. Though the door to the ship's galley stood open as well as the windows, Marius could feel his eyes burning. His heart raced.

He spoke quietly, almost too quiet. They'd have to get close to the crack to hear, putting their faces into the smoke of the witchweed.

"Do you know what happens to people who smoke too much?"

He could tell by their silence that they did.

Marius continued, "Tell me wh-where the wizard is."

He could hear a hard scrabbling on the wooden floorboards as the two backed into the cupboard. The ship rolled back and forth on the waves. The room itself swayed in Marius's vision. The witchweed was affecting him too.

"You'll tell me," said Marius. "Whether you do it before or after you lose your minds is up to you."

He emptied his bindle onto the smoking pile of witchweed. The flame licked it up, belching out thick smoke that Marius waved under the door.

Fists beat on the cupboard. Marius thought he heard a strange, staccato rhythm in the thumps. He found his shoulders twitching back and forth. He wanted to dance.

He started humming a tune, "Where's the wi-zard. Where's the wi-zard? Find the wi-zard. Find the wi-zard."

Barn and Pithy joined in the song. Marius was glad they'd finally gotten into the spirit. He tried to harmonize with their discordant screams.

* * *

Late into the night, Marius wandered the streets of Seatown. The oil lanterns left streaks in the air as he passed them. The lantern poles multiplied as solid as their numerous shadows. Marius thought he could trace words forming in the cracks in the paving stones. Though he didn't know how to read, the words spoke to him.

The assassins and their swords had completely flown from his mind. Marius thought he might fly too, light as his thoughts felt that night.

He found himself in the rotary that formed the center of life in Seatown. The statue of the Lady stared out to sea. The dove on her outstretched fingers cooed. The flame in her lantern flashed a coded pattern to the ships, telling them where the rich fish slipped silently through the sea. Her white robe billowed behind her, blown gently on the breeze.

Marius and the Lady were the only two people alive in the square. The entire city had fallen silent in the night.

The Lady turned her head toward Marius, observing him.

"Speak to me, Lady," said Marius.

"I speak to you every day." Her voice sounded like the breeze that tips over the morning waves, pushing them toward the beach.

"Then why can I never hear you?"

"You will one day," said the Lady.

"When?"

"When all seems lost. When you lay below the ground facing death eternal, imprisoned within a prison, then you and I will speak again."

"Bummer," said Marius.

The Lady smiled.

* * *

He didn't see her head turn. She looked again out over the ocean. He didn't know how long he'd been standing in the same spot. His knees ached. His legs felt rigid. The morning mist coated his clothing, wetting the shoulders of his rust-red tunic.

Marius felt hungry, he felt ravenous. He also felt something else, a more primal urge. He had to see Clarion.

Marching up the hill, Marius saw the first signs of the sunrise. All around him, the sounds of morning came to life. Servants were moving in the courtyards, preparing for the day.

The dew on the walls made the colors pop even brighter.

Marius felt the spirit of the witchweed leaving him. He felt a profound sense of appreciation for life, but at the same time doubted whether he'd ever try the stuff again. People who lived on witchweed tended to think the visions they saw more real than life itself. They missed the truly important things.

Marius slapped his forehead, just as he'd missed something important last night.

He knew the location of the wizard. He'd missed a chance for revenge.

But the wizard would still be there. Marius had time. No reason to be hasty.

Marius was glad he'd given orders before using the witchweed against Barn and Pithy. The maternal little Sparrow would have carried them out by now he felt sure.

Marius paused outside the light-blue wall that bounded House Fluctus trying to remember why he had come.

He'd wanted something.

His stomach rumbled.

Well, some breakfast wouldn't be amiss, thought Marius, and he could check on Iatro.

The gate in the wall opened. Marius brushed at his tunic, wondering if he looked presentable enough to gain entrance.

A boy passed through the gate at speed, wearing the aquamarine tunic of the house. He collided with Marius, sending them both to the ground.

Marius remembered his first day in Seatown when Clarion had bowled him over.

He recognized her fair hair and blue eyes in her son, Jank.

Marius wondered where the boy was going in such a hurry.

"Marius," the boy gasped, "they're gone." He took a short breath and repeated himself. "They're gone."

"Who's gone?"

"They're all gone," Jank said. "Mother and Iatro and the girl."

"Fira?"

Jank nodded.

Marius felt the solid ground under him tilting and knew that, this time, it wasn't the witchweed. The only question was who had taken them? There were too many options: the wizard Malconus, the assassins hired by House Marcel, Carra—formerly known as Secundus, or maybe a new enemy, like the witch whose shack he'd ruined.

One thing he did know. Something very bad had happened in Seatown. Marius didn't need Old Mad Maude, the witch in the alley, to tell him that, though she'd no doubt try.

Chapter Sixteen

Marius trudged through the streets of Seatown, aware of nothing but the mechanical rise and fall of his feet.

He had not found Clarion or the others at the Sparrows' Nest, nor had he expected to. The three closest things he had to friends in Seatown had been taken during the night, out of a walled, if not heavily fortified home.

He hadn't a clue as to where they'd been taken. His only solid lead came from the directions Barn and Pithy had given him to the wizard's lair. He didn't know if he could trust their directions, having forced the information out of them during a drug induced stupor.

Perhaps the wizard had Marius's friends and perhaps he didn't. Marius had nothing else to go on.

He'd been intending to visit the wizard anyway, but with a different agenda in mind, namely the death of Malconus. Now, his mission of revenge had turned into a rescue.

Marius had hoped to confront the wizard with more panache, more cunning.

He'd spent the better part of the day wandering around the city, looking for any clue, hoping he'd find his friends, trying to come up with a better plan, one that was a little less suicidal. He didn't trust the plan his brain had invented, not when his hair and skin still reeked of witchweed. The slave tunic had been rendered unwearable by the foul smoke. Marius adjusted the sleeve of his colorful jester's costume.

He stalked through the town, not pausing when he passed the statue of the Lady in the rotary. Nor did he stop to examine his handiwork in the black market. He walked past the stinking warehouse and the narrow opening to the alleys that lead to the Sparrows' Nest.

The slave quarter arose before him in all its squalid glory. Marius had seen it the day he arrived in Seatown. He'd seen the slaves being auctioned off, heard the clatter of their chains.

Having been born into slavery, Marius had never seen the more sordid side of the system. As a boy, he hadn't been allowed near the slave market in the capital city, Zeno.

The slave quarter in Seatown seemed to be doing steady business in the late afternoon. Many ships had arrived in anticipation of the fair. These had cargo from ports to the South, including slaves.

The weather would soon change, making the run between Arovia and the lands to the South more treacherous. The ships arriving in Seatown would either winter in the city or move farther north along the peninsula.

Even now, Notori's ship might be sitting among all the masts that had turned the docks into an undulating forest.

Finding Notori seemed a distant task to the one now facing Marius. He thought of his planned escape from Arovia and from the Jester's Curse and how unlikely either possibility now seemed.

Cargoes of slaves had arrived with the fleet of merchant vessels. They lined the wharf, men and women bound in chains and bound in even deeper misery.

These were men and women who had once known freedom, the opposite of Marius who'd had freedom unwillingly thrust upon him. As a slave, he'd known where each meal would come from and exactly what was expected of him.

He knew, for instance, that, as a slave, he would never have been called on to confront a dangerous wizard in the attempt to free three captives.

Almost, just almost, Marius envied the slaves lined up on the docks. Most were going to a life he knew well. Others—well, others might be going to the mines or to the houses of pleasure. Marius didn't envy them.

Securing the assassin's sword that was currently serving as a stick for his bindle, Marius elbowed his way through the crowds that had come for the slave auction and would stay for the fair. Bringing the sword had seemed like a good idea, though Marius didn't know how effective he might be with it.

Marius pushed through the assembly, ignoring a merchant hawking a slave the way Mortimer might sell a fish.

As the crowd thinned, Marius came to a grand building as solid as the ground itself and as tall as the neighboring slave houses, though it was evident that no slaves dwelt in this house. Two white columns rose into the sky, supporting an ornately carved frieze featuring men and fantastical creatures the likes of which Marius had never seen.

Had events turned out otherwise, Marius might have lurked outside this house, hiding in the shadows, looking for a chance to strike Malconus.

Instead, Marius walked to the door, took up the knocker held in the teeth of a fearsome gargoyle, and struck three resounding blows.

The arching stone doors swung silently open, framing in the doorway the white robes and crooked nose of Malconus, the wizard who had cast the Jester's Curse.

Behind the wizard, wearing a sheer dress that left little to the imagination, stood Carra, the second son lately turned second daughter of House Ponti. The red sash tied around her waist bore the weight of a thin rapier.

"Come in, Marius," said Malconus. "We've been waiting for you."

Marius entered. The stone doors swung shut, closing with an ominous thud.

* * *

The view from the third-story window looked out over the bay. The ships, which had been little more than a collection of masts from the wharf, could be seen individually at this distance. The various shapes and designs called to Marius's mind the wonder of the world and of all the places he'd never see.

The view might have been pleasant were it not for the sight of the slave auction in the street below profiting from the trade in human flesh; or had it not been for the presence of the odious wizard in whose house Marius now stood; not to mention the way Carra kept looking at Marius as though she could see through the quilted folds of his jester's costume. He found her gaze both upsetting and confusing.

More unpleasant, however, than the slavery, or the wizard, or the staring, were the three figures lying supine on settees in the middle of the room.

Clarion, Iatro, and Fira looked as though they were having the most gruesome dreams, not terribly surprising since they'd been entranced by Malconus. He only did "nice" magic for a fee or by order of the Emperor. In everything else, even his kindest mercies were cruel.

Marius hadn't known that Malconus had the captives. Of course, that explained why the wizard had been waiting for Marius to arrive. Only, now that he'd arrived, Marius didn't know what he was supposed to do. What exactly did the wizard want from him?

Standing with his back to the large windows overlooking the bay, Marius resisted the urge to take out the brass knuckles or to unshoulder the sword holding the bindle.

Carra broke the silence. "You've been bad for business, Jester. Had it not been against the wizard's wishes, I would have killed you long ago."

Not as though she hadn't tried, thought Marius. Carra had ordered Barn and Pithy to murder him and had later tried to run him through with the rapier that even now hung from the sash at her side.

The wizard seemed content to let the woman talk. Marius was happy to oblige since every moment of conversation was another moment he stayed alive.

"Why are you k-kidnapping people? What's the p-point?"

Carra shrugged her shoulders, tilting her head to the side, as though the lives of those she'd taken were nothing more than toys in a game.

Marius addressed the wizard directly, "Why?"

The wizard sniffed, as though deciding whether to answer the question. "What we of the White Tower do may seem simple to a fool like you, but curses like yours are not easy. They must be studied."

"B-but why not use slaves? Why must your victims b-be willing?" Marius remembered Barn and Pithy saying as much.

"You ask many questions for a man in your position," said the wizard. "Still, the answer is simple enough. Greed makes them easier to bend. You are living proof that those who resist are more...difficult. But even they must eventually succumb, just as you are doing."

Carra tittered; her nasal laugh rang through the large hall.

A look of defiance came over Marius's face. He wouldn't see his friends Clarion and Fira and Iatro become the wizard's playthings.

"Release my f-friends."

A hand fluttered to Carra's mouth as though the demand shocked her. The wizard merely smiled, though it looked more like a snarl.

Malconus spoke, "I can see why you like this one."

It took Marius a moment to realize that the wizard hadn't addressed Carra. He was speaking to someone else, someone standing in a doorway, a doorway he hadn't noticed upon entering, cleverly concealed as it was behind a tapestry.

Having begun the bluff, Marius blustered his way through, though his nerves were badly shaken by the appearance (or lack of appearance) of the unseen third party.

"These p-people are under my protection."

Carra smiled. "Yet it was so easy to take them. Especially Once I'd suggested to her master how unwise it was for the woman to continue cooking his meals when her bastard son stood in direct succession. As a protector, you failed."

So, she'd taken them out of House Fluctus with the full approval of the master. No wonder the walls hadn't secured them. The enemy was already inside.

Marius buried his anger, "I was b-busy."

"I heard," said Carra. "How are Barn and Pithy by the way?"

It was Marius's turn to smile. "They're on a slow boat to Machoo by now. Turns out kidnapping is a sport anyone can play. I might even be better at it than you."

"Superb," the wizard interrupted. "You really are some of my finest work."

Marius glared at the man, standing so secure and confident in his white robes. "Then how come I've been f-fighting it and w-winning?"

"Do you really think so?" said the wizard. "How very interesting. I see you've had some help."

Marius clutched at the charmed ring Asadal had given him. It had kept the curse at bay during his time in Seatown. But as the grass faded, so did the power of the ring. Marius hoped it would last long enough to survive this encounter.

The wizard, however, wasn't looking at the ring. He stared at the prone form of Iatro.

"I'm warning you for the l-last t-time."

"Enough," said the wizard. "I tire of this. My experiments go unattended while this fool blathers about things he knows not of." Turning to Marius, he added, "It has been a pleasure to see you, fool, and by you I mean, of course, my work growing and blossoming within you."

He tapped a finger to the side of his nose, thoughtfully, "I would say within the week. Yes," he added, "within a week its work should be complete."

"B-but," Marius stammered, "in Amok you said a year."

The wizard smiled his crooked smile, "Did I? But then again, in Amok you were fighting it."

Marius replied, "I still am."

"Are you?" said the wizard. "Do you still not understand the nature of the curse? Oh, it is subtle. Some of my best work. Really. And that is saying something. Now," Malconus turned toward the concealed doorway, "goodbye, fool. Forever I think."

Marius watched the tapestry intently, trying to guess who might be behind it; the assassins perhaps.

But why would Malconus want him dead? The answer to his question sprang immediately to mind: because the Jester's Curse had run its course. The experiment was nearly complete. He said so himself.

Yet, how was that even possible, thought Marius. Aside from the return of his stutter, Marius hadn't had the overbearing urge to act the fool. The ring Asadal made had worked. The Jester's Curse left him alone. It had even helped him—

That's when Marius realized. His countenance fell.

The wizard clapped his hands. "You see it now, don't you? The Jester's Curse has remade you in its image. If you act the fool it allows it, because you are acting in its image. If you act with ironic cruelty, it allows you, because that too is in its nature. If you resist, it may take longer. But you are no longer resisting. You and the Jester's Curse are becoming one."

"No!" Marius shouted.

"Your friends tell me otherwise," said Malconus, his lips twisted into a smirk. "The boys who betrayed you, what happened to them?"

Marius shook his head, "No."

"The witch in the black market? Carra's ignorant pirates?"

Images of the past few days flashed through his mind: Demari hit by Fira's stone, Rebius doubled over by a blow from the brass knuckles, the witch's screams as her shack collapsed, Barn and Pithy shrieking to be let out as their minds broke apart. And in the background each time, the Jester's Curse laughing and Marius laughing with it.

The wizard was right.

Something within him still resisted. An image of the statue of the Lady filled his mind, as alive as she'd been in his drugged hallucination the night before.

Marius spoke slowly, "What I d-did, I did to s-save my friends." Marius pointed at the three figures lying on the settees. "I'll d-do the s-same to you if you don't w-wake them up."

"Wake them up?" the wizard clapped his hands. "I should have thought of that already. They would hate to have missed this, to not know why they were sacrificed and for what a worthless cause."

Malconus waved a hand.

The three figures stirred.

They sat up but did not rise further.

"It will take a moment for them to recover," Malconus spoke more to himself than to anyone else in the room, "these friends of yours," he said, "of whom you know as little as they about you."

"I know them," said Marius.

The wizard cast an accusatory glance at Marius, "You have no idea what this one would have become had you never entered her life." He pointed at Clarion. "Greatness in her future, Marius, and you took that away."

Marius struggled to understand how Clarion, a kitchen slave, could have greatness ahead of her.

"And this one," Malconus pointed at Fira. "She bears a curse even more powerful than yours. It is an ancient magic."

"What are you talking about?"

"Destined never to age. Ever the child."

Suddenly, Marius realized why Fira always covered her face. He'd seen something in her eyes the night they escaped from the assassins. They looked so old compared to her youthful visage.

He wondered how long she'd been with the Sparrows, perhaps changing names and hair styles. The children always grew up and moved on, who would notice a child that never left the Nest? Asadal would. Maybe that's why he trusted her.

"This one is my personal favorite," said Malconus, pointing a wizened finger at Iatro. "You really don't know who this is? You don't recognize the auburn hair or the shape of his eyes or," Malconus paused, "the magic that seeps out of him, making everything around him better?"

Marius's stomach fell as the realization sank in of what the wizard was about to reveal. "He can't be—"

"Oh, but he is. The brother of the little whore the church stole from me in Amok."

Iatro was Irina's brother. The one she had told Marius about. The one that had been kicked out of House Marcel, forced to make his way in the world alone, all for being born like Marius.

He should have known. He should have realized. Oh, Iatro, thought Marius. What a bummer.

Clarion, Fira, and Iatro stared at Marius, seeking some confirmation of what the wizard had said.

"Yes," Malconus waved a hand, directing their attention toward Marius. "Behold the man with the Jester's Curse. See how he tries to resist it and how it consumes him. How delicious. Behold the runaway slave who ruined your lives to save his own."

"I never—" Marius's head fell. His chin hit his chest.

"Tut, tut," said Malconus, "is there anything sadder than a weeping fool? Sing a song for us, jester. Do a funny little dance. Compose a dirty rhyme."

"No." Marius

"No?" replied Malconus. He gestured toward the hidden door. "He bores me. Take him away."

A skin-tight suit of black armor bearing the red star of an Astor appeared, Lespa, followed closely by the hulking form of Bithius who barely fit through doorway.

The Astors had returned to claim him.

Chapter Seventeen

Had a white dove flown by the third-story window of the wizard's house at that exact instant, it would have seen Lespa the Astor, standing with her hand planted squarely on her hip, smiling at Marius's obvious discomfort.

It would have seen her companion Bithius shuffling uncomfortably from foot to foot as though he loathed being inside a house so fine and feared he might break an expensive antiquity.

The dove would also have seen the way the seated figures of Clarion, Fira, and Iatro scooted away from the Astors in fright. Fira and Iatro as members of a criminal gang had good reason. Clarion too, though she did not know it, had aided a fugitive slave.

The dove might have seen the triumphant look on the wizard Malconus's face and the look of lust on the face of his creation, Carra, as she stared back and forth, eyes darting between the leather backsides of both Bithius and Lespa.

A dove could have seen all this if it had flown past the window at that moment.

And who is to say a dove didn't do exactly that?

* * *

Lespa addressed Marius, "We've still got work to do, fool. But first, we've got to get one thing sorted." She turned to Malconus. "Wizard, fix that blasted stutter."

Malconus's white robes ruffled as though the Astor's offensive tone had physically affected him. "A Wizard of the White Tower does not take orders from an Astor."

Lespa turned to face him, her hand on the hilt of her dagger. Marius wondered whether she could draw it before Malconus cursed her. Of course, to curse an Astor would be an affront to all Astors and maybe to the Emperor as well.

"If you serve the Emperor," said Lespa, "you'll do it."

"Would you ask Moncarno the Blind to alter a single brush stroke of his mural celebrating the Third Great War?"

"If it offended me personally," said Lespa, "yes. And if he didn't," she added, "I'd break every finger on his painting hand."

Malconus visibly flinched either because of the threat or because of the woman's barbaric view toward fine art.

"Very well, though it diminishes one of my finest works." He waved a hand at Marius.

Something within Marius gave way. He felt relief, as though a large and very necessary belch had cleared a bubble of gas from his stomach.

Putting a hand to his throat, Marius tested his voice, "Ah, ah, ah." He said the first thing that came to mind, "time to turn the turnips." He looked at Lespa, "I'm—"

She nodded, "Less of a fool."

"Make him remove the curse."

She grimaced. Her hand never moved from the hilt of her knife. Its wickedly curved blade lay beneath a simple piece of leather.

"An Astor doesn't take orders from a fool."

"Except for the Emperor?"

"I could kill you for such impertinence!"

"I'm dead already. The wizard says the curse will take me by the end of the week," said Marius. "A witch told me a Walker would die by the turn of the new tide. Why fight the inevitable?"

Marius brandished his sword, dropping the bindle from its tip. He swung it, not at the Astor but, turning, punched the blade through the window. Glass rained down. Shouts and curses arose from the street.

The entire slave quarter looked toward the commotion and saw a jester in fully colored garb threatening to jump from a third-story window. Now, there was entertainment! And the fair hadn't even started yet.

Turning to face Lespa, Marius shouted, "You need me to get Asadal. I can find him. I know how."

Lespa spoke out of the side of her mouth, "Do something, wizard."

Malconus shrugged. "I work magic. Apprehending a fugitive is an Astor's job."

Lespa cursed. She added calmly to Marius, "I don't negotiate."

"Of course you do." Marius took a step back with his hands outstretched ready to fall.

"Say what you want then, fool?"

"I want my friends released."

Carra butted in, earning a reproachful stare from Lespa. "We could take them again at any time."

"That's as may be," said Marius, glad—though the situation seemed dire—to have free use of his voice without the constant interruption of his stutter. "I only ask that you release them now, and—"

"And?" said Lespa, "There's more?"

"And," Marius continued, "I want the wizard to fix the girl's curse."

Again, Malconus's robes ruffled. "I don't—"

Marius took another step back. The wind rippled through his hair.

"Do it," said Lespa.

"He's bluffing," said Bithius.

"So what?" said Lespa. "Do it, wizard. Fixing curses is wizard's work."

Malconus frowned, "It's a shame to disrupt such old magic. There's so little left of it in the world."

Lespa pulled the curved knife from its sheath. "Fix the girl."

Malconus wave his hand. Fira doubled over. She sat back with a look of astonishment on her face. She must have felt something similar to the relief he'd felt when his stutter had been removed.

Secretly, he was glad that she hadn't suddenly aged all at once, wrinkling and turning to dust. He wouldn't have put such a stunt past the evil wizard.

Marius breathed a sigh of relief. He had been bluffing, a bit. But he'd also seen the look in Lespa's eyes when she ordered the wizard to fix his stutter. She liked ordering the wizard around. He'd used that to help Fira.

Fira examined her hands as though they might change. They didn't. She pulled the hair away from a face that remained young except for the ancient eyes.

Marius was happy for her. She would be able to live an entire life now.

"Let the women go," Lespa ordered.

"But," Marius began to protest. He wanted all the captives to go free, including Iatro.

Lespa crossed over to Clarion and Fira, grabbing them by their tunics, she threw them off the settees and onto the floor. "Go. Run if you know what's good for you."

She placed the dagger to Iatro's throat.

"The boy stays. You jump and he dies before your head bloodies the pavement."

Clarion and Fira huddled together. They stood in the room unsure of what to do.

"Go," said Marius. "I'll see to Iatro."

Without looking back, they hurried out of the room, their heads disappearing down the marble staircase that ran up the interior of the house.

Carra watched them go. She fingered the hilt of her rapier.

Lespa mocked Marius, "You can do nothing for the boy unless you tell me where to find Asadal."

"You're right as always, Lespa," said Marius. "I can't do anything. There is one more thing though."

"What's that, fool? Make it quick, my hand tires." Her knife pressed closer to Iatro's neck. A touch from its razor sharp blade would slice through the boy's skin.

"You remember the bounty that House Marcel put on my head?"

"What of it?"

"There's a group of assassins in Seatown. They must have blended in with the crowds coming in for the fair. They're here to collect. Tried to kill me two nights ago."

"And you want our protection," Lespa sneered. "You are bold, fool."

"No," said Marius, "I only thought it fair to warn you that they're looking for me—for someone wearing a colorful jester's outfit just like mine."

Marius looked over his shoulder at the crowd that had gathered to watch the spectacle.

Someone shouted an encouragement. "Jump!"

"Do a back flip!" added another.

Marius ignored them because, at that moment, an assassin rappelled from the rooftop, bursting through the window to his right. Another burst through the window to his left. Grabbing his bindle, Marius rolled across the floor as a third assassin came through the window he'd just vacated.

Marius came up in a guarded stance with the sword protecting his head. Through the doorway he could see more assassins coming up the stairs.

His great plan had materialized. Marius had been wearing the jester's uniform as he walked through Seatown that day, hoping the assassins would see him, hoping they would come. Now, all he had to do was survive their second meeting.

The crowd outside, witnessing a fight, erupted into a swelling cheer. Marius thought he could hear bets being placed: Astors versus Assassins versus the Wizard versus the Fool.

He imagined the odds on his own survival were pretty low. Even a fool wouldn't bet on Marius.

* * *

In the split-second, as Marius rolled to his knees, holding the sword above his head, the room seemed frozen in time.

Fragments of glass hung suspended in the air, glittering, reflecting the sun as it set across the waves, reaching across the sky, across the world to enter the third-floor room of the wizard's manse.

Marius saw Lespa pulling a wicked short sword from its sheath. Her knife had already flown from her hand, bursting through a cluster of dust and glass as it sped toward the heart of an assassin.

Bithius stood planted mid-stride, his bulging muscles rippling under the black leather and red star of the Astor's armor, his hands flexing as though he intended to rip his enemies apart.

Erect and poised, her rapier forming a perfect extension of her arm, Carra had turned, awaiting the assassins rushing up the stairs.

Malconus had a nasty snarl on his lips and a spell on his tongue. His white robes swirled as he raised his arms, his hands cocked at an awkward angle, his fingers splayed and outstretched, ready to unleash the power of the White Tower on the intruders.

Beyond the wizard, still sitting on the settee, a single word formed on Iatro's lips.

"Bummer."

As if that word were itself a powerful spell, the room snapped into action.

Lespa's dagger hit the assassin in the chest, the force of it hurling him back through a broken window. Bithius caught another by the wrist, pulling him off the floor, swinging him into the wall with a crack that broke the plaster and the assassin's skull.

The third assassin's black tunic collapsed in on itself. Marius blinked. The wizard must have amplified the assassin's ability to hide so much that the man's body disappeared.

More assassins came through the windows. Others rushed up the stairs and into the room. Carra's thin sword flashed. It swam like a fish in the sea, taking the leader in the throat and another through the chest. Carra didn't retrieve it quickly enough and caught a backhanded blow to the side of her head. She fell to the carpet.

Marius abandoned all pretense of fighting. The assassins were trained and well-armed. Yet the Astors and the wizard cut through them. Bodies hit the floor. One of them belonged to Marius.

Dropping the sword, Marius crawled on his hands and knees. He reached Iatro's seat, grabbed the boy by the arm, and pulled him to the floor just as an assassin's dagger flew overhead, ruffling the boy's hair.

Irina shone so clearly through her brother, Iatro, that Marius wondered how he'd never noticed it before. They had the same auburn hair and the same set of the mouth. Marius couldn't believe that he'd found Irina's brother. She told him the boy had been lost to her forever. Marius could return him to her. The church at Amok would surely take him in. Marius would be a hero. Irina would embrace him, thanking him with a kiss.

Marius was brought back to reality as a body tilted over the settee landing in the awkward, broken pose of death.

Marius spoke into Iatro's ear, having to shout to make himself heard over the clash of sword against sword and the screams of the dying. "F-follow me."

Not waiting to see if the boy understood, he crawled toward the hidden door, the one behind the tapestry. There was a chance the assassins, like Marius, hadn't noticed it on entering the room, preoccupied as they were with the swords and knives and spells flying about.

Iatro followed.

They crawled through the battle and around combatants locked in deadly struggle.

An assassin fell backwards over Marius, a dagger stuck in his chest. Marius turned his shoulders, dumping the man's twitching legs onto the floor.

He saw the wizard Malconus, just a few steps away, his back to them, casting spells. His hands moved in a blur. He twisted to the side as a knife flew past his shoulder.

Three assassins ran toward him. The wizard's back lay exposed. Even if the wizard took the three assassins, Marius saw a chance, a chance to have his revenge.

He pulled the dagger from the assassin's chest. The man groaned, clutching feebly at Marius's wrist. Then a more firm grip took his arm.

Iatro held his hand, with a look of pleading in his eyes, he shook his head, no.

Marius understood. Part of him, the sane part of him, knew they should leave, escape while the battle raged, while their enemies were distracted, leave while they still had a chance.

But he had to try. He might never get another chance to kill Malconus. The wizard had to die for what he'd done to Marius and to countless others. Marius couldn't trust the assassins to do it. One had already fallen and the other two hesitated, only for a moment, though it would cost them their lives.

Marius sprung forward. He plunged the dagger into the wizard's billowing robes, aiming for the heart, hoping for a kidney.

At the same moment, the wizard stepped forward to meet the oncoming assassins, his hands wielding fingernails the size and shape of daggers.

Marius's knife plunged through the robes, becoming entangled in the folds. It tore loose from Marius's hand.

The wizard didn't even feel Marius's attack. Malconus sliced through the assassins' blades, then through their throats with his hardened nails.

Marius stood dumbfounded, his mouth hanging open. He'd been so close. He looked at his empty hand.

Pressure on his back caused him to turn, to remember that he stood exposed in a room bristling with blades, a colorful target on a killing room floor.

Iatro stood back to back with Marius.

Marius felt a spark of pride. They were fighting together.

But something felt wrong.

Iatro slid toward the floor. Marius saw in one horrible instant: an assassin across the room with his arm extended and Iatro clutching a knife to his chest.

The boy had saved him. He'd blocked the assassin's throwing knife with his body.

Marius locked eyes with the assassin. Then the man was crushed against the wall in a death embrace by Bithius.

Marius caught Iatro as he fell to the floor, cradling Iatro's head in his arm.

Iatro looked into Marius's eyes. A dribble of blood ran from his mouth. He spoke softly, "Jesser, is the L-lady real?"

Marius could feel tears forming in the corners of his eyes. He didn't know what to say. He wanted to comfort the boy. A small lie wouldn't matter. "She is," he said. "I saw her myself last night."

Iatro closed his eyes.

The assassin struggled in Bithius's grasp. Marius heard the man's bones snap. The big Astor looked at Marius, nodding his head toward the hidden door.

"Run!"

Marius picked up Iatro's body, looping a hand behind his head and one under his legs, Marius lurched toward the concealed door. His legs stepped erratically.

The Jester's Curse was reasserting itself. Iatro's death must have removed whatever protection the boy's magic had been providing.

It hadn't been the ring after all, or perhaps it had helped a little. Really, the curse had been deflected by Iatro's magic, a magic that bled out of him with every drop of blood.

The urge to urinate overwhelmed Marius as the curse pressed in on his bladder, picking the most inconvenient time possible.

The Jester's Curse was back to its old tricks.

Marius stumbled from the room and into the secret passage that the Astors had used. He stepped gingerly, trying to keep from peeing, trying to keep the curse from desecrating the body of his friend by dropping it down the stairs or banging his head against a wall.

At the realization of his sorry state, feeling in his bones the malevolent juxtaposition between the curse's foul humor and Marius's all-encompassing sorrow, Marius began to sob. He truly was a fool, through and through. A slave to his foolishness just as High Priest Campri had said.

If he'd joined the church and taken vows he might never have come to Seatown. Iatro might still be alive. Instead, Marius lived, his own man, but in an inwardly crippled body, unable to do the things he ought to do and unable to stop doing the things he didn't want to do. He lived every day in a body of death and had only a week to live before the curse took him permanently; yet Iatro had died for him. What an incredible and irrational waste, thought Marius. What a waste.

Clutching Iatro's body to his chest, He stumbled onto a landing and pressed through a low door that exited into an alley behind the wizard's house. Pausing to get his bearings, Marius flew as best he could toward the Sparrows' Nest.

Chapter Eighteen

A small hand shook him. Marius opened his eyes. No matter how fervently he wished it, the scene hadn't changed. Why wouldn't they leave him alone, he wondered? He wanted to die, or if not to die then to sleep the sleep of the dead.

"Marius?"

Fira's voice called him back to the land of the living. Snapping into focus, his eyes beheld the inside of the Sparrows' Nest, lit by a hundred misshapen candles that had once seemed so comical. Now their bent forms felt fitting, an act of reverence toward the body of the fallen Sparrow that lay on the table in the middle of the common room.

He looked so much like Irina.

A hand tugged insistently at his elbow. "Marius, you have to leave."

She had been saying this to him for hours. And he hadn't listened. He didn't intend to listen.

But Fira wouldn't be put off.

Marius sat on the dirty floor of the Nest with his back against the wall. Fira sat beside him, while Clarion looked after the children, assisting them in their mourning, making the necessary arrangements, and saying all the right things.

The Sparrows finally had a mother.

"Marius, listen to me. You have to leave Seatown."

"And go where?" Marius replied.

Fira had brushed her unruly hair and tied it up with a ribbon. Her ancient eyes looked up at him from her childlike face. She had been cursed, same as him. But her curse had been removed, while his threatened to consume him. The wizard said he had a week at the most.

"Clarion told me about Notori. We could help you find him. I've already sent Sparrows to the docks to search for his ship."

Why did it matter, thought Marius? Iatro lay dead. The wizard yet lived. The Jester's Curse held his soul in its grinning jaws, ready to devour him.

What did it matter where he went? In a week's time the curse would finally take control. Why did it matter if it happened in Arovia or at sea? It would be better to avoid Notori. After all, the curse couldn't betray someone it had never met.

After a week, Marius wouldn't be Marius anymore. He would be the jester incarnate. He hoped the assassins, if any still lived, found him before then.

Marius looked at the stupid grass ring on his finger. To think he'd believed it had done him some good.

He ripped it off, dropping it to the floor. The ring might have helped, initially, but it had been Iatro, blessed with the same magic as his sister Irina, who had really prevented the curse from manifesting.

Though neither he nor Irina had known it at the time, Irina had helped Marius survive the curse while he stayed in Amok. She had a way about her, something that made him want to be a better man.

Iatro had exerted a calming influence on him. He thought it was just because he didn't have to act foolish around a fool. But Iatro had been no more a fool than Marius; a lot less of one in fact.

Wisdom, Marius realized, didn't have anything to do with how smart someone was but with how they lived their life. Iatro had been loyal and a friend, right up to the end.

Tears formed in the corners of his eyes. Marius wiped them away, too ashamed to cry in front of Fira and the others, too ashamed to weep again over a death that had been his fault.

"I can't believe he's dead." Fira said what Marius had been thinking. Her blue eyes gazed toward the body of the boy.

How long had she been a Sparrow, Marius wondered? How long had she walked the world and how much death had she already seen?

Fira had been doomed never to age. Marius wished time would stop for him as well. He wished the next week might never come. Or that time would roll back. Then he could undo everything he'd done wrong.

"He did it for me," said Marius.

He'd already told them the story, had blabbed like a baby when he returned to the Nest with Iatro's dead body. His conscience and his guilt and his shame poured out.

Now, he said it more as a mantra, something repeated so many times that it no longer made sense. He wanted to lose the meaning of the words. "He died for me."

"I know."

"Why?"

Fira sat still, her face lit by the orange-red glow of the candlelight. Only her lips moved. "Because he loved you."

Marius sniffed derisively. As if there was anything to love about a fool like him. What a pointless waste of life. The Marius everyone knew would be dead in a week when the curse took over his body.

Thinking of death, Marius mulled over the prediction of the witch in the alley.

She'd said a Walker would die before the new tide turned. Maybe she hadn't meant literally. Perhaps a figurative death, the death of his soul, would be enough. Of course, to fulfill her prophecy, it would have to take place within a day. But Marius no longer cared when it happened, if in a day or in a week.

Fira laid a small hand on his arm. "Are you worrying about what the wizard said about the Jester's Curse? I know what it's like to be cursed."

It felt strange being comforted by a child. He ought to be the one comforting her, though he knew in his heart that Fira was much more than a child.

"No, you don't know what it's like." Marius lashed out. "You were just, I don't know," Marius waved his hands, "cursed, but mine takes over. I have to watch it consume me bit by bit."

He remembered his stutter and how it had made him seem eternally stupid. At least that aspect of the curse was gone.

"The wizard said you were fighting it."

Marius wanted to scream. "I have a been fighting it. At least I thought I was. If I acted foolish then the curse left me alone. I thought that I was fighting it. But the curse didn't care. If I acted stupid it was just doing the curse's job for it. If I was fighting it, it doesn't matter, because it's back now. I can feel it." Marius's shoulders sagged in defeat. "How do you fight a curse?"

Clarion answered. Stepping away from her work for a moment, she joined the pair on the dirty floor. Clarion ran a finger through the dust, examining it as she spoke, "You fight it the way you fight any kind of evil. By refusing to do nothing. By standing up to it."

Marius shook his head, "But I—"

Clarion interrupted. "I heard what you said, and this is what I think. I think you acted the fool as a way of standing up to the curse, refusing to let it work its evil through you. You sacrificed your pride. You became humble enough to become a fool. I think," said Clarion, "that the wizard was lying."

"He said—" Marius began to protest, only to be cut off again, this time by Fira.

"He might have told part of the truth, Marius, but Clarion is right. Wizards lie. It's what they do. They don't even know they're lying because lies are their native language—they're like babies brought up in it."

Clarion chimed in, "Every spell is a lie told about the person or object. They believe it and convince the world to believe it."

Fira shook her head in disagreement. A far-away look came over her eyes as though she were remembering a dream. She repeated a line from a poem in a sing-song chant:

Long ago, I walked the world and this is what I learned: they call a thing a name it's not, a name it never earned. While dancers dance to foolish tunes, to notes by false flutes played, the players never match the beat, no matter how the dancers sway.

Clarion cocked her head to the side, "That's from the Book of the Wind. I've never heard it translated that way before."

"That's how I received the song, from the Lady herself."

Clarion slapped her arm, "You're not that old!"

"Perhaps," said Fira, "perhaps not." Fira smiled.

Marius grew agitated. "Will you two speak plainly for once? What are you saying," said Marius. "that I'm not really cursed? It's all just in my imagination?"

"No," said Clarion. She wiped her dirty finger across her apron. "She is saying that the wizards don't believe their own spells, something I'd can hardly imagine."

Fira took Clarion's hand, "Because you have a true heart."

"Am I cursed or not?" said Marius. "Because I feel cursed."

Clarion's warm smile at Fira's compliment turned to a frown. "You are cursed, Marius. And not just the way you think you are. Cursed within a curse. Imprisoned within a prison."

Marius stared at her. She'd said the same thing as the statue of the Lady. Marius started to speak, to ask Clarion what she meant, where she'd heard the phrase, but a commotion outside interrupted their conversation. A series of whistles broke through the silence of the night.

Fira looked up, listening intently. The whistles sounded again. "The Nest is under attack."

* * *

In the square beyond the red door, where the alleys bled into the warehouse district, whistles and shouts were drowned out by the crash of stones hitting the ground.

Marius, Fira, and Clarion stared into the dark, waiting to see who would emerge from the alleys, the Sparrows or their assailants.

Marius wondered who was attacking. Who had prevailed in the fight: the assassins or the Astors or maybe the wizard and his strange companion? A frontal assault on the Sparrows' Nest didn't seem like Malconus's style. And last Marius had seen of Carra, she hadn't looked as though she would recover quickly from such a nasty blow to the head, if she didn't get a sword through the heart in the bargain.

Marius turned to Fira. "Shouldn't you run? Isn't that what Sparrows do? Whistle," he said. "Tell them to stop fighting. Tell them to run."

It was Clarion that responded, resting a hand on Marius's shoulder. "It's their home. Let them defend it."

"Last time we weren't prepared," said Fira. "And the assassins knew the pass codes."

Shaking Clarion's hand off his arm, Marius challenged Fira, "This time you are prepared? Prepared for a gang of assassins or for a pair of Astors?"

Fira didn't reply.

The sound of falling rocks grew closer.

Marius squinted into the alley. His bindle sat on his shoulder, tied onto the familiar staff. He wore the brass knuckles. Fira held his knife.

Clarion had found a knife of her own in the Sparrows' Nest, though Marius imagined she missed her own familiar blade from the kitchen.

She might retrieve it, he thought, and be tempted to slice it through her master's pudgy chins for betraying her to Carra of House Ponti.

But a person as religious as Clarion might not take revenge, no matter how deserved it might be or how better the world would be because of it. That was their weakness, and Marius aimed to avoid it by refusing to follow the Lady.

Though if he hadn't sought revenge on the wizard... The thought crashed down on him like a palpable weight on his chest. Iatro had died for his stupid revenge. Even if he killed the wizard, would Iatro's sacrifice have been worth it?

Marius shook his head. He sounded like Clarion now. She'd thought Marius had been ruining his own life, seeking revenge.

He would never again risk someone else's life. But maybe that was the same way she felt about him. The paradox made his brain hurt. Shouldn't he be even more concerned than Clarion about ruining his own life?

In the alley, a figure began to take shape. Stones rained down, but it moved too quickly, almost faster than Marius's eye could follow, stepping out of the way, avoiding each stone.

"Call off the children or they're going to get hurt!"

Marius recognized the voice. The face appeared a moment later.

Lespa.

Behind her strode Bithius, holding an enormous arm over his head, ignoring the rocks that rained down on him, bouncing off his armor. He appeared to be munching on a purple fruit, completely unconcerned.

Marius sighed. "Tell them to stop, Fira."

She put a hand to her mouth, but before Fira could whistle, Lespa bounded up the walls of the narrow alley, jumping from wall to wall as she went.

Reaching the roof, Lespa snatched a stone out of a little girl's hand. Lespa bared her teeth. Her head darted toward the girl, causing the child to flinch and to flee, wailing in terror.

"That's more like it," said Lespa, "more like the respect we Astors deserve."

Marius could see that Lespa wore a bandage on one arm. Her armor also had been cut away from her ribs. A bloodied cloth ran around her waist beneath the black leather.

The Astors had not come through the fight unscathed; yet they were alive. Marius was certain the same thing could not be said for the assassins.

Putting on his best manners, Marius called up to Lespa, "Glad to see you made it."

Lespa coughed out a laugh as she slipped down to the street. "No you aren't, fool. But that's the thing I like about you."

"And the wizard?" Marius didn't ask after Carra. Frankly, he didn't care.

"He lives."

Marius's heart sank. He had been hoping—

"It takes more than a sharp blade to kill a wizard," said Lespa. "The swipe you took at him took guts. I was almost rooting for you."

"It got my friend killed."

Lespa shrugged.

Marius saw it from her perspective. A lot of people had died that day, many at her own hands. The death of a child she didn't know meant nothing to her.

"He was the brother of the bursar at House Marcel," Marius added. "If you're ever in Amok—"

"Astor's don't—"

"I know," Marius said quickly. "But if you ever—"

Bithius spoke. His voice, unnaturally low, sounded like the growl of a bear. "He died bravely. If we're in Amok, we'll take the news to House Marcel."

Bithius had killed the assassin responsible for Iatro's death and had told Marius to run. He wondered why. Perhaps the Astor wanted to keep him alive so they could find him afterward, which they had.

Marius took a step forward. "I'm ready then."

"Ready for what?" said Lespa.

Marius looked her in the eye. "Ready to die."

The square went silent. The small eyes of the Sparrows were on Marius. Behind him, Clarion gasped. Fira, however, joined him, taking his hand.

How many souls had Fira walked toward death, never able to go with them?

Lespa laughed. "Not today, Walker."

Marius paused mid-step, his brow knit in surprise. He'd been so sure they'd come to kill him.

Lespa continued. "It's time to finish what we started."

"You heard the wizard," said Marius. "I've got a week before the curse takes over. Why would I help you?"

Lespa frowned, "Where's your spunk? Your zest for life?"

"Even if I did want to help you, which I don't," said Marius. "Asadal isn't here. He left Seatown a week ago."

The big man, Bithius, growled, "He's here. Got back yesterday."

Lespa looked from Bithius to Marius. "Why do you think we're here, fool? We're here to collect on the debt you owe me for not killing you."

Asadal had been back since yesterday. Marius couldn't believe it. Where had he been when the assassins attacked or when Marius confronted the wizard?

Lespa continued, "At the wizard's place you said you have a way of contacting Asadal."

"What if I do?" Marius responded with his usual abruptness. Inside, he shook with anger. He tried to keep his fingers from quivering. Asadal had betrayed him all over again, using Marius to draw out the kidnappers, then disappearing when things got too dangerous. At least he hadn't stolen all of Marius's worldly possessions this time.

Lespa took her time considering. She pulled the carved dagger from her belt. "If you do know how to contact him, you should thank your lucky stars," said Lespa. "Because if you don't, you're forcing us to kill every single one of these children."

Fira spoke, "You wouldn't."

"We would, old girl," Lespa looked down her nose at Fira. She'd heard about Fira's curse and been instrumental in removing it. Yet no compassion touched her eyes. "Every one of these children have broken the law."

Marius responded, "If they've broken the law then why don't you go ahead and do it? Or are you a hypocrite?"

"Marius!" Fira gripped his hand tighter.

Lespa snarled. "I am no hypocrite. I wouldn't let a child die for me and then act as though my life meant nothing."

"How dare you!" Marius released Fira's hand. He ran across the square with his fist raised, ready to hit Lespa in her smug jaw.

The Jester's Curse intervened. Marius tripped on a loose stone that had been thrown from the roof. He did an involuntary somersault.

Bithius caught him mid-spin, picking him up by an ankle as though he weighed less than the smallest Sparrow.

"That's better," said Lespa. "That's the old Marius I've come to know and love." She called out to Fira, "Call your children home. We'll spend a cozy night together. Wouldn't want anyone to get ideas about warning the old man."

Marius twisted toward Lespa. Hanging upside down, it was difficult to maintain his dignity. "She's not in charge of them."

Lespa shot him a look. "If you believe that, you're more foolish that I thought, and my estimation is already low." She waved Bithius toward the Sparrows' Nest. "Let's get out of the weather. It's raining rocks tonight. And we need to explain to this fool how he is going to help us capture the most elusive spy in the kingdom."

Chapter Nineteen

Morning had barely broken, yet the rotary that sat at the center of Seatown teemed with visitors who had come for the fair. They traveled from the neighboring districts, and poured in from the sea as well, bringing goods to sell and gold to spend. Booths lined the busy streets and the wharf.

Performers like Marius staked out small spots where the foot traffic might draw in an audience, but not where it was too crowded. Otherwise, the onlookers might feel forced to move on before the show finished. No one paid for a show they didn't finish, as Marius well knew.

Some of the performers displayed real talent. There were the fake wizards, the jugglers and acrobats. There was even a man with a red beard and mad hair who verbally abused the audience. Far from chasing him out of town, the objects of his wrath only laughed, showering him with coins.

Marius wondered whether news of his own performance in Amok had spread. If this man was evidence, Marius might have invented a new show. There might be money in it. Surely the Jester's Curse could come up with more creative insults than Red Beard.

A sigh crossed his lips. The Jester's Curse. How many days, how many hours, did he have before it took him? He wondered if he would notice when it did. Marius remembered the performance in Amok at House Marcel, when he'd given himself fully to the curse. It felt as though he was outside himself, watching.

It might feel like that, trapped in his own body, unable to do anything, a passenger on a slow boat to idiot-town.

Marius looked around the rotary.

Merchants like Mortimer fought to maintain the little corners they'd occupied for years.

No one had come to the market to buy fish, however. They had come for the fair. So, the merchants, adaptable as ever, lined their carts with local trinkets, ornaments the travelers could take home with them in remembrance of Seatown: a pretty seashell, the jagged tooth of a great fish, the shriveled tail of a mermaid.

The tail was no larger than Marius's hand and, he suspected, had been appropriated from a former catch of the day.

Other merchants had converted their stalls into makeshift food carts, complete with narrow tables and three-legged stools.

Mortimer presided over such an impromptu establishment. He brushed flour from his green vest before dusting a fillet of fish in a mixture of flour and salt. He dropped it into an iron pot full of oil.

The glorious smells of food cooking at the fair and the sweets lining the merchant's carts—pies and puddings—

almost drove away the stench of fish guts that normally lingered over Seatown.

Marius would normally have sat by the town message board. But there was no place to sit today. Every inch of the rotary was taken by vendors or customers.

One of the stools at Mortimer's booth came open. Marius darted for it, beating out a fat seaman who looked angry enough to eat Marius instead of the deep-fried fish he'd so obviously been craving.

The Jester's Curse chuckled.

Mortimer pulled at his bushy mustache, "Paying customers only, Jester." He had his eyes set on the great big belly of the sailor, looking as though he'd like to land a catch like that. The seaman would eat enough to pay for a small villa.

Marius plunked a coin down on the narrow table.

"Fish please." Before the man could ask, Marius added, "No skin flutes."

Mortimer registered the money and gave the seaman a resigned shrug that said, what could he do, the young man paid for the seat.

A plate full of golden, flaky fish appeared at Marius's elbow. No fork was offered. He would have to eat with his hands.

The smell of the fish reminded Marius that he was still alive and hungry. He took a bite. The meat of the fish melted in his mouth, a sharp bone stuck into his tongue—the curse again at work. Marius had nearly forgotten how difficult the curse made it to eat.

Mortimer spoke over the crackle of the frying pan. "Shouldn't you be performing?"

"The big acts don't go on till later," he said.

In truth, Marius was already performing. His act entailed wearing the old bindle wrapped around his arm, the sign he and Asadal had arranged in the event of an emergency. He acted as though he needed the old Walker's help. Then he would betray Asadal to Lespa, just as the old man had once done to him.

Marius had told Asadal on the way to Seatown that he wouldn't turn him over to the Astors. That was before they'd threatened to annihilate the Sparrows' Nest. Asadal would have done the same.

Iatro was already dead because of Marius. He couldn't have any more blood on his hands.

He thought of Clarion. He'd left her in the Sparrows' Nest, cooking breakfast for the children. Marius thought she might actually have to cook less for the Sparrows than for her corpulent master.

Her master had given her over to be used in the wizard's experiments. If it had been Marius, he would have returned to House Fluctus to take revenge. After all, Carra said that if the master of House Fluctus died, Clarion's boy Jank, his bastard son, would inherit the whole lot.

He tossed the idea aside. Clarion wasn't like that. She had religion.

Helping Clarion in serving breakfast had been Fira, so young and yet so old. The two women seemed to have formed a close connection after being taken captive by the wizard and Carra.

According to Lespa, Fira ran the Sparrows. He wouldn't have thought it possible. After all, Marius had displaced Rebius and Demari, the titular leaders of the gang.

Yet it had been Fira that cast the first stone.

It made sense. Children came and went from the Sparrows' Nest. A pecking order would be established for a while, but always there was Fira in the background, making sure the Nest remained functional, that it served as a place where the homeless or unwanted children of Seatown could hide until they hatched into adults.

He hadn't said goodbye to either of them when he left. The last thing he'd done was to pay his respects to Iatro's body, which lay in state at the Nest. Clarion had said they couldn't afford to take care of the body till after the fair.

Marius remembered the cemetery in Amok marked by the lamps hanging over the graves of the wealthy, while wind chimes or cultivated trees marked the other places of burial. The place felt peaceful.

Fira wanted to bury Iatro properly.

Sparrows were no strangers to death. Many had lost their families to disease or the sea or had simply been abandoned. Fira said they needed to see what sacrifice and loyalty looked like.

Marius hoped that Clarion and Fira understood that he wasn't coming back to the Nest. They must have seen him take his bindle. They must have known what that meant.

He couldn't bear to face them, to have them look him in the eyes as he went to betray Asadal.

Not that the old man didn't deserve it. He'd been in Seatown for two days and hadn't shown himself, hadn't helped. He hadn't even said goodbye when he left or told Marius where he was going.

Marius took another bite of fish and licked his fingers. He intended to make the plate last. Marius had nowhere he needed to be. The meal would have been more comfortable though, had the fat sailor moved on to another booth instead of standing over him like the opposite of a scarecrow.

Of course, Lespa, was also watching hungrily from a concealed location. She was in for a similar disappointment, thought Marius.

Asadal wouldn't be showing up.

Marius had worn the bindle once before, after learning that Malconus had engineered the kidnappings.

Asadal hadn't come then. He wouldn't come now.

Of course, if what Lespa said could be trusted, Asadal hadn't been in Seatown that day. Today, he might be watching the rotary, checking in on Marius and the Sparrows.

Marius hoped Asadal didn't go to the Nest first.

Bithius had been left behind against such a possibility. If Asadal had to die, it would be better to be skewered by Lespa's blade than pulled apart by Bithius.

There was simply no way Asadal would fall for the trap though. He was the church's master spy. He would no doubt see through the ploy and skip town again.

When Asadal didn't arrive, Marius would find some excuse to slip away and meet Notori.

Even if he had only a week to live, that time would be better spent away from the Sparrows, who'd already faced assassins and a pair of brutal Astors because of him.

Besides, thought Marius, Lespa had been right. He wasn't inclined to give up. It might be that Notori could help him. Carra had mentioned amulets that could combat the effects of a curse. Maybe Notori had access to a magic amulet. Carra said they were expensive, but maybe

Notori would take him on as an indentured worker till he could pay off the cost.

Marius silently cursed himself for not paying better attention when he robbed the witch in the black market. Maybe she'd had just such an object in her shop. It wasn't as though she'd miss it among the wreckage of her shack, assuming she'd survived the fall.

Marius formed a plan. He would lose Lespa in the crush of the fair and meet Notori. He seriously doubted the Astor would really kill all the children. Marius, meanwhile, would be gone from Seatown and the entire Kingdom of Arovia. If the curse wanted to overtake him, it would have to chase him.

All he had to do was wait for Asadal, who would never arrive, and look for an opportunity to slip away.

Marius turned his back on the sailor and bent over his plate, concentrating on the fish.

A stool beside Marius opened up. The sailor would finally get satisfaction, thought Marius, inwardly calculating how much he would have to move to make way for a man whose girth almost put Clarion's master to shame.

Again, the sailor proved too slow. Another man got to the stool first.

Mortimer repeated his speech, "Paying customers only."

The edge of a coin rapped on the table. "I'll have what he's having."

A familiar voice with an island accent addressed Mortimer. Marius looked up from his plate and into the face of Asadal the Walker.

* * *

A fly buzzed over Marius's plate of fried fish, nearly landing in his wide-open mouth.

Behind him, he could hear the muttered curses of the sailor as he abandoned his quest for fish and moved, less than delicately, through the crowded market in search of more attainable fare.

The morning sun had climbed into the sky and beat down on the back of Marius's neck.

He felt acutely aware of a cascade of emotions racing through his mind as he registered the presence of the old Walker, the man who'd saved him from starvation, then betrayed him to the Astors, then saved him from drowning, only to run off again leaving him high and dry in Seatown. Yet here Asadal sat, having responded to the signal of the bindle wrapped around Marius's arm.

Words tumbled out of Marius's open mouth along with bits of unchewed fish. "You shouldn't have come. It's a trap."

"I know."

"Then what are you—?" Marius paused. There were more important things to say. "Lespa's somewhere in the crowd."

"She can wait," said Asadal, rubbing his hands together as Mortimer slid a plate in front of him. "This fish, however, cannot." His eyes closed in pleasure as he took a bite.

Coming from an island, Marius figured Asadal would have had his fill of fish. Yet he seemed to take genuine pleasure in Mortimer's plain offering.

Out of respect for the moment, pushing back his mounting frustration, Marius waited till Asadal swallowed before continuing. "Where have you been?"

Asadal's already swarthy face darkened into a frown. His always-visible teeth disappeared. "You aren't the only person who needs me, Marius. Besides, Fira has been keeping me informed, like about this trap."

"Fira? How? We were together all night."

Asadal shrugged. "We have ways of communicating. Sometimes, silence says more than words."

"Then you know what's been happening?"

Asadal nodded.

"Why didn't you do something?"

"I did," said Asadal. "I told Fira to keep an eye on you. She couldn't save you from yourself—"

Marius had a sudden vision of his less than graceful exit over the wall of House Ponti.

Asadal continued, "But she did keep the assassins from killing you in your sleep."

"But the wizard—"

Asadal's voice took on a chiding tone, "All you had to do was wait one week for Notori to arrive. But, no, you had to take revenge." Asadal's smile could never say buried long, though. It eventually won out. "Still, it looks like you survived the wizard as well."

"Iatro died."

Asadal froze, a bit of fish hung in his hand, never reaching his mouth. He sighed, "I didn't know."

So, thought Marius, the master spy wasn't omniscient. He knew about the trap. He must have heard about the dust up at the wizard's house in the slave quarters. But Asadal didn't know all the details.

"His death must have been especially hard on you," said Asadal.

Marius realized that the old man had made the connection between Iatro and Irina. Of course he had, thought Marius, Asadal would have known all about Iat-

ro, where he'd come from. Things Marius hadn't bothered to ask.

Marius had to get something off his chest. "When I
confronted the wizard—"

"Your stutter is improved."

"What? Oh, the wizard fixed it."

"Did he now?"

"On Lespa's orders."

"How interesting."

Marius grabbed the man's arm. "Let me finish. The
wizard said it's only a few days till the Jester's Curse
takes over. Iatro died saving me. He died for nothing.
Can't you do something? Make me another ring? Help
me." Marius realized the irony of begging a favor from
the man he'd come to betray.

Asadal examined Marius, looking at him intently for
some time before he spoke. The gray tips of his long,
black hair had been tied up in a bit of string. The wrinkles around his eyes had deepened. Marius hadn't noticed how much Asadal had aged since they first met on
the road to Amok.

"You're in no danger of that."

"Of what?"

"Of the curse taking over." Asadal patted Marius on
the back.

Marius's heart leapt into his throat. He felt hopeful
for the first time in days.

"It has grown stronger," Asadal cautioned. "But the
curse can never really take over, so long as you fight it."

"I've been trying to fight it," said Marius, "but I can't
do it on my own."

"Truer words were never spoken."

"Tell me what should I do?"

Asadal paused, hesitating before he spoke. "You know what I think already."

"Join the church?"

"No. Not the church. The Lady. Follow the Lady."

"But I can't—"

Asadal sighed. "Marius there's been something I've been wanting to ask you."

Marius wondered what he, with his curse, could offer Asadal.

"I'm getting too old for this, Marius." Asadal waived a hand in the air melodramatically. "It's time that I turned the reigns over to someone younger."

Marius couldn't believe his ears. Asadal was trying to recruit Marius into his spy ring, and not as a low-level grunt. He wanted Marius to take his place, to take over as spy master for the church. Could anything be more ridiculous? Marius nearly laughed. He had to refuse.

"If you hadn't noticed, I'm kind of cursed."

Asadal blinked. "I was going to say," said Asadal, "that I was thinking of asking Fira. I wanted to get your opinion."

Marius's chest collapsed, instantly humbled. He recovered quickly, "She's—"

Asadal added awkwardly, "Not that you aren't, um, couldn't do it. But she already knows the network, and she believes in the Lady—"

Marius cut in, "Fira's great, really." A moment of silence followed. Asadal took the bite of fish he'd been postponing since learning of Iatro's death.

Marius added quietly, "I saw the Lady."

"Hmmm?"

"The other night, the statue of the Lady came alive," he pointed over his shoulder, down the street to the rotary and the image of the Lady it contained. "She said she would see me again, at the end, when I faced death below the ground, imprisoned within a prison."

"Remarkable," said Asadal. He looked at Marius with something bordering on awe.

"Of course, I was high on witchweed at the time."

"Ah!" said Asadal. "Still, many of the ancient mystics burned certain herbs to commune with spirits. If the Lady spoke to you, you should listen."

They sat together quietly, each man consumed by his own thoughts, picking at the fish on their plates, ignoring Mortimer's more obvious hints that they should vacate their stools.

Asadal broke the silence, "Notori is in Seatown. His boat is called the Minstrel. He'll be expecting you. There will be a test."

"What kind of test?"

"Don't worry. You'll pass. But you know, Marius, you don't have to go," said Asadal. "You don't have to leave Arovia."

"How could I stay?" said Marius. "What would I tell Irina next time I saw her?" He looked fervently at Asadal, "You will tell her for me won't you?" Marius didn't see how he could stand to do it himself.

"She'll miss you. And so will I." said Asadal. He broke into a sad grin, "But of course I'll tell her, right after Lespa executes me."

"Oh!" said Marius. They'd been eating together and conversing so normally that he'd nearly forgotten that their meeting was a trap waiting to be sprung.

Asadal asked casually, "What exactly is the plan?"

"I'm supposed to make you walk back to the Nest with me."

Asadal finished his last bite of fish and stood. "Shall we go?"

Marius hesitated before standing. He didn't want to go. His legs felt like lead. His knees didn't want to bend properly. Of course, that might have been the result of sitting for so long on a stool or it might have been a by-product of the curse.

Mortimer called after Marius as he stepped away, "Jester, remember. You promised to let me in on your act."

Marius nodded and waved back at the man.

He had no intention of performing in Seatown. He had no plans at all beyond each footfall. He and Asadal made their way toward the opening of an alley leading to the Nest.

Marius's future had constricted to the size of that narrow opening, hemmed in on both sides by the high walls of the warehouses.

The next few moments would decide his fate and Asadal's as well.

* * *

The walls of the alley closed around them, swallowing Marius and Asadal. The sounds of the fair died away, replaced by the drip of water splashing into a series of foul puddles that they studiously avoided. The fresh smell of baked pies was replaced by the cloying scent of mold and rot.

"As fitting a place as any to die," Asadal commented.

"Depressing more like," Marius glanced behind them, to see whether Lespa had entered the alley.

They proceeded deeper into the alleys, heading for the Sparrows' Nest. Still Lespa did not appear.

"Maybe she got lost," Marius suggested.

A dry, feminine voice cut through the silence of the alley. "Not likely, fool."

A door in the wall opened behind them. Lespa stepped through.

"Asadal, by edict of the Emperor, you are ordered to submit to the laws of the kingdom—"

While Lespa spoke, Asadal whispered to Marius. "Find Notori on the ship called the Minstrel. And I am sorry about this."

Marius whispered back, "About what?"

Asadal shoved Marius toward the Astor.

Marius stumbled into the woman's chest, collapsing in a heap in the alley. Lespa shoved him aside, drawing her knife. The split second head-start saw Asadal running down the alleys as swiftly and as comfortably as a rabbit in the tall grass.

Turning at the nearest intersection, Asadal and the Astor raced out of sight.

Marius found himself alone in the alley with his bindle in hand. The silver rings hung from the end of his staff, swaying side by side, clinking together.

Marius was free. Free from the Astors, free from the wizard; still enslaved by the curse, but that was nothing new. He'd done what the Astors had asked of him. The Sparrows were safe.

Marius could find Notori and escape the peninsula, provided he passed the man's test, whatever that happened to be.

Yet Marius didn't immediately run to the docks. He stood in the alley.

Asadal had saved him countless times, yet Marius had betrayed the old Walker, something that went against their entire code.

Asadal had known about the trap and had sprung it willingly, just to save him.

Marius thought of Iatro, lying in his arms with a dagger in his chest. Marius couldn't let another person die for him. Not if he could help it.

Marius hobbled through the alleys, running as fast as he and the curse could manage, looking like a cat and a dog doing a three-legged race.

At the first intersection Marius paused. Asadal had turned toward the Sparrows' Nest, but obviously he wouldn't lead the Astor back toward the children. Where would Asadal go? Marius tried to think.

To the fair, Marius realized. Asadal would double back to the market and try to get lost in the crowd. It's what Marius would have done.

Marius didn't follow the Walker and Astor. Instead, he pictured the alleys in his mind, trying to figure out where Asadal might come out.

He went left instead and, in a moment, found himself racing beside a warehouse that held stacks of ropes. Great bales of rope hung overhead. Old strands, left to rot in the elements, hung from lines suspended between the walls of the alley. The ropes covered his shoulders, obscuring his view.

Clawing his way through the rope curtain, Marius came to another intersection.

He heard a scuffle taking place around the corner.

Marius crouched behind a bundle of rope. He peered around the corner.

A deep growl echoed off the walls of the alley. "Stand still and take it like a man."

Marius saw Bithius. He had Asadal's hair clutched in one enormous fist. The Walker squirmed, trying to get away.

"Stop moving, it won't hurt."

Bithius put another hand around Asadal's throat. His fingers reached all the way around Asadal's neck.

Marius jumped out. This was no time to hide. He had to do something before the big Astor broke Asadal's neck. "No!"

Asadal's eyes fixed on him. "Marius, run!"

Bithius squeezed.

Marius heard a snap.

He saw Asadal's limp body hit the paving stones, his arms and legs splayed at an awkward angle.

Bithius turned toward Marius. Marius backed away, unable to believe his eyes. First Iatro and now Asadal. He remembered the warning of the witch: before the new tide turned, a Walker would die.

Behind Bithius, Marius saw movement: Fira running in the opposite direction. She'd seen the whole thing.

Bithius advanced, covering three of Marius's steps with one of his own. "Marius, stop," he said. "Wait."

Not likely, thought Marius. He turned and raced around the corner, pulling down stacks of rope as he went, as if those would stop the Astor.

Putting his forearm up to protect his face and eyes, Marius raced through the curtain of ropes hoping the curse wouldn't find a way to hang him.

When he made it through, Marius dropped his arm. Lespa stood in front of him.

He heard Bithius approaching from behind.

Lespa looked winded, as though she'd been sprinting. She held her curved dagger in her hand.

"Out of the way, fool, or you really will die this time."

"You're too late," said Marius.

"He's not escaped yet!" said Lespa.

"He's dead." Marius wiped a sleeve across his eyes and his nose, surprised to find them both damp. "Bithius killed him."

"Did he now?" Lespa frowned as she sheathed the knife.

Bithius emerged from the frayed curtain of old ropes.

"Well?" said Lespa.

"It's done," said the big man.

Lespa clapped her hands, "Years of work over, just like that. Amazing how that happens."

Bithius didn't respond. Neither did Marius.

"Don't look so glum, fool. This is no time for tears but a time for celebration. After all those years, such a long chase, I think we deserve a little something. Don't you, Bithius?"

Bithius shrugged.

"I'll tell you what I want," said Lespa. "I want to see your act, fool."

Marius blinked.

"I've heard so much about your legendary performance in Amok. I want to see you sing and dance and juggle."

"I don't sing or dance—" Marius protested.

Marius felt the weight of the bindle on his shoulder and heard the rings gently clinking. He had just lost his friend, Iatro, to an assassin's blade, and he had lost his mentor, Asadal, to the cold-blooded grip of an Astor. Yet Lespa wanted him to play the fool, to laugh and be merry.

Lespa persisted. She took the knife back out of its sheath, whirling its tip in the air as though she were painting a canvas, "I want to see your show. And if it is not the best performance I've ever seen in my life," Lespa looked at him with death in her eyes, "then your life is forfeit."

Lespa turned on her heel, "Let's return to the market. I'm going to enjoy this."

She hadn't been the one to kill Asadal, Marius realized. Blood lust consumed her. Lespa was looking for an excuse to kill him and wanted a creative murder, not a sportless stab in a rope-strewn alley.

She wanted people to witness her craft, as though they hadn't seen it on display when the Astors fought the assassins. Marius knew that it didn't matter how well he performed, his act would end with his death at the Astor's hands.

With a shove, Bithius hurried Marius along after Lespa, forcing him to move step by step toward his own demise.

The witch at the top of the hill had been wrong, Marius thought. The new tide would witness not the death of one Walker but two.

Chapter Twenty

P eople of Seatown!" Lespa called out to the crowd. A large circle formed around the three figures standing in the rotary. The entrance of two Astors had caused a stir. The raucous crowd that had been enjoying the fair suddenly shuffled aside like a miser who'd spied a beggar. Those guilty of some crime or who simply had a bad conscience slipped away down one of the many streets that connected to the rotary.

Lespa shoved Marius toward the statue of the Lady that stood serenely in the middle of town.

"This fool is going to perform for us," said Lespa. "And if I don't like it," she corrected herself, with a magnanimous gesture to the audience, adding, "if we all don't like it, then I will give you some entertainment."

A smattering of applause met her announcement. A few high-pitched whistles emphasized their approval.

Lespa drew her sword for emphasis, "This fool will perform, or I will execute him for crimes against the kingdom."

More people applauded the dispensation of rough justice.

Marius saw the looks in their eyes. They thought he'd been caught committing a crime during the fair, picking a pocket or worse. They appreciated the security the Astors afforded. The criminal element would put off their wicked trade while the people enjoyed the fair in safety.

Lespa whipped her sword over her head, rallying the crowd, encouraging their cheers.

Marius realized that he would have to perform, otherwise she would end him on the spot just to please the crowd. He saw no way out.

Turning his back on the crowd, Marius fished the cod-piece out of his bindle. He had yet to use it in Seatown, a fact he'd earlier regretted. He had no intention of letting the Jester's Curse score another low-blow.

Fingers pointed and tongues wagged as Marius adjusted the piece of metal in the front of his pants. He knew how it looked to the crowd. He didn't care. The cod-piece guarded his manhood.

Marius took the three juggling rings off the bindle and dropped the fabric and stick onto the pavement. He wouldn't need it. He turned the rings over in his hand, practicing the maneuver that would lock them into a solid chain.

Marius jumped as a sharp slap landed on his backside. Turning, he saw Lespa raising her sword for another blow with the flat of the blade. The crowd howled with laughter. Marius thought he saw money changing hands, betting on whether he would perform well enough to save his life.

Something inside him snapped. Iatro lay dead in the Sparrows' Nest. Asadal's broken body littered the refuse-strewn alley. The wizard, Malconus, sat in his mansion overlooking the slave auctions. Dozens of innocent people had been subjected to the wizard's evil experiments. The rich sat in their colorful houses on the hill overlooking the suffering of the poor below. All the while, Seatown laughed.

Asadal had given his life for the jeering mob. Iatro had fought and died to save them. Now Marius's own life hung in the balance.

And they laughed and pointed and drank and placed bets.

Enough, thought Marius.

He felt the wind blow. Felt the statue of the Lady sheltering him. Her shadow covered him.

But she would not help him. She might come to life in pipe dreams, but not when it mattered most.

Marius had promised Asadal that he would help with the danger to Seatown. Now, Marius saw that danger to Seatown was Seatown itself: the people of Seatown, the people who let the young Sparrows, orphans, fend for themselves.

He would help them all right. Just as he'd agreed to do.

Marius looked deep inside himself. He found the Jester's Curse waiting, approving. Together they would help Seatown.

Marius shook his head, clearing his mind. This was the path to madness. He couldn't let the curse take control! Asadal said that the curse couldn't consume him so long as he resisted.

The curse argued with him. What was the point? Lespa intended to kill him if he didn't give her the show of her life. She would likely kill him anyway. Marius couldn't do it alone. The juggling routines and false magic wouldn't impress her. He needed to pull out all the stops. He needed the curse.

But Marius had seen the curse in action, when he punished Demari and Rebius, when he sent the witch plummeting to the surf and rocks, when he pushed Barn and Pithy past the brink of madness. That had been the curse's doing, the curse acting within him.

He looked out at the faces in the crowd. What would the curse do to them? Marius held up his hands in a show of surrender.

Lespa sneered. She pointed the sword at his face. The crowd jeered. They howled for his blood. Few faces in the crowd held any compassion. Mortimer stroked his mustache. Marius had promised him a starring role. Marius couldn't tell whether the merchant was concerned about Marius's life or his own, should the Jester implicate him in the performance.

The only other look of concern came as a shock. Bithius the Astor, Lespa's burly companion, gave him a silent nod of encouragement.

He hadn't expected compassion from the man who'd just killed Asadal. But he remembered how Bithius hadn't stolen from him in the forest and how he'd crushed the assassin that struck down Iatro, giving Marius the chance to escape. No one else in the crowd cared.

A piece of rotten fruit hit Marius in the face, the sickening sweet smell of its wet flesh slid down Marius's cheek and mouth.

He clenched his fists. The people of Seatown wanted a show? A show they would get.

A flash of white caught the corner of his eye, a dove landing on the roof of a nearby stall. Backspace, reminding him of the dove on the statue of the Lady that stood behind him. Marius stepped out of her shadow.

He made his choice.

The Jester's Curse responded with glee, shoving its way to the forefront of his mind. The curse loved an audience and had never seen such a large group of people gathered to see him perform. The curse had to do something spectacular.

In his mind, Marius gladly took a step back, content to stop feeling, to stop thinking, if only for a moment. To forget Iatro and Asadal, to forget Lespa, to forget his wretched life.

The Jester of Zeno bowed to the audience, which now included Marius himself.

* * *

The Jester boldly strode forward, his hands raised, his fingers wagging, pleading for silence. Lespa gave way. A hush fell over the crowd.

He began to recite:

People of Seatown lend me your ears.

My account it seems is in arrears.

The Jester patted his bottom, thrusting his hips forward. The cod-piece stuck out provocatively. A few of the women tittered.

He sidled toward Mortimer's cart as he spoke.

I owe you for everything you've given me,

I'll give you your payment right now if you please.

Flourishing a hand, the Jester bowed low. When he did, his hand landed with a splash in a bucket.

The Jester looked at his arm, astonished to find it soaked to the elbow. He sought to remove it from the bucket, but something appeared to keep his hand stuck firmly to the bottom. The simple mime act drew a few smiles.

He grabbed the elbow of his trapped arm, pulling vigorously. Bending his knees and putting his back into it, the bucket came up, with his hand still inside.

Those standing near the Jester gasped. Through no means they could perceive, the bucket stayed attached to his hand. They leaned in closer, trying to spy out his trick.

The Jester removed his free hand from his elbow, placing it on his hips in a look of consternation. He tapped his foot and scratched his head.

Finally, holding a finger aloft, as though he'd gotten a brilliant idea, the Jester began to pivot on his heel, swinging the bucket in a circle.

Cold water splashed out of the bucket, dousing the curious onlookers and causing the others to laugh. The sailor, who'd been hungrily eying Marius's stool earlier, slapped his wet friend on the back.

The bucket came loose from Marius's hand, hitting the sailor in his face.

He fell back into the crowd, crushing several of them, unable to rise unassisted.

It was his friend's turn to laugh.

A woman put her hand to her mouth. The rest of the crowd drew a collective breath.

The Jester's hand and arm were covered in pink slimy things. Skin flutes.

He shook his hand. They didn't come loose.

He pulled at one. It came away, leaving a trickle of blood. The skin flutes had attached themselves like leeches. Mortimer hadn't been kidding about them biting.

The Jester tossed the skin flute over his shoulder absentmindedly. It landed in a woman's massive hairdo. She shrieked.

Another and another came away. He tossed these high into the air as he removed their friends.

Soon he had the little suckers flying through the air, seven at a time. They squirted out of his hands as quick as he touched them.

He added the first ring. Flipping it end over end into the sky, the Jester cycled the seven squirts one after the other, shooting them like arrows though the heart of the spinning ring. At its apogee the ring slowed, catching the sunlight. Then it fell.

The crowd roared as he caught the ring, holding it like a hoop for the skin flutes to pass through as they fell back toward the ground, only to be caught and sent back up into the sky.

Applause broke out. The audience had seen juggling that day from the many performers lining the streets. But they had never seen anyone as deft as the Jester of Zeno.

As the skin flutes descended, the Jester raised the silver ring to shoulder height and sighted through it with one eye.

The crowd squinted, trying to guess at his next trick.

He flashed the skin flutes through the ring in quick succession, spinning again as he tossed.

Each squirt hit an onlooker square on the nose. Their little teeth sunk into flesh and soft cartilage. Their new owners crossed their eyes, beholding with terror the things dangling from their noses. Some pulled gingerly at the creatures while the rest of the crowd, as yet untargeted, pointed and laughed.

The Jester cried out to the proprietor of the stall, "Mortimer, your fattest fish, good sir. And hurry!"

Mortimer, clad in the green vest that fought valiantly to contain his belly, bent over to retrieve a fish. He had to lift with two hands, it was so large.

"I was saving these for—"

The Jester interrupted, "Toss them to me, my good man!"

"Well, I want to know who's going to pay—"

The crowd yelled, "Toss it!"

A piece of rotten fruit hit Mortimer, staining his green vest and splattering his bushy mustache.

Sensing the potential for violence rippling through the crowd, Mortimer tossed the fish.

The Jester extended a ring. The fish slid into the ring, up to its neck, and held fast.

"Another!" cried the Jester.

Mortimer complied.

The Jester trapped the fish in another of his rings.

His arms swung low with the weight of the two great fish wedged within the rings.

"Another!"

Mortimer heaved. A third fish flew through the air.

Swinging his arms back and forth to gain momentum, the Jester threw the two fish into the air and trapped the third.

This he added to the first two, flinging them into the air. They wiggled and swerved as though they swam upstream only to be pushed back to earth by a strong current.

The fish swam toward the sun and fell, again and again, swimming higher and higher each time.

The crowd gasped.

The Jester gave one last enormous toss.

The fish flew, soaring so high that, at last, they slipped through the silver rings and into the air the way a baby escapes its mother.

The crowd stamped and cheered.

The rings and the fish fell back toward the ground.

The Jester caught the rings on his arms, they clanked together at his shoulders. Two fish he caught, but not with his fingers, their gaping mouths swallowed his hands up to his elbows.

The third fish never landed, or if it did, the crowd never saw where. They were too distracted by the man running around the circle with two large fish for hands, slapping every face in sight.

The Jester sprinted around the gathering, shaking his arms, trying to free the great fish. The tails of the fish slapped everyone he passed.

Lespa took a slimy blow to the face.

She turned to the Jester, her lip bleeding. She advanced toward him with her sword held at the ready.

The crowd was of two minds, some pushing back while others pushed forward to see the imminent violence.

The Jester held his hands up apologetically, waving them, nodding his head toward the fish as though trying to explain.

The injured Astor did not accept the apology.

She swung her sword. As she did, the Jester winked.

Lespa blinked. The blow went wide, parried off the thick scales of the fish attached to the Jester's hands,

Furious, the Astor swung again. The Jester parried her blow, swinging both fish through the air between

them, the weight of them nearly knocking the sword
from her hand.

She kicked out, taking the Jester in the crotch.

He stumbled back, grimacing. Then he smiled. His
knuckle rapped on the codpiece.

The crowd called out encouragement. Some for the
Astor and, even more amazingly, some for the Jester.

She raised the sword to strike again, circling it around
menacingly in one hand.

The Jester raised his fish and in a mocking parody,
twisted their tails in a small circle.

Lespa charged, swinging her blade. The Jester
charged too, waving the fish.

They clashed and passed one another.

Lespa held her blade by two hands, its tip toward her
feet, still extended from the force of the strike.

The Jester held nothing. The severed tails of the fish
lay at his feet. Blood covered the paving stones.

The mouths of the fish still circled the jester's forearm. He looked in shock at the severed stumps where his
hands should be.

Chapter Twenty-one

M arius shifted in his mind. He looked passively at the two bloody ends of his arms. The Jester's Curse had been driving his body, putting on a show for the crowd. Marius was just another onlooker.

He felt he should care about the fact that he'd just lost his hands. Marius stirred, but the Jester's Curse pushed him back. It was in charge, and it wasn't done yet.

Lespa's smirk returned.

She shouldered her blade, obviously waiting for the Jester to fall to his knees in shock at the loss of limbs and blood. She could then decide at her leisure whether to end his suffering with a merciful blow to the neck.

Not likely.

The Jester, meanwhile, staggered forward. His feet hit the slimy tails of the fish. He lurched, sliding on the greasy skin and entrails across the rotary toward the Astor.

He held his severed arms up imploringly, asking her to help him, to arrest his movement.

Lespa stepped aside, motioning as though she was opening a door.

The Jester looked horrified.

The Astor's smug face betrayed no sympathy.

At the last moment, as he slid past by the Astor, slipping on fish guts and blood, the Jester looked at his arms and back at the Astor.

His hands popped out of the severed fish heads, one after the other.

He smiled and blew her a kiss.

Lespa seethed. She swung her sword.

The Jester quickly joined the silver rings into a chain, blocking Lespa's sword.

The crowd cheered.

She readied to attack again, but he had gone past, out of reach.

In fact, the Jester had not stopped sliding. He slipped into Mortimer's stall, upsetting a stool, colliding with the thin table, tumbling over it and into the cooking fire.

The large oil pot Mortimer had been using to fry fish overturned. The Jester watched as the golden liquid, turned a rust colored brown by the iron and the remnants of fish batter, poured over the lip of the upturned pot.

The oil struck the fire beneath, which gratefully accepted the gift, belching out flames as tall as the Jester himself.

The oil spread across the stones, the fire trailing as though it was a game of chase, the opposite of freeze tag, whatever it touched burned.

The stall next to Mortimer's erupted in flames.

Shops and stalls lined the rotary, tucked close together to accommodate the crowd gathered for the fair. They suddenly bristled with fire.

The faces of the crowd, having been poised to witness the death of the fool, then appreciating his wit, took a moment to adjust to the new reality.

Seatown was burning.

Abandoning the show, the onlookers rushed in every direction. The merchants ran toward their stalls, trying to salvage whatever they could from the flames.

The Jester saw Mortimer through the smoke. His stall had been spared as the flaming oil snaked toward his neighbor. Mortimer grabbed his money and bolted.

The more civic minded began to organize, forming a bucket brigade to fight the fire.

They lined up past the Lady toward the ocean and its jagged rocks. Water passed swiftly between them.

The Jester had all but been forgotten in the wake of the disaster.

He appeared now at the head of the bucket brigade.

He took the first bucket of water.

Instead of pouring it onto the raging fire, he raised it to his lips and took a sip.

He spat it out. "So thirsty! Must drink!"

Angry shouts arose. The merchant, whose stall was burning while the Jester dithered, ran at the Jester as though he meant to choke him.

The merchant found himself holding an empty bucket.

He dropped it, reaching for the Jester. Only to find it replaced by another bucket, this one full.

Another of the fire crew attacked the Jester, who, turning to receive a new water bucket, put it into his attacker's surprised hands.

"Well?" said the Jester, pointing and shouting. "What are you waiting for? There's a fire!"

A group of men broke away from the bucket brigade. Their angry eyes reflected the burning city.

The Jester giggled. He ran down the street, chasing the spreading fire. The men, and some women, chased after him.

The Jester's Curse laughed and laughed, louder and more fully than the audience had laughed at him. The people of Seatown were getting what they deserved. The curse longed to bend over, grab Marius's belly, and laugh itself sick.

Marius himself, in the recesses of his mind, sat up and took note of his surroundings. They entered the black market. Flames quickly engulfed the shacks that hung out over the seawall.

The witch's collapsed shack served as a lucky fire break for the sea side of the street. The shops across the way weren't so lucky. Fire rushed through them toward the warehouse district.

Marius thought of the Sparrows' Nest. The children sheltered there might die in the fire.

The Jester's curse responded: the city needs to burn.

But not the children, thought Marius, surely not the Sparrows and sweet Clarion and clever Fira.

The curse spat, using Marius's own mouth to do so. It could care less about those precious fools. The fire might spread to the wizard's house and kill him. Hadn't Marius thought about that?

And take the slave quarter with it, Marius replied.

The curse scoffed. Some might be criminals.

Stop, Marius thought, but the word wouldn't reach his lips.

The Jester's Curse had control.

Marius fought it.

The curse resisted. It beat him down saying, this is what you wanted.

No. It wasn't. Marius mustered his willpower. Asadal had said the curse couldn't take over if he resisted. Now, it was him being resisted by the curse.

He thought of the children.

He needed help. By the Lady, he couldn't do it. The curse would burn the city to the ground, innocent and guilty alike.

Help, he thought.

A cool breeze stirred, hitting Marius in the face as he ran, refreshing him, giving him hope.

Marius pushed against the curse.

He broke through.

The Jester's Curse retreated, licking its wounds and laughing. You can't save them, it said. You can't even save yourself.

Looking around, Marius saw that he'd run all the way through the black market. He saw the section of the sea wall that he and Asadal had climbed after being thrown into the ocean by the kidnappers and that he and Fira had used to retreat from the assassins.

To his back stood the maze of alleys that led to the Sparrows' Nest. To his left stood the noxious warehouse containing chemicals ready to be shipped to mines overseas. To his right, an angry mob raced toward him and with them came the fire.

Marius backed up, running up against the corner of the warehouse's rough, wooden wall.

Without thinking, Marius scaled the wall moving with the alacrity of a cat being chased by a rabid dog. He arrived on top of an overhanging porch unaware of how he'd physically gotten there.

He looked at the crowd gathered below and dodged the stones they threw.

The fire leapt from the final shop in the black market onto the wooden wall of the warehouse. Marius was keenly aware of the way it spread up the side of the wall.

The mob stepped back, reaching the same conclusion as Marius. He would be burned alive by the fire without them having to dirty their hands. They stood back and watched.

Marius stood on the roof of the porch with his back against the front of the warehouse, flames flickering at its sides.

In a moment of stillness in the mad rush, Marius looked out over the oceanfront of Seatown.

The market burned as did the black market. Great plumes of yellow and green smoke rose out of the witches' shacks in the black market, contraband and spells burning in the fire. The familiar smell of witchweed filled his nostrils.

On the ocean, the seagoing vessels were alight with flame. It leapt from ship to ship like a boarding party full of pyromaniacs.

Sailors struggled to move their boats into the middle of the port away from the flames.

Over his shoulder, a great commotion arose in the slave quarters as the masters tried to move their prized cattle only to be met with resistance.

A revolt started. The sound of a small battle carried over the roar of the fire now churning within the warehouse.

Marius realized he had only moments to live.

He thought he'd been ready to die when the Astors found him at the Sparrows' Nest. He could have given up his life for the children. But Lespa had been right about one thing, he clung to life fervently, not willing to quit it, especially for nothing and going to nothing. What would happen when he died, Marius wondered?

Then he thought of the Lady and her promise to meet him again, at the end, under the ground, imprisoned within a prison.

It had been just another empty promise. Unless she meant to show up when he was already dead and buried—not that there would be much left to bury when the fire finished with him, and not that anyone would care about him enough to look after his charred remains. He might even be hung from the city gates as an example.

A smell arose, coming from all around him, stinking as though someone had urinated on a smoldering campfire.

Marius's nose scrunched involuntarily at the stench. He put an arm to his mouth to protect his lungs from the fumes.

A series of pops and crackles burst behind him. Foul smoke hit his eyes, causing them to smart and to water. He looked around but could not see. His entire world went gray with smoke and ashes. He could not breathe.

Marius had almost drowned in the ocean that first night in Seatown. He'd never considered the possibility of drowning on land.

Then his world turned upside down.

The building exploded as the flames finally embraced the chemicals within.

Marius found himself flying through the air, turning end over end like a juggled fish. He flew out over the ocean.

As he spun, head over heels, he looked down on the city of Seatown and saw it lit not by the sun but by fire. The swirling rainbow of the houses on the hill blended into the rippling flames dancing across the skyline.

At the heart of the fire, instead of light, Marius saw the deepest, darkest blackness and knew at that moment, as consciousness faded, his own soul.

Chapter Twenty-two

Marius?"

A voice came out of the darkness, insistent, calling to him.

Marius didn't want to wake. He'd been having such pleasant dreams. He dreamt he was dead.

"Marius!"

A hand slapped his face.

His cheek stung. Salty water erupted from his mouth. Water clogged every opening in his face. His lungs burned.

Eyes finally opening, Marius looked at a red star painted across a massive chest. A pair of eyes stared back at him over top of the star.

Marius understood the Walker's sign for the Astors, a star set below open eyes.

Bithius the Astor knelt above him.

Marius wondered why he was still alive. The explosion should have killed him, and if not the explosion or the subsequent dunking in the ocean, then Bithius should have killed him.

Maybe the big man wanted him awake before passing sentence, part of his code of honor or something.

Marius didn't feel like cooperating in his own death. He lay unmoving on the uncomfortable ground. Sharp rocks poked into his back.

"Kiss him again, Bithius!" an amused voice came out of the darkness.

Marius tried to find the source, but his head hurt too much to move. Water sloshed around inside his ears making him dizzy.

"I didn't kiss him, I—" Bithius sounded even more disgruntled than usual.

Marius disrupted the argument by vomiting another bellyful of salt water.

He managed to croak, "What happened? And why—" Marius tried to sit up and failed.

Bithius growled, "Take it easy." To his companion he added, "Did you bring a lantern?" He paused. His companion must have replied because Bithius added, "Then do something useful and light it."

As Marius settled back onto the sharp rocks, he felt the wet ocean tugging at his ankles. He longed to put a finger into his ears to scoop out the water that had accumulated.

Bithius continued, "What happened is you damn near burned down the city."

Marius found that he didn't feel too bad about that. They'd had it coming. But not everybody. "The Sparrows?"

"Safe," said Bithius. "When you blew up the mining warehouse, it put a big gap between the warehouses and the market. The fire stopped there. If it hadn't been for

the new fires started during the slave riots, it might not
have been so bad."

"Riot?"

"The slaves didn't like the idea of burning to death in
prison. So they let themselves out. You're not the only
runaway slave on this side of the peninsula tonight."

Marius looked up at the big man, "Why are you telling me all this? Why aren't you killing or arresting me or
something?"

Bithius chuckled, "Lespa always did like your pluck."

Marius shivered.

"Don't worry," said Bithius, "she's not here. Out chasing slaves I imagine. Thinks you're dead."

The feeble light of a lantern being coaxed to life
bathed the shore in a dull orange glow not dissimilar to
the one he now noticed on the horizon: the embers of
Seatown, he imagined.

Marius coughed. He tried to spit up more water but
his stomach held none. He heaved a great deal of nothing
onto the rocks. The thick taste of stomach bile coated his
tongue. His stomach cramped.

Bithius's friend cackled, "He pulled you out of the
ocean like a fish. Then slipped you the tongue."

"I did not," Bithius protested. "He needed air. I saved
him."

Marius wanted to shout. All he could manage was a
feeble croak, "You're no savior. You're a murderer. You
killed Asadal!"

The unseen companion laughed all the harder, "Did
he now?"

"I saw him," said Marius.

"Did you?"

Marius began to speak. He thought back to the alley near the rope warehouse. He had seen Bithius snap Asadal's neck like a twig, had seen his legs and arms splayed on the ground.

"Yes," Marius concluded. "I saw Asadal die."

"Then I hope you aren't afraid of ghosts."

The lantern came nearer, its light falling across a familiar set of white teeth framed in a swarthy face.

Asadal lived.

"Alive?" was all Marius could manage. He shook the water from his ears like a dog with wet fur.

"Yes," said Asadal, he squatted, sitting on his haunches next to Marius, the lantern dangling in his hand.

Marius finally recognized the familiar accent of the island-born man.

"But how? The witch on the hill said a Walker would die!"

Asadal smiled even more broadly. "Of course she did. I paid her a small fortune to say that."

Marius rose to his elbows, the blank look he gave Asadal communicated his complete lack of understanding.

"I told her to give every Walker she saw that warning. Now, everyone thinks I'm dead, just like she predicted. Very convenient."

Marius thought of Fira running down the alley, away from Asadal's prone body. She'd seen the same thing Marius had and would have reached the same conclusion. Everyone would think Asadal was dead, including Lespa. He wondered if Asadal had told Fira the truth. Or maybe he planned to retire, forcing her to take over his role as the head of the church's spy network. If she thought Asadal dead, Fira wouldn't have much choice.

The stick Asadal perpetually carried waved up and down in the lantern light. "Of course they think you're dead too." Asadal sighed. "I'm told you put on quite a show."

"Not me, the Jester's Curse."

"If that were entirely true you wouldn't be here," said Asadal. "You must have fought it."

Marius's cheeks burned. He couldn't meet Asadal's gaze, so he looked at the big Astor instead. "I thought Bithius wanted you dead."

Asadal shook his head. "Not every Astor is like Lespa."

"But he works for her!"

Scowling, Bithius crossed his arms. He walked a few paces down the shoreline.

Asadal said gently, "What better place than beside a sworn enemy? I only wish I could get a spy that close to Malconus. The wizard trusts no one but himself. Well, he's out of business in Seatown now, him and his Lady friend."

"I don't understand," said Marius.

"You will," said Asadal. "You will, in time."

Marius let out a deep breath. "What about the curse? The wizard said I only had a week before it took over."

"The curse is much weaker than it was earlier today," said Asadal. "You fought it marvelously. But even if you lost the curse you would still be cursed."

High Priest Campri had said something similar. Marius recognized the sales pitch for the Lady. He chose to ignore it.

"What should I do?"

"You've been touched by the Lady, Marius. How else can you explain your survival? Join us in fighting alongside her," said Asadal. "Stay in Arovia. There's much you could do."

The thought of seeing Irina sprang to mind making Marius's skin turn hot and cold. How could he ever face her again? Her brother, Iatro, would not be returning from the grave as Asadal had done. Marius had no desire to stay in Arovia.

"Notori?" he asked, wondering whether the man's ship had burned with the others.

Asadal sighed. "The Minstrel sets sail with the tide."

Marius raised his eyebrows, asking the obvious question.

"A bit after breakfast," said Asadal. He added, "Notori saw your display. He says you passed the test and may come aboard."

"What test?" said Marius. "What does he do?"

Asadal, still seated in a crouching position, shifted his weight. He considered a moment before answering. "Tries to make the world a better place, same as the Lady though not by the same means."

Marius opened his mouth to ask another question but was interrupted by the return of Bithius.

His low growl rumbled over the breaking waves, "Lights on the shore. Guards coming, searching for slaves." Bithius tossed Marius his bindle. "Picked this up for you."

"Thanks," said Marius genuinely overcome by emotion. He never thought he'd see the bindle again. Marius looped the rings, which he'd amazingly managed to retain through the explosion and the dunking in the ocean, over the end of the bindle's stout staff.

Bithius looked over his hulking shoulder. "Better change into your slave tunic. A bit dangerous this night but worse if you tried to walk into town as the infamous Jester of Zeno."

Marius imagined the townsmen might string him up on the spot at the first sign of his colorful outfit.

Asadal took him by the hand, helping Marius rise to his feet. Asadal held the grip, letting it linger.

"This is goodbye then."

Marius nodded.

"Go with the Lady," said Asadal.

Marius merely shook the man's hand in return. He wouldn't be going anywhere with the Lady, as the only place fitting for her was hell, and that wasn't his immediate destination.

* * *

The rising sun cast its rays on the wall guarding the entrance to Seatown. The city beyond the wall lay smoldering, smoke rising to the heavens. In the distance, Marius could hear the rhythmic sound of axes falling, chopping down the charred timbers that had once supported homes and businesses. The smell hanging around Seatown reminded Marius of the campfires he'd shared with the family of tinkers in a time that felt so long ago.

Marius adjusted the rust colored tunic that marked him as a house slave. It still reeked of witchweed. He hadn't worn the uniform much in the past few months. He noticed the places where it no longer fit. He had grown so much since leaving House Cervix, both physically and in so many other ways.

He'd left a cushy life of slavery to take up the bindle of a Walker, a lonely path full of uncertainty. And he bore in his soul the stamp of the Jester's Curse, waiting to re-awaken. For now it slept as uneasily as the citizens of the city below. If the others were to be believed, he bore the mark of the Lady as well. Much good it had done him.

Standing back, Marius examined his handiwork. Scratched into the city wall stood a new marking: a hat with three large tassels, the mark of the Jester.

Below it he had drawn a crude boat. Let no one look for him on the shores of Arovia any longer, he thought. Today he would put to sea with Notori.

As a Walker, no one cared if he lived or died, but if they could read his sign, they would at least recognize that he'd once been alive.

"Hey."

A feminine voice called out to him. Marius tensed, preparing to run, fearing he'd been recognized. He hoped it wasn't Clarion or Fira, or heaven forbid, Jank, whose voice had yet to drop and who could sound a lot like his mother.

Marius turned slowly and, he hoped, casually. He gripped his bindle tight. The rings clattered.

A girl waved at him. He recognized her as the skinny Walker he'd seen in the market days earlier.

She walked over, examining his mark. "I seen it around," she pointed at the jester's hat. "That you?"

Her bindle was made of soft pink fabric. She smelled of crushed grass in the summer. Her angular face ran toward the thin side, but that's how it was being a Walker, not knowing where your next meal might come from.

"Yeah," said Marius. "That's me."

"The Jester, huh?" she smiled. "People talking about a jester, say he burned down Seatown."

Marius shrugged, growing uncomfortable. "People talk," he said.

"It's kind of great though, isn't it?" She looked wistfully into the sky. "Man's a legend."

"He is?"

"You are," she said, eying him levelly.

"I—" Marius stammered.

"I'm Quinny." The girl stuck out her hand, waiting for an introduction.

"I'm Marius."

The girl nodded as though she'd known all along, as though she had a mystic streak.

"Nice to meet you, Marius the Jester. I'll be seeing you around."

Had she not read his symbol, Marius wondered, or perhaps not understood it? It clearly indicated that he was going to sea. Still, he didn't disabuse her of the notion. The less people who knew his whereabouts, the better.

"Sure... Quinny." He repeated her name as though he had a chance of actually remembering it.

"Gotta go," she said. "It's a long way home."

Marius cocked his head, "The only place a Walker can never go is home."

Hadn't Asadal taught him that as the first rule of the Walkers? Maybe she hadn't understood that either.

She smiled. Her teeth were a little crooked but in a way that only added to her charm. "You'll learn."

"Learn what?"

"You'll see," she said. And with that enigmatic answer, Quinny walked down the road, heading away from Seatown, as so many would that day. The fair was over, closed early. The whole city was almost over, thought Marius. Rebuilding would take a long time and cost a fortune.

Through the gate, hardly more than a week after he first entered the city, Marius walked down the hill of Seatown, as changed as the city itself, free but at a terrible cost.

He passed by the light-blue wall of Clarion's old house without pausing. She no longer worked there, and he didn't want to see her again anyway. He had eyes only for the tall masts of the sailing ships and a vessel called the Minstrel.

A firm hand grabbed Marius's wrist. He looked down into the familiar blue eyes and wrinkled face of the witch who lived on the hill.

"Are you a Walker?" she asked, her voice rattling.

"No," said Marius. "I'm a sailor."

She released his wrist and gave him a curt nod as if to say, of course you are.

Marius turned his back on the witch, and on Seatown, and on Arovia itself. He would set sail. And he would never stop. Not until he or the Jester's Curse lay buried at sea.

Thanks!

Thanks for reading the book. I hope you liked it. If you want to know more about Marius and company, sign up for my mailing list. I'll let you know when the next installment comes out:

tinyurl.com/hergotlist

Also, please consider adding a review over at Amazon or Goodreads. Honest reviews really help independent authors connect to new readers.

About the Author

Hans Hergot is the penname of, well, me. I've lived in Korea for the better part of the last decade, and I enjoy writing science fiction and fantasy with a redemptive message. If you liked this book, you might also check out my other fantasy work, *The Moondial*.

You can drop me a line at:

www.hanshergot.com

The original Hans Hergot lived nearly five hundred years ago. He was a writer, a pamphleteer, and a book seller who wandered from village to village bringing knowledge and truth. He was burned alive for speaking a wisdom that the world could not understand.

Deo vindice

www.ingramcontent.com/pod-product-compliance
Lightning Source LLC
Chambersburg PA
CBHW020554260626
47157CB00003B/701